DEAD SECRET

A gripping detective thriller full of suspense

JANICE FROST

Published 2015 by Joffe Books, London.

www.joffebooks.com

© Janice Frost

ISBN-13: 978-1514622933

Chapter 1

The mud-streaked legs of Amy Hill brought a lump to the throat of DS Ava Merry. They protruded from a makeshift tent that was being erected around her lifeless body to protect it from the elements. Ava turned away to give herself a moment to recover her composure, and was just in time to see her boss squelching his way across the sodden common to where she stood, gloved and suited, ready to begin a preliminary examination of the crime scene.

Ava shivered. She was damp to her bones from the persistent early morning drizzle that was slowly but steadily turning to rain. It had rained every day for weeks now, but this morning, whether because of the early hour and the lack of light, or because of the grim business at hand, the weather seemed more than usually depressing.

Better late than never, thought Ava, as DI Neal approached. She hadn't been working with him long enough to speak the words out loud, however. Besides, her focus now was on bringing the young victim's killer to justice.

"Sorry I'm late," Jim Neal muttered, "bloody lumbering goods train eighteen carriages long. What other city would hold its traffic to ransom in the middle of the rush hour by sticking a level crossing right across its busiest high street?"

"Advantage of living on the south side of town, sir. Took me no time to get here. Forensics arrived about fifteen minutes ago and Dr Hunt's on his way." Neal shot her a dour look, as if to say he didn't need any smug reminders that he was practically the last member of the team to arrive on the scene.

"Body was discovered by an amateur treasure hunter, I understand?"

"That's right. Albert Lichfield. He was out at first light despite the weather. Apparently, the boggy conditions make a find more likely."

"Some bloody find," Neal commented.

"Most days, half the city's joggers would have been tripping over the body at that time of the morning," Ava said, looking down at the soggy grass, rain dripping off the end of her nose.

September had been a miserable month, officially the wettest since records began. Early autumn gales and flash floods had transformed the city's low lying South Common into a muddy swamp interspersed with puddles as big as small lakes, discouraging walkers and joggers alike. Had it not been for Albert Lichfield's dogged enthusiasm for his hobby, Amy Hill's body might have lain undiscovered in the waterlogged earth for much longer.

Ava ducked under the yellow and black caution tape after Neal, and they bent to take a closer look at what they had.

The victim was petite, surely not much over five feet two inches. Lying pressed into the saturated ground in her skinny jeans and pink-sequined ballet pumps, her matted blonde hair curling around a pretty, doll-like face; she looked much younger than her nineteen years. How easy it must have been to crush the life out of her, Ava thought, noting the livid bruising around her throat.

"Must have snapped her like a twig."

Ava herself wasn't big, just a fairly average five six, but she was athletic, strong and fit and a competent kick boxer; altogether a tougher twig to snap.

"How does it feel to be right?" Neal asked.

"I'd rather have been proven wrong," Ava confessed, thinking back to their phone conversation of the previous day.

Neal had been sceptical. "So, what makes you think this is anything more than just a young woman spending the night with a boyfriend, or someone she met last night and decided to go home with?" he had asked.

"Her flatmate, Becci, told me they were supposed to be going to Seventh Heaven this afternoon." Pause. "It's a health spa, sir. It's very popular. Expensive too — out of my range, not that it's really the sort of thing I go in for anyway."

"Bit pricey for a pair of students, then?" Neal had asked.

"You'd think so, sir, but Amy'd landed lucky. Won some vouchers in a prize draw, or so she told her flatmate." It was Ava's turn to sound sceptical.

"It's a two hour drive away, sir, and they were supposed to leave by midday at the latest. A one-night stand would have to be pretty special to make you risk missing an afternoon of top of the range spa treatments."

"Thought you said it wasn't your thing."

"I wouldn't pass up the opportunity if it was free. I'm not averse to a bit of pampering."

But she had failed to convince him. Ava wondered if Neal regretted not listening to her now. Of course, he had been right to point out that Amy Hill had been missing for less than twenty-four hours, and it was more than likely she had met someone and stayed over. In the end, Ava had to accept this explanation. She had told herself that she'd merely been picking up on Becci's anxiety. Would it have made any difference to Neal's decision, or Amy's outcome, if she'd been more insistent?

"Morning folks!" Dr Ashley Hunt's greeting seemed much too cheerful in light of the circumstances. But his face fell when he caught sight of the victim. Ava remembered that he had a teenage daughter.

"Well, I hardly need to tell you that she's been dead for at least twenty-four hours," he said after a cursory examination of the body. "Cause of death is pretty obvious. Do you need me to spell it out?"

"Asphyxiation due to strangulation by a ligature," Ava said in a monotone.

Hunt nodded, "That just about covers it. No immediate sign of sexual assault. Of course we can't be sure of anything 'til I get the poor lass on the table. If you don't need me, I have another call — suspected suicide. All this dreary weather, no doubt," he said, with a glance at Ava, who was aware she must look like the proverbial drowned rat.

The forensics team were unpacking their equipment. Ava shared a glance with one of the team, Dan, a slightly geeky guy she'd got talking to at a colleague's retirement party a couple of weeks ago. He'd reminded her of her younger brother, Oliver, shy and awkward with a self-deprecating manner that was quite attractive. He even wore the same black plastic glasses. Ava smiled at his blush; his clumsy attempts at chatting her up had been quite charming.

Although she found forensic science intriguing, and admired the team's skill as they went through the minutiae of each case, Ava was of the same mind as her DI. When it came to solving a crime, it was the living, not the dead, who would yield up their secrets. They would tell how and why the victim had died; but even more, how she had lived; her passions and desires, loves and hates and secrets, and the people she had known. Jim Neal swore that in all his years as an investigator, it had always been human frailty that had led in the end to a successful arrest and conviction. Ava was not about to disagree with that.

Ava had been working with Neal for less than six months, and as yet, neither had the measure of the other. Jim Neal had a reputation as a bit of a wonder boy, having risen through the ranks to his present status in record time. But she would have preferred to have been assigned to someone more experienced.

No doubt he held the same opinion about her — the bit about more experience anyway; she had been a DS for only six months. Ava knew she wasn't intellectually in the same league as Neal, but she did believe she had other talents. She was committed and passionate and she believed that she had a sort of sixth sense about people that helped her sniff out a crime. And she was attractive, which she knew gave her an advantage in interacting with other people. Sometimes she worried about this; it made her gender politics seem questionable; she was too willing to assert herself through a kind of overt femininity that was more girl power than feminism. Other times she felt that as a woman in a profession still dominated by men, she was justified in taking advantage of every stratagem at her disposal.

"Not much chance of being lucky with footprints," said Neal, nodding at the mud churned up around the body. "Looks like everybody and their auntie's been stomping around the crime scene. Your treasure hunter's obviously not a big fan of CSI."

"Albert Lichfield? I doubt he's even got a telly, sir. A bit eccentric. I took a statement from him but he wasn't a lot of help. Poor bloke was really shaken up. I sent one of the uniforms home with him."

"Let's give HQ an update and find out about the victim's next of kin. And we'll need to interview the flatmate, Becci is it?"

"Rebecca Jones, sir. She told me Amy's mother lives six miles out of town, in Shelton. Amy moved away from home when she started at the Uni. Apparently Mrs Hill was a tad over- protective and Amy wanted some independence."

Neal sighed. Ava knew that he had a young son, of whom he was fiercely protective. In this line of work, who wouldn't be over-protective of loved ones?

"She looks so young, so innocent, doesn't she, sir? Like a sleeping princess," Ava said, immediately embarrassed at her choice of simile.

"Innocence is the preserve of the very young, Sergeant. I doubt that's what we're looking at here," Neal said in his soft Scottish accent.

Ava looked at him in surprise. Was he implying that Amy had somehow invited her fate? She dismissed the thought immediately. Even after such a short association with Neal, she knew him better than that.

* * *

Once Neal was satisfied that the crime scene had been secured and the collection of forensic evidence was under way, he and Ava left the common and drove back into the city, this time — to Neal's obvious relief — clearing the level crossing without delay.

Having to break the news of a child's death to a parent was one of the most distressing aspects of police work, and the thought of informing Nancy Hill about her daughter's murder filled Ava with dread. She had yet to master the emotional detachment that allowed some of her colleagues to do their job without drowning in their own emotions.

"Let's get this over with,' Neal said, his hand hovering on the polished brass door handle of 'In Stitches,' Nancy Hill's needlecraft and knitting shop. They had driven to the historic Uphill area of town, beneath the city's magnificent, brooding, gothic cathedral. Nancy Hill's shop was one of a host of trendy shops, cafes and galleries located in the cluster of narrow streets that radiated out from its shadow.

"That's pretty," said Ava, pointing at the embroidered sign that read, 'Open.' She stepped over the threshold behind Neal, to the sound of a jingly bell that brought the proprietor out from the back of the shop with a breezy, "Good morning."

Not for much longer.

"Good morning," said Neal, approaching the counter. Nancy Hill did not seem at all fazed when he flashed his identity card and made the necessary introductions. Ava watched her face closely, aware that the poor woman's whole world was about to fall apart. *Don't look at me*, she thought, *don't read the bad news in my eyes first.*

"Nancy Hill?" Neal asked. There was little about the woman behind the counter that spoke of a biological tie to Amy. She had a round, smooth-skinned face and dark, almost black hair. Although she was short — like Amy, thought Ava — everything else about Nancy Hill was large. Nancy had none of Amy's fragility; her colouring was entirely different, though Ava suspected that the raven hair was no longer natural. If she had once been blonde like Amy, no hint of it remained.

"Good morning, Inspector," Nancy Hill said. "How may I help you? Was there a break in or vandalism over the weekend, perhaps? I haven't seen any broken windows or any other signs of damage, and Mrs Kelso from the cheese shop didn't say anything when I saw her earlier this morning; she's usually the first to hear if something's been happening . . ."

Even as she chattered on, it seemed to dawn on her that the county constabulary would not be sending its finest just to investigate a burglary. And then Nancy Hill did catch the look in Ava's eye, and her hand went straight to her throat, eyes widening in fear. She took a step back, instinctively retreating from the coming bad news.

"Is there somewhere we can talk privately, Ms Hill?" Neal enquired gently. Ava had already observed that he had a soothing way of dealing with distressed people.

7

Taking Nancy Hill by the arm, he led her towards the back room, leaving Ava to flip the 'open' sign on the door to 'closed.'

Ava joined them in the tiny back room that doubled as stockroom and office — judging by the array of catalogues, needlecraft and knitting patterns and kits arranged neatly on shelves around the room (the floor space appeared to be reserved for boxes of materials and tools). Nancy was sitting, deathly pale behind her desk.

Ava looked around for a kettle. The traditional nice cup of tea really did help in cases of shock. Ava also needed to position herself where she would be able to observe Nancy Hill's reaction to the news of her daughter's murder, which was standing behind Neal who occupied the only other chair in the room.

"I'm deeply sorry to have to bring you this news, Ms Hill," Neal began. Nancy gasped, and her left hand, still hovering at her neck, went to her throat. Neal paused a moment to allow her time to steel herself against the blow.

"A body was discovered early this morning on the South Common. It was that of a young woman whom we believe to be your daughter Amy."

Despite the slightly formal mode of delivery, Neal's soft, Edinburgh accent prevented his words from sounding harsh or uncaring. Ava admired his skill. She had yet to work out whether emotional detachment stemmed from lack of empathy or from over-sensitivity; from coldness, or self-protection in the face of suffering. Looking at Neal; his quiet proficiency and calm, reassuring manner, she could only guess at what he was feeling at this moment, but his next move gave her a hint.

Leaning across the table, Neal touched the distraught woman's hand once, lightly, the slightest of physical contact but more, Ava knew, than most officers would be willing to risk for fear of their gesture being misinterpreted.

Ava cleared her throat. "I'll put the kettle on, shall I?" She found some teabags and cups on a shelf and, after locating the kettle on a shelf beside a stack of knitting patterns, busied herself preparing drinks, glad of the distraction. She heaped two spoonfuls of sugar into a mug that bore the motto, 'sew far, sew good.'

"Ms Hill, I know you're in shock and the last thing you want is to be bombarded with questions . . ." Neal said.

"It's alright, Inspector," Nancy Hill said, though clearly it was not. "You're only doing your job, and I want to do what I can to help you find the person who . . ." The unfinished sentence hung in the air.

Neal nodded, and then, when Nancy's sobs had subsided asked, "when did you last see your daughter, Ms Hill?"

"Last Thursday," Nancy said, tears welling up in her eyes again, "we had afternoon tea at the new patisserie."

"Did she seem her normal self?"

"Yes, apart from being too thin, like most girls her age. A year ago I'd have said something to her about it but I've learned not to interfere. Amy often accuses me of being overprotective. She thought I'd be nagging her every time she was late home for tea if she stayed on at home, so she took a flat in town. She hates — hated me fussing over her, liked her independence."

"And you realised she was missing, when?" Neal pushed.

"Her flatmate, Becci, phoned me late on Saturday evening to say Amy hadn't returned to the flat after a night out. It was gone midnight and she hadn't said anything to Becci about staying over anywhere, and her mobile was turned off.

Ironically, I was the one to reassure Becci. At first when Amy left, I worried all the time but I had to learn to stop or I would have gone out of my mind. It was probably good for both of us for Amy to move out. I should have worried though, shouldn't I?" Nancy's eyes flitted from one to the other of them, seeking what? Reassurance? Blame?

Ava felt for her. Nancy Hill had no reason to blame herself. Amy's flight from the nest had clearly benefited both — Amy had gained her freedom, and Nancy, the peace of mind that came with no longer being able to worry about what her daughter was up to.

"I threw myself into the shop when Amy left home," Nancy said, looking around at the crowded but orderly room, "Amy always came first. I opened fewer hours, and fitted work around her needs."

Neal and Ava exchanged glances. No doubt Nancy needed to talk, but time was moving on. Ava caught Neal sneaking a look at his watch.

Nancy dabbed at her tears with a pretty, embroidered handkerchief. Her immaculate, glossy black bob was still perfect, but it now framed a face that was blotchy and pallid, streaky foundation caking in the fine lines under her eyes.

Neal asked about Amy's father.

"I . . . I hardly knew him," Nancy said, "I haven't seen him since before Amy was born." She dabbed at her nose and eyes with the pretty handkerchief. Hiding behind it, Ava thought. Nancy's eyes were wide with fear.

"We'll need to contact him," Ava said.

"I don't think that's possible. I don't even remember his name. He doesn't live in this country. Amy was the result of a one-night stand. Her father doesn't even know she exists."

Ava looked at Neal and he shook his head, indicating that later would do.

"May I see her?" Nancy asked, looking from one to the other of them, pleadingly.

"We need someone to make a positive identification of Amy's body. When you're ready, Sergeant Merry and I will take you," Neal answered.

Thus far, Nancy had requested no details about the circumstances of her daughter's murder. And, other than the evident cause of death, there was little they could have told her. There had been no obvious indications of rape or sexual assault but, of course, these could not yet be ruled out. "Did she suffer?"

Neal said simply, "She would have died quickly," and Ava was relieved that Nancy did not ask for further details.

"Is there someone we can call for you, Ms Hill?" Neal asked. "A relative, perhaps, or a friend who could come with you? You shouldn't be alone at a time like this."

Nancy nodded. "My friend, Anna Foster. She owns the second-hand bookshop down the hill from here."

* * *

At a nod from Neal, Ava left the shop and walked along to a crossroads. The cobbled Castlegate was still quiet; a hush foreign to most large towns. To the right, the street led to the cathedral, to the left was the medieval castle built by William the Conqueror as he plundered his way southwards. Ava walked straight ahead. She seldom came to this part of the city, except as a tourist when friends came to visit. It was the cultural centre of Stromford, and more to Jim Neal's taste than hers. Ava preferred her culture popular, and was unimpressed by what the aptly named Long Hill area had to offer in the way of craft shops and restaurants, galleries and museums. She supposed the narrow hill had a certain charm, with its harmonious jumble of half-timbered medieval houses and elegant Georgian architecture, but for a good night out, she'd head for the bars and restaurants at the other end of town any day of the week. That's where the life was.

The bookshop to which she had been directed was about halfway down the hill. A sign on the door promised the browser thousands of titles inside, but from the outside it looked tiny. A chime announced Ava's arrival as she stepped inside. The shop was a labyrinth of small interconnecting rooms and meandering, over-stocked bookcases.

"Hello!" she called, peering round a dark oak bookcase laden with used paperbacks.

A voice answered, "Coming!" and a fresh-faced, forty-something, auburn-haired woman appeared, apologising profusely,

"I'm so sorry, I was next door sorting through some books I picked up at a library sale at the weekend; I wasn't expecting a rush."

Ava looked around, and then realised that the remark was humorous.

"Are you looking for something in particular or just browsing?"

"Actually I'm looking for you," Ava explained.

"Oh, well, that's nice. Are you a rep, or looking for a job perhaps, because I'm afraid I don't stock a lot of new titles and I'm not looking for extra help at the moment."

Ava shook her head and showed the woman her ID.

"Oh," the woman said again, "is something wrong?"

"Poor Nancy," she sighed, when Ava finished explaining the reason for her visit. "Just when she was beginning to sort her life out a bit. She worshipped that daughter of hers."

Had Ava imagined it, or had Anna Foster intended to imply that Amy Hill was not worthy of her mother's adoration?

"Did you know Amy Hill, Ms Foster?" Ava asked.

Anna Foster shook her head, and her hair swished.

"Not that well. I met her a couple of times. Pretty girl, but . . ." Ava arched an eyebrow, "well, she was inclined to be rather selfish. I didn't like the way she spoke to her mother. Then again, how many teenagers respect their parents these days? Not many."

She sighed, "it's unkind, isn't it, speaking ill of the dead? Nancy was devoted to Amy, she must be devastated."

Ava nodded, thinking that 'speaking ill of the dead,' was often a help in a murder investigation.

Anna agreed immediately to offer her support to Nancy.

"Is it alright if I grab a few things before we go? And I need to call my son to see if he can mind the shop while I'm gone."

Ava followed Anna Foster along a passage narrowed by bookcases on either side, with doors leading off to further small rooms stacked with books. The floor was uneven in places and tripping hazards were indicated by large red arrows pointing downwards. Pondering the nightmares a risk assessment might raise, Ava concentrated on watching her feet as Anna Foster led her to the rear of the shop, and through a door opening into a small square hallway with stairs leading steeply upwards.

"Do you live here?"

Anna Foster smiled. "There's a small flat upstairs." Ava waited in the hallway while Anna Foster hurried upstairs to collect her belongings. The woman's voice could be heard talking on the telephone.

Ava picked a book at random from one of the shelves on a small pine bookcase in the space under the stairs, and leafed through it.

"Do you like poetry?" asked Anna Foster moments later.

Ava replaced the slim volume hurriedly, muttering, "no, not my thing really. I prefer a good thriller. Or horror, you know, Stephen King's good. Are you ready?"

"I've just been phoning my son. He's coming to keep shop. I'll lock up behind us. He has his own keys."

Ava noticed that Anna Foster had replaced the bright red shirt she had been wearing with something darker. She had clasped her abundant hair away from her face, emphasising her hazel eyes. With her full lips and striking looks, she resembled a sultry French actress whose name Ava had forgotten. One of her ex's had been a big fan.

"What did you mean just now when you said that you didn't like the way Amy Hill spoke to her mother?"

Anna Foster shrugged, "I really don't want to speak ill of the dead. It's just that Amy was always asking for money, and nothing her mother did for her was ever good enough. When Nancy opened the shop Amy refused to help out. Once I heard her making fun of her mother's business. I think she was put out to discover that her mother had an interest in her life other than her daughter."

"Did they fall out? Were they estranged?"

"Oh no, nothing like that. For all I know they were the kind of arguments that mothers and daughters engage in all the time. Most young people are selfish, aren't they, Sergeant?"

Ava was much closer in age to the hapless Amy than she was to Anna Foster.

* * *

They had arrived at Nancy's shop. Anna Foster walked straight into the back room and embraced her friend, prompting a fresh shedding of tears. Neal and Ava excused themselves and waited in the shop's more cheerful interior.

"I hated sewing at school," Ava remarked picking up a kit containing all you needed to create a cushion cover of Van Gogh's 'Sunflowers' painting in needlepoint. "Nice design though, would go well with my bedroom curtains."

"We need to interview Amy's flatmate as soon as possible; the one who reported her missing," Neal commented.

"Becci Jones?" Ava said, "I spoke with her briefly on Saturday evening, remember?" It was as close as she would permit herself to come to saying, "'I told you so.'"

They were interrupted by the hesitant appearance of Anna Foster at the stockroom door.

"Nancy's ready," she said, and Neal nodded. A few moments later, they stepped outside into the sombre light

14

of late morning, Neal and Anna Foster supporting Nancy up the hill to where Ava's car was parked in a side street, outside the pedestrian zone. Ava walked slightly ahead of them in the drizzling rain, conscious of the heavy weight of sorrow following in her footsteps.

Chapter 2

Ava wished Becci Jones would stop sending those critical looks in her direction.

"If your lot had listened to me on Saturday evening when I first reported her missing, Amy might still be alive," the girl complained, shaking her head. Ava felt herself redden. She didn't dare look at Neal. In the circumstances, explaining that most people who failed to return home on a Saturday night usually turned up safe and sound the next day seemed inappropriate.

Becci obviously needed someone to vent her anger on, but Ava wished she hadn't chosen her. Then again, she had promised Becci she would do all she could to ensure that Amy's disappearance would be properly investigated. Well, Amy's disappearance would certainly be investigated. Along with her death. In fact, Amy Hill's short life and her death were about to be given the highest police priority, but it was too little too late as far as Becci Jones was concerned. Neal cleared his throat, and Ava was grateful for his words.

"Perhaps we need to focus on how we can help bring your friend's murderer to justice."

For a moment, it seemed that Becci Jones hadn't heard. Then, she simply nodded and sat down. "Yes, I suppose you're right. It's just so overwhelming, you know? I can't believe I'll never see Ames again. I keep hoping she'll just walk in the door and like, laugh her head off at us all for getting so worked up."

Ava felt a pang of pity for the girl. And not only for her grief, but also her thinness, the pinched, slightly undernourished look, like a waif. She was dressed in a blue crop top and skinny jeans that hung low on her jutting hips, leaving her white midriff bare. A silver ring pierced the skin around her navel. Fine, heat-straightened hair hung limply around a plain, unremarkable face. She could be pretty, Ava thought; she had the kind of face that could be transformed with the right amount of colour, like a blank canvas.

"Had you and Amy been friends for long?" Neal was asking.

"Since school. We got this flat share together after we both got accepted at the Uni."

Becci's eyes filled with tears. Perhaps she was remembering her first day at school, the uncertainty she and Amy shared, the first stirrings of friendship.

"Had you noticed any changes in your friend recently? In her appearance or her behaviour?" Neal asked.

"No. She was just Amy."

"Did Amy confide in you, Becci? Would she have told you if she were in any sort of trouble?" Ava asked.

"We were best mates. We told each other everything. She wasn't in any kind of trouble."

"What about boyfriends? Was Amy seeing anyone?"

"She wasn't seeing anyone seriously. There was a boy who pestered her a bit to go out with him, but she didn't fancy him."

"Can you remember his name?" Ava asked.

"Bradley Turner," Becci said, looking up. "His dad, Richard, is Amy's mum's boyfriend. Amy thought it a bit

17

pervy him asking her out as they'd practically grown up together, even though they're not actually related."

Ava caught Neal's eye and saw his eyebrow arch. No doubt he was wondering, as she was, why Nancy Hill hadn't asked for this Richard instead of Anna Foster when they'd broken the news about her daughter's murder.

Before Ava had a chance to ask her next question, Becci said, "There was another guy interested in her but he never asked her out. Amy wouldn't tell me his name. Apparently he just came up to her out of the blue one day and told her that she didn't have to worry about anything; that he'd look after her. After that, she said, he'd followed her a few times, at a distance, kind of like he was looking out for her. I thought it was a bit creepy but Amy was convinced he was harmless. I think she kind of liked the attention."

Ava's jaw dropped open. Beside her, Neal was frowning.

"You said you thought it was 'a bit creepy' this guy following Amy; did you think he might be stalking her?"

Becci shrugged, "Maybe. Ames didn't think so. She said she could tell he wasn't a threat."

Ava was about to ask how on earth Amy could possibly know that, when Neal stepped in, as though he'd read her thoughts.

"Becci, is there anything you can tell us about this person? Did you ever see him yourself, or did Amy ever describe him to you? How could she know he didn't pose a threat to her?"

"She said he was quite good-looking. Tall and dark, sort of shy and gentle."

"Gentle?" Neal asked, his eyebrow arching again.

"That's what she said. She called him her BFG. You know, her Big Friendly Giant, like in the Roald Dahl story?"

Ava snorted, earning a glare from her DI.

"Had Amy quarrelled with anyone recently? Did she have any enemies?" Neal asked.

Becci shook her head impatiently. "I don't know of any quarrels. Amy didn't have any enemies and I don't know why anyone would want to kill her."

Ava and Neal exchanged glances. Clearly the interview was going to yield no further results.

"What am I going to do now?" Becci sniffed.

At first, Ava thought she spoke in grief.

"The landlord will stick some stranger in here with me — I can't afford to pay the rent myself. I gave up the chance of a room in halls to move in with Ames."

Ava handed her a tissue from a box on a beech coffee table by the two-seater sofa where she sat surrounded by needlepoint cushions. Nancy Hill had been busy. Looking around, Ava suspected that Nancy had also been generous in helping her daughter and her friend set up house, for the furnishings, though not expensive, were modern and recently purchased, probably from one of the trendy Scandinavian stores. Bookcases in the same light shade as the coffee table lined the walls, and deep-pile shaggy rugs in different shades of pink relieved the bareness of the laminated floor. All very chic and comfortable; it wasn't hard to see why Becci was worried about having to move out.

"We need to take a look at Amy's bedroom," Neal said.

"It's locked," Becci said, quickly, "We always lock our doors when we go out. The landlord said it was better for insurance reasons, or something."

"You don't have a spare key?" Neal asked. Becci shook her head. Neal sighed, "There's no point in breaking down the door. " Turning to Ava, he said, "Search Amy's possessions for her house keys and come back in the morning." Ava nodded.

"Becci," she said gently, extending a card, "I'm going to leave you my contact details. If you think of anything,

anything at all that you think might help with our investigation, please get in touch immediately."

Becci saw them to the door, still clutching the card. Ava looked back as she and Neal walked down the path towards the gate and caught the girl already frantically pressing buttons on her mobile phone as she closed the door.

"She was keeping something from us," Neal observed. "Something to do with Amy's recent behaviour or appearance. Or about this mysterious benign stalker, perhaps. We'll need to set up interviews with Amy's other friends, tutors, anyone who knew her. If Becci isn't prepared to give us information, someone else will." Neal suddenly looked around, "Fancy a coffee?"

They were standing on the pavement outside Becci and Amy's house, one of a row of terraced houses, two-ups and two-downs which had been bought up to let to students when the university was in its planning stages.

The opening of the city's new university eight years ago had given the local economy a boost and had created a lively atmosphere in parts of town that had previously settled into dreary inner city decline. The street where Amy had lived was in one such area.

The effect on this street had been striking. Wooden doors leading to the passageways linking one house with another were painted in cheerful primary colours, foliage plants graced windowsills, and wind chimes dangled against panes of glass, adding colour and character to the rows of grey stone terraces. Cafés and clubs and pubs had sprung up all over the city seemingly overnight, along with shops selling merchandise aimed at the student population. Across the street was one such café, and it had been a long time since breakfast. Ava nodded and they crossed the road.

* * *

"Like the stripy sofa," Ava commented as she took in the café's cosy interior. It was furnished with mismatched armchairs and sofas strewn with cushions, a refreshing change from the city centre chains. There were small side tables and long coffee tables on which were scattered a selection of magazines, and flyers advertising local alternative businesses such as suppliers of organic produce and complementary therapists.

"Grab a seat, then; I'll get the drinks," said Neal, "anything to eat?"

Ava looked longingly at the mouth-watering selection of Danish pastries and cakes arranged temptingly under glass domes on the counter, but she shook her head.

She settled into the pink and white striped sofa by the window, and with a quick glance at the grungily-attired man behind the counter, elevated her aching foot on the side of the coffee table. No one told her off. She'd injured her foot a couple of weeks ago, and it was still giving her jip; it was bliss to take the weight off it from time to time. Neal joined her with two steaming mugs of coffee and an outsize cinnamon Danish. She watched as he spooned two sugars into his cup, marvelling at his slim, almost skinny frame. He caught her watching.

"What?" he asked. "Isn't this what everyone thinks cops are supposed to do? Drink coffee and eat pastries?"

"Only in cheesy American cop shows. And it's doughnuts."

Neal tore his Danish in two and offered half to Ava, with a, "Go on, you know you want to."

There was no arguing with that, and for a couple of minutes they ate and drank companionably, watching the traffic stop and start at the traffic lights on the road outside.

"How's Archie?" Ava asked, wiping a pastry crumb from the side of her mouth and sitting back contentedly. Archie was Neal's ten-year-old son.

"He's good. He'll be pissed at me for letting him down this morning."

Ava looked at her boss questioningly.

"We were supposed to be going cycling. It's half term, remember? I'd booked a couple of days off."

"I knew about the leave, but I'd forgotten it was half term."

"Sometimes I wish he were less understanding about my job and the hours I have to put in. I wouldn't feel so guilty. When the call came this morning, all he said was, 'they've found that girl, haven't they? You'll have to go to work then, Dad.' He must have heard me talking to Maggie about Amy at the weekend."

Ava nodded in sympathy. She had never met Archie, or Neal's younger sister Maggie, who was on an extended 'visit' to her brother's house following a relationship break-up. Neal rarely talked about his domestic arrangements, and she realised that he must be feeling particularly bad about disappointing his son.

"You'll make it up to him," she said, knowing that Archie might have a long wait. She thought suddenly of her own father, whom she remembered as a shadowy presence in her early childhood, before he left his family for good. Archie should be counting his blessings.

"Anyway, it's good he understands about your job, isn't it? He's probably dead proud of his dad being a big shot in the force."

"Hardly a big shot," Neal commented dryly.

"You know you're destined for great things," Ava pointed out, and cleared her throat. Neal hadn't appreciated the compliment. "Do you think it was Nancy Hill who provided all the posh bits and pieces for her daughter's flat? Did you notice the fancy rugs and cushions? Amy was the only child of a single parent. Can't blame her mother for over-indulging her, I suppose." As soon as the words were out, Ava realised she'd made a further gaffe. "Not that I think all single parents of only

22

children ruin them," she added hastily. "Far from it, I mean I'm sure Archie's not the least bit spoilt." Ava blushed crimson, and was relieved to see an amused smile on Neal's lips.

"Anyway, to come back to the point; from what Anna Foster had to say, Amy wasn't exactly grateful for what she received." She told Neal what Anna Foster had said about Amy.

For a moment Jim Neal appeared to be deep in thought, but when he spoke, it was to say, "Nice lady."

Ava shot him a quizzical look.

"Anna Foster."

Ava was perplexed. The female population of the station had dismissed Jim Neal as a lost cause. With his dark brooding good looks, his soft Scots accent and reserved manner, he attracted the attention of many of his female (and some male) colleagues, but he was also something of a dark horse; a family man, devoted to his young son. Of his past, little was known, except that there had been some tragedy involving his wife, and it was commonly assumed he was a widower. Jim Neal was not the sort of man who invited questions about his personal life.

"She has a son at the university," Ava said.

"Did he know Amy?"

"It's very possible, given that their mothers are friends. We'd better add him to the list of people to interview." Her words earned a nod of approval from Neal.

As they stood to go, Neal sighed, "I do worry, you know, about not spending enough time with Archie. I'll go home this evening and we'll spend some 'quality time,' together but it's never enough. Archie'll survive, of course, but we busy parents miss out in the long run. I can look forward to spending other days with Archie the teenager, Archie the student, Archie the young man, but the Archie I love to be with, to tease and chase and build Lego models with will have moved on. You can't book time in the future to spend in the past, Sergeant."

Ava nodded, thinking again of her own family, and how awful it would be if either of her parents ever showed an interest in her life. Neal was right; you can't revisit the past, but in her case, that wasn't such a bad thing. She was doing just fine without their input. Still, she couldn't help feeling a thrill of pleasure at this rare glimpse into her boss's inner life. If they were going to work together successfully, she wanted to know him as a person as well as a colleague.

* * *

After work, Ava didn't feel like going straight home. Often in the evenings, she would run around the south common or swim laps at the pool, or visit the gym for a workout. Keeping her body in peak condition was an interest that bordered on obsession with Ava Merry.

If anyone asked her why she needed to run five miles or work up a sweat at the gym, or clock up eighty or more lengths of the pool every day, before she could let herself relax, she would claim that she was an athlete, and besides physical fitness was important for the job. The fact that she was no longer a competing athlete, and had never had to chase a crook on foot was neither here nor there. The real reason why she kept pushing herself was that she simply couldn't stop.

Missing a session at the gym or a visit to the pool caused Ava to feel uneasy, and she had never asked herself why. Exercise was anathema to her studious younger brother, Oliver, and he liked to tease her about her OCD tendencies. Running was out of the question today with her aching foot, so Ava took off for the pool, where she churned up and down, emptying her mind of the events of the day for an hour, her arms splicing the yielding water.

Images of Amy Hill's lifeless form returned to her as she stood under the shower, enjoying the massage of hot water that beat on her neck and shoulders. Absurdly, it was the memory of the mud that bothered her most; the dirty streaks on the girl's legs and arms, and her soiled clothing. She was supposed to have been at the spa, being pampered and perfumed, and clean, not left to rot in the muck.

The sight of the girl's pinched face and staring eyes had eradicated any satisfaction she might have felt about being right about her disappearance.

Ava had stared at death before, of course, and it was always the same; bewilderment at the loss of that mysterious sense of presence living beings had. And it was especially so when, as in Amy's case, the victim had been so young.

* * *

Energised by the physical activity (another justification for her exercise addiction) Ava was reluctant to go home. Her car was parked at the station half a mile distant and after collecting it, she drove to the Long Hill area of town and parked in the side street where she had left her car that morning when she and Neal had visited Nancy's shop to deliver the news of Amy's death.

She found herself walking past Nancy Hill's shop. On any day it would be closed at this time of the evening, but today the darkness that lay beyond its locked door made Ava shudder involuntarily. She wasn't sure why she had come here instead of driving straight home. It was already dark and the rain, which had dried up in the afternoon, could be felt at the back of a moist wind that was whipping up the usual sounds of the night on the empty hill, a mingling of squeaking shop signs, and water running from downpipes and gutters into waiting drains.

Looking down the hill, Ava was surprised to see Anna Foster, standing on the pavement near her property, coat collar pulled up against the wind. She was not alone. A tall young man was waiting by her side. He was dark-haired with downy whiskers on his chin and upper lip and he was wearing the geeky black-rimmed specs that seemed to be all the rage these days.

"Good evening, Detective Sergeant," Anna said as Ava approached. "This is my son, Simon. Simon, Detective Sergeant Ava Merry."

Ava and Simon Foster exchanged polite nods. He seemed to be shy.

"How was Nancy when you left her?" Ava enquired. It didn't escape her attention that Simon Foster stiffened at the mention of Nancy's name.

"I'm afraid she broke down badly," Anna answered.

"She was very brave this morning, answering our questions. A lot of people can't, you know, because of the shock. For others, the full impact hits them a little while afterwards," said Ava.

"Yes, I think that's what happened with Nancy."

"Is anyone with her now?"

"Her partner, Richard Turner. He was out of town this morning but was due to return this afternoon. I called him and stayed with Nancy until he arrived."

"Did you know Nancy or Amy?" Ava asked Simon.

"I met Nancy once or twice at my mother's book group. I knew Amy by sight, but that's all." On her coffee table at home, Ava had a book about how to spot when someone is lying to you, but she'd only opened it twice and both times she had fallen asleep without getting past the first chapter, which debunked all the usual myths about fidgeting and avoiding eye contact. She therefore had to trust her gut instinct, and at that moment she would have bet money that Simon wasn't being truthful.

"Are we under investigation, Sergeant?" Anna Foster asked, her tone suggesting mild amusement even though her look was guarded. "How exciting."

"I'm off duty," Ava replied. Then, because Anna's tone had irritated her ever so slightly, she added, "Still, I suppose there's no harm in asking what you were doing last Saturday evening?"

"We were at home, sorting through some books from the library sale I mentioned to you earlier today."

"We?"

"Simon and I."

Not a lot of point in pursuing that one, thought Ava.

Instead she said, "I've often thought of joining a book group. I quite enjoy reading; but as I said before, Stephen King's about as intellectual as I get, although I did read, 'Lord of the Flies' at school. Cracking book. What about you, Simon? You a reader?"

"Yes," Simon answered guardedly.

Ava waited but he didn't elaborate.

"All those little boys running wild on that island. It's not surprising it ended in tragedy," she went on. "I wonder what would have happened if they'd been girls instead?"

Anna Foster smiled, indulgently. "You're welcome to come along to my book group, Sergeant. I'm sure my members would love to debate that topic."

Ava looked at Simon and was surprised to see that he looked as if he was almost on the point of tears. He couldn't be crying for Nancy's loss, surely. For whom, then? Amy?

"I might just do that," she said. "You guys have a good evening."

Anna Foster smiled and wished Ava the same. Simon nodded, politely.

Ava returned to her car and headed home. She cooked a light supper and curled up with her fat tortoiseshell cat, Camden, to watch TV for an hour. Before going to bed she did fifty press-ups and set her alarm for five thirty just in case her ankle was feeling up to a run in the morning.

Chapter 3

Nancy Hill's cottage was located in a quiet village only twenty minutes' drive from the centre of town. Making the move from London all those years ago had been a wrench, and it was a long time before she was able to appreciate the pleasures that village life had to offer. Several times in those early days Nancy had asked herself whether the anonymity of city life might not have suited her needs better than the intrusive closeness of the community she had entered unprepared, as a single mother, with a secret that was sometimes too oppressive to bear.

She had expected to be judged and found guilty of the sin of single motherhood. In reality she had found that Shelton, an expanding commuter village with a rapidly changing population, was not the kind of closed-minded community that she had feared it might be. For every member of the old guard there was a new type of villager who hailed, typically, from an urban area, attracted by Shelton's relatively rural character and its proximity to a city that was enjoying a renaissance in jobs and culture that had culminated in the building of the country's first new university in many years. Far from being the only stranger in their midst, Nancy had found herself simply one among many.

With a young child to care for, it would have been impractical to keep herself entirely to herself, though this was exactly what Nancy had hoped for when she moved into the small cottage on the outskirts of the village, which she had first rented, then bought when her landlord put it up for sale.

Babies, they say, open doors, and this had certainly been the case for Nancy, not least because Amy had been such a beautiful child. People would stop Nancy in the street and exclaim at her daughter's cornflower blue eyes, her fair hair and delicate features.

"You must be so proud," they would comment, and Nancy could hear the words they left unsaid: 'she must take after her father,' for nothing of Amy's Nordic beauty was evident in her mother.

At first she had been afraid to talk to people, for fear of letting her guard down, of letting too much slip out. She was careful never to elaborate on her basic story, never to reveal anything or invent anything that would not stand up to scrutiny, or that could be shown conclusively to be false.

Along with others' acceptance of her back-story came some sense of security; if others could believe in it, then so could she. As time passed, invention and reality seemed to merge, to the point where she could barely distinguish where one ended and the other began.

For Amy's sake Nancy suppressed her impulse to live a reclusive existence. As long as she did not deviate from the half-invented past she had fabricated for herself and her daughter out of a painstaking mix of fact and fiction, she could feel, on certain good days, that she had nothing to fear, either from the past or in what the future might hold.

Over the years, Nancy had made friends and settled into a way of life, which, even if it was not the one she had planned, had its own compensations, not the least of which was her love for Amy. No sacrifice was too great where her daughter was concerned.

All through her childhood, Amy was seldom out of Nancy's sight. For the two years that her daughter attended the local playgroup, Nancy volunteered as a playgroup assistant, thereby delaying the separation she knew would come when Amy started school.

Then, by a stroke of good luck, a vacancy arose for a classroom assistant at the local school, and on Amy's first day in reception class, Nancy walked through the door holding her daughter's hand, and went to work in the classroom next door, where she remained for the following six years, never further than a few doors away from Amy. Nancy had begun to panic whenever Amy was out of her sight for too long.

For that reason, even brief separations, such as school trips, (onto which Nancy usually managed to wangle her way), and later, sleepovers at friends' houses, were planned with meticulous care, and unavoidably, some of Nancy's anxiety communicated itself to her daughter.

"You never let me go anywhere!" became the recurrent refrain of Amy's teenage years as she battled for her independence in the face of her mother's stifling over-protectiveness. Nancy reached a point when she began to accept that things could not go on as they were. Nevertheless, the split, when it came, all but broke her heart.

* * *

A couple of days after Amy's murder, Nancy was roused from a feverish mid-morning sleep by the sound of soft but persistent knocking on her door. With a gargantuan effort she heaved herself upright and walked like a zombie to the door. It was most likely another well-wisher come to offer condolences, thought Nancy, wishing they would just leave her alone

"Thank you," she said, accepting the card proffered by the nervous young woman on her doorstep, whom she recognised as one of her daughter's former classmates, one who had not gone to university, but had taken a job as an apprentice receptionist at the village health centre — and stayed alive.

"I'd just like to say how sorry I am. Amy was a mate."

Nancy nodded, taking in the girl's pretty face and despising herself for wishing that this girl, any girl, could take her daughter's place. She did not encourage her to linger, and closed the door before she had even turned her back.

The house was bursting with cards and flowers. Some of the cards had been opened and arranged along the mantelpiece, on windowsills, and the polished surface of a heavy oak merchant's chest standing in an alcove. The rest lay in a heap on the coffee table where Nancy tossed this latest offering, not bothering to open it. It landed on the pile, then slid to the carpet. Nancy walked over it as she went back to the sofa where she had been lying most of the night and all of the morning until the girl's timid knocking disturbed her.

She had lost all sense of time since Anna Foster and DS Merry had driven her home from that horrid place where they had taken her to identify her daughter's body. Afterwards, at her insistence, they had left her alone to come to terms with her loss. As if she ever could. Anna had promised to visit the following day. The young sergeant had said that she would be in touch. Nancy did not want visitors, and besides, aren't people secretly relieved when a bereaved person reassures them that there is nothing they can do?

From her prone position on the sofa, Nancy heard a key turning in the back door. *Oh dear God, not Richard.*

"Nancy! Love, why didn't you call me?"

Though she had dreaded him coming, Nancy suddenly realised that his familiar face was all she wanted to see.

Speechless, she turned to him, her eyes brimming with tears. Of course she had wanted to call him. In the eight years that she had known Richard Turner, there had been scores of times when she had wanted to call him and blurt out the truth about her past, why she would not marry and settle down with him like normal people do. Any other man would have given up on her by now, but not Richard.

A little older than Nancy, divorced, with two teenage children of his own, rarely seen when they were small, Richard had no doubt harboured hopes of starting a new family with her, but she had made it clear from the beginning that marriage and children were not on her agenda.

Over the years, he had come to accept the terms of their relationship, but her unwillingness to share was, she knew, a constant source of frustration for him. Above all, he could not understand why she still refused to live with him.

"Amy's dead," she heard herself wailing.

"I know."

"Who would do such a thing?"

"You know I loved her like a daughter, don't you?" Richard asked. There were tears in his eyes too, she realised. Nancy sniffed. It was true. She looked at Richard, thinking that he deserved to know the truth at last, and fearing that once he did, she would lose him forever.

"Sit down," she said. Richard, who had been kneeling on the floor beside her, heaved himself tiredly onto the sofa. "There's something you should know."

Richard regarded her quizzically. At that moment, Nancy had been sure she would tell him, but when she spoke, her words were a shock to them both.

"When all this is over, when they've found Amy's killer and he's safely behind bars, then we'll get married."

Chapter 4

Jim Neal was re-reading the medical report on the cause of Amy Hill's death. It contained no surprises, and only confirmed what was evident that bleak morning on the common; that she had been strangled to death.

Technically, Ava had been correct in saying that Amy's killer had snapped her like a twig, for the tiny hyoid bone in her neck had been crushed, the most likely cause being a ligature of some sort, tightened around the girl's throat by a man, or even a woman with enough strength to overpower the petite victim.

Ava Merry interrupted his thoughts, rapping impatiently on the glazed panel of his office door.

At his nod, she barged into the room, saying, "Foot soldiers have come up with a lead, sir. A girl answering to Amy Hill's description was seen outside the Odeon cinema at around ten forty-five on Saturday evening with a lad aged around eighteen to twenty years old with dark hair, black plastic-rimmed specs and a mild case of acne."

Before Neal had a chance to point out that half the town's student population would fit that description, Ava's smug expression gave her away.

"Do you know something I don't, Sergeant Merry?" he asked patiently, then listened, frowning as Ava described her impromptu meeting with Anna Foster and her son.

"Simon denied knowing Amy but the description fits. He could be Amy's stalker, sir. Predictably, your fancy woman shoved an alibi his way; claimed they were at her place sorting through some books on Saturday evening, but what mother wouldn't lie to protect her child?"

Neal let Ava's remark go without comment, but he cursed himself for his indiscretion in revealing his thoughts about Anna Foster in the café. It had been a tiny slip, but Merry was sharp, damn her. He was well aware of the speculation that went on at the station about his personal life, particularly amongst the female staff, and let it pass. He had two lives, and it was vital to his sense of balance that they remain separate.

Archie knew what his father did for a living and when he was younger he had often asked Neal to tell him stories about real-life criminals. Neal had told imaginary tales, sweetened versions of the real thing that would not give his son nightmares. Maggie often accused him of being over-protective, but he had seen enough of what happened to unprotected children to worry about damaging his son with too much kindness. And his sex life — or lack of it — was none of their damn business.

"Let's not leap ahead of ourselves, Sergeant," he said dryly, adding, "Find out where Simon Foster lives at the university. We need to question him as soon as possible. And while you're at it, see if you can find out anything about that other lad, Bradley Turner. We'll need to question him as well, and his father."

* * *

The complex of buildings that made up the new university campus and student village had sprouted up on former brownfield land, which in the city's past had been the site of a sizeable goods yard for railway freight, taking in disused railway sidings, warehouses and buildings that had long ago lapsed into various stages of dilapidation and disrepair. After a big clean-up operation that had included decontaminating the site and demolishing or renovating a substantial number of buildings, the whole southern aspect of the Stromford Pool area had been transformed. The area was now vibrant and modern; several of the new and renovated buildings had won prestigious awards for their daring design and architectural style. There were ambitious plans for sports facilities, a theatre and an arts centre.

Across the water, on the north bank of the Stromford Pool, (or the Marina, as the modest lake was increasingly referred to nowadays) restaurants, hotels and a new Cineplex had sprung up.

Many saw the regeneration of the area as a new golden era for the small city, an opportunity to reclaim some of the prestige and grandeur it had enjoyed in its glory days in Medieval times, when it had been a religious and commercial hub. Certainly the university was attracting private investment that would otherwise have passed the city by, enabling the planners to think big and long term.

Of course, there were others who were against the whole venture; who had seen the redevelopment as an abomination, but even they would sometimes now admit, albeit grudgingly, that on a good day, it fitted in well with the town's older and more prestigious edifices — the cathedral and castle to the north.

Stromford had been an important destination for tourists and visitors even before the coming of the University, thanks to its rich Roman and Medieval heritage. It had long been a site of significance. Archaeological remains confirmed its early importance in pre-Roman times as an iron-age settlement and capital for the Celtic tribe that inhabited the area at the time of the Roman invasion.

Neal remembered taking Archie to the city museum to see the canoes and other artefacts that had been hauled out of the silt along the banks of the River Strom, and how eager his son had been to touch and admire the skilfully crafted swords, daggers and shields of another age. Whichever way he looked, north or south of the river, Neal saw much to celebrate in his adopted city.

Neal and Ava parked in one of the university car parks and walked to the 'student village;' clusters of student residences, shops and eating-places that zigzagged along the south bank of the river. The residences were modern three or four storey buildings with recessed windows and blue and silver cladding, which harmonised pleasingly with the watery hues of the marina. Neal and Ava paused a moment outside Simon Foster's block to take in the view of the Pool; longboats, river cruisers and swans jostled for space on the crowded expanse of water where the river Strom broadened before narrowing again to wind through the city centre.

Simon Foster lived on the second floor of one of the newest residences, known as Cathedral; so new that as Neal and Ava entered the reception area, they almost collided with a group of surveyors and contractors in business suits and hard hats waiting for the lift.

As the group stepped into the lift, Ava hung back for a moment, then, seeing that Neal was following them, squeezed in last of all. The group of men, who had been discussing snagging on the roof in loud voices, fell silent and the atmosphere was suddenly charged with sexual tension.

No one was impolite enough to stare at Ava, but there was a lot of throat clearing, and the men looked around as though the walls of the lift were suddenly fascinating. Neal smiled inwardly, thinking how awkwardly men always behaved in the presence of an attractive woman.

If anything, Ava played down her looks on the job, preferring to dress in trainers or flat shoes, with jeans and casual jackets but as Neal had occasionally observed, she wasn't averse to using her looks to her advantage. Today, she was wearing a snug red cashmere sweater with skinny jeans tucked into knee length tan leather boots. Over the sweater, she was wearing a beige fur-lined gilet. Her blonde hair was swept back from her face and tied in a ponytail, loose strands tucked behind her ears. Ordinary enough, yet she looked stunning.

The lift jolted to a halt on the third floor and as they stepped out, all eyes turned to the window to admire the view of the Cathedral after which the residence had been named. Neal and Ava trod springy new carpeting down a long corridor until they came to Simon Foster's flat. Loud music boomed from within; Brandon Flowers singing about Mr Brightside. Ava began to sing and from the sound of it, at least three male voices inside the room were doing the same. The sound was ratcheted up for the chorus:

"Destiny is calling me
Open up my eager eyes
'Cause I'm Mr Brightside"

"God, Archie played this non-stop for weeks," Neal groaned.

"Reminds me of my student days, this place," Ava remarked.

Neal was aware that Ava had completed one and a half years of a degree course in London before opting for a career in the force. When questioned at her interview about why she abandoned her studies, Ava had replied that it was not because she was academically weak, nor was she the type of person who gave up easily, but she felt that what she was studying no longer had any relevance to her or to the world that she lived in, and that she had quite literally woken up one morning knowing exactly what she wanted to do with the rest of her life. Neal hadn't been convinced of this, but he had no worries about her conviction. In the interview, her enthusiasm — and naivety — had come across strongly. He recalled her saying that her reason for wanting to be a police officer was, 'so that she could make a difference.'

It had been different for Neal. At the age of eighteen he had received offers from all the best Scottish universities, and he'd had his sights set on a law degree. Becoming a policeman could not have been further from his thoughts, or desires. A year later he was a single father with a child to support, and his dreams of becoming a lawyer seemed suddenly extravagant.

As he had faced up to his responsibilities and embarked on the daily grind of earning a living as a policeman, there had been no time to mourn his bankrupt future. He had never expected to like the job, but gradually it had taken hold of him, and now he could barely remember a time when he had wished to do anything else. Nor had he missed out on his education; he had a first class Open University degree under his belt and was studying part time for a Masters in Criminology. And he had never regretted being a father. "Sorry. Time to stop the music," he said to Ava, rapping loudly on the door.

"Who is it?"

"Police. Open the door."

"Just a minute!"

Neal and Ava exchanged glances. "I expect they're tidying up for us, sir," Ava said, her tone ironic. Neal rolled his eyes.

"Come on lads. We haven't got all day," he called, impatiently. The door opened and they were invited in by a young man in black skinny jeans and a T-shirt bearing one of those slogans about keeping calm and carrying on.

"Good vibes boys," Ava commented as she stepped into the communal kitchen, which was surprisingly clean and tidy; so much for students' unsanitary living habits. There were no piles of unwashed dishes, no rubbish overflowing from the bin, and Neal was sure he could detect the faint odour of a chemical air freshener.

Two lads were seated at the kitchen table; another was turning the music off. The one who had answered the door looked Ava up and down and asked if they'd like a drink.

"We're on duty," Ava said, eyeing the half-empty bottle of scotch on the table.

"I meant a cup of tea," the lad said. Ava shook her head. She explained the reason for their visit.

"Sy's not here," one of the lads said.

"Your name is?" Ava asked.

"Ray Agorini." Ava wrote his name down and asked each of the others in turn for their names, jotting them all down in her notebook.

"Is Sy in some sort of trouble? "asked a gangly lad with a black goatee beard, who'd identified himself as Gary. As he spoke, he sat down abruptly, clearly attempting to cover an ashtray with his elbow, only succeeding in drawing attention to the burned-out end of a joint. Neal resisted the urge to sigh.

"It's alright. Your mate's not in any trouble, not at this stage anyway. We just want to ask him a few questions, that's all." Ava reassured them.

"This hasn't got something to do with that dead girl, has it?" asked one of the lads, called Ric.

"Amy Hill. Did you know her?" Neal asked. There was a collective shaking of heads.

"Are you sure, not even to look at?" asked Ava, flashing them a photo of Amy on her smartphone.

"I might have seen her around," said Gary, "she looks sort of familiar. This isn't a huge campus; you get to know people by sight."

"Yeah," she does look a bit familiar, probably seen her in the bar or somewhere," Ric agreed. After looking more closely at Amy's picture, the others agreed.

"What about Simon Foster. Did he know Amy?" Ava asked. They thought not, but no one knew for certain.

"Does Simon have a girlfriend, or has he mentioned recently that he's been seeing anyone?" Neal asked.

"There's girls he likes, same as all of us," Gary said, seeming embarrassed.

"Simon's kinda quiet, shy, you know," said Ray.

"I think he did like Amy," the fourth flat member, Dan, said, "like I was with him in the bar once and she was there with a group of friends. I asked him which one he fancied and he pointed Amy out." Dan looked at Ava as he spoke; blushing bright red, he added, "Funny thing was, he said he didn't like her *that* way."

"In what way do you think he did like her?" Neal asked, with a raised eyebrow.

Dan shrugged, "Dunno. Maybe he thought she was too good for him. Amy was hot."

The others nodded in agreement. Neal sighed.

"Which room is Simon's?" he asked. The lads looked at each other and Gary pointed down the hallway at a door on the left. Neal tried the handle and was unsurprised to find it locked.

"Are you going to kick the door in?" Dan asked, sounding excited.

"Sorry lads, that only happens in the movies," Ava answered, smiling, "The warden will have a master key. Much simpler."

Simon's flatmates could offer no further information. They seemed relieved when Neal nodded to Ava that it was time to leave. He did not need to look back to know that all four lads had their eyes on Ava's backside as she walked down the hallway towards the door.

"Has Simon done a runner, do you think?" Ava asked as they made their way to the car park. Neal shrugged.

"Probably keeping a low profile. He must know he would have been spotted with Amy on Saturday evening."

They reached the car and Ava slipped into the driver's seat. "I take it we're going to pay Anna Foster a visit?" she asked, putting the car into gear and barely waiting for an answer before heading towards the Turning Leaves Bookshop.

* * *

When Neal and Ava walked through the front door, Anna Foster was busy at her desk in a draught-protected alcove behind the entrance to her bookshop, tapping busily on her keyboard. Was it his imagination, or did she seem displeased to see them? Neal came straight to the point.

"My son doesn't live here, Inspector," Anna Foster replied in answer to Neal's enquiry concerning Simon's whereabouts. "Yes, this is his home and he has a room here, and he occasionally stays over, but we both agreed it would be good for him to be with people his own age when he went to university. No doubt at this time of day, he'll be hard at work in the library. He's very studious. He's exceptional, in fact." An image of the young man Ava had described flashed into Neal's mind. There didn't seem to be anything particularly exceptional about him. Clearly Anna Foster was a besotted mother. Neal smiled at this, for of course, in his eyes Archie was the most exceptional young man he had ever met.

He cleared his throat. He had been looking steadily at Anna Foster as she spoke and his professional detachment had begun to slip. Today her auburn hair was loose about her shoulders and she was wearing wide black linen trousers and a silky blouse in a floaty material that was practically see-through. If there was a type Neal preferred, Anna Foster fit the profile. There was the small matter of the age difference between them, which he thought might be as much as ten years, but was that really an issue?

"When did you last see your son, Ms Foster?" Neal enquired, after explaining that they had checked the university library and Simon's flat.

"On Monday evening." Anna turned to Ava. "We had supper at a bistro on the long hill after we bumped into

41

you, Sergeant, and afterwards Simon went back to his flat at the university. I'm stocktaking this evening; he's supposed to be coming by to give me a hand."

"Is he often out of touch for this long?" Neal asked.

"This long? It's barely been a day, Inspector. Simon's a student; he has his own life. I don't expect him to check in with me every day. "

"But he does work for you?" Neal prompted.

"On an informal basis. Simon loves books; he likes to help out. And of course he finds the money useful, although I think he'd help out even if I didn't pay him; he's that kind of person."

Again, that glowing maternal admiration and pride. Neal wondered how objective Anna Foster was capable of being when it came to her son. Probably about as objective as he was about Archie.

"Why are you so interested in Simon? Do you think he's got something to do with Amy Hill's murder? I've already told Sergeant Merry that Simon was with me on Saturday evening."

Neal dropped his bombshell, in the gentlest of tones; his eyes followed Anna Foster's reaction closely.

"Ms Foster. A young man answering to your son's description was seen outside the Odeon cinema with Amy Hill at approximately ten forty-five on the night of her murder. Please think carefully before reaffirming that Simon did indeed spend the entire evening with you."

Anna Foster paled visibly but she answered without hesitation. "It wasn't Simon. It couldn't have been. He was with me all evening. We were going through the books from the library sale."

Neal nodded solemnly. His sergeant made a noise that sounded like a snort hastily disguised as a cough. *Need to have a word with her about that*, Neal thought, irritably.

"Is it possible Simon may be staying with family or friends?"

42

"Simon doesn't have any other family." Anna fidgeted with her mouse lifting it slightly off the mat and replacing it, an action that she repeated several times, before standing up and confronting them.

"Simon is my adopted son. His birth mother is dead," she said, flatly. "His father is . . . he's inside."

"He's in prison?" asked Ava, surprised.

"He's doing life for murder."

"For killing Simon's mother?" Neal asked, taking a leap.

"Beat her and left her for dead. Simon's sister, Emily, disappeared and his father, Wade Bolan, was accused of killing her and hiding the body."

"And Simon, how did he escape?" Neal asked.

"He was hiding in a wardrobe in his mother's bedroom. No one is sure how much he witnessed. He doesn't remember anything about it."

"How old was he when you adopted him?" Neal asked, gently.

"He was six. He was fostered for a while after the tragedy. I already knew him from when his class visited the library I worked in, and I had always been quite taken with him. He was a very bright child, eager for books. His teacher told me he'd been taken into care because there was no other family to offer him a home, so I made some enquiries."

"It can't have been easy, taking on a child from such a background," Neal remarked.

"Simon's behaviour was sometimes . . . difficult. Challenging I suppose is the politically correct term now, but his intelligence helped him overcome a lot of his problems."

"That, and your care and influence I would imagine."

Anna Foster coloured faintly at Neal's compliment. "He was easy to love, Inspector," she said in a whisper, her eyes clouding over as she gazed at her computer screen to avoid looking at Neal or Ava.

43

Neal dared not look at Ava. He had a lump in his throat. Was she aware that Archie was his Achilles heel? That, because of Archie, he could not bear the thought of any child being neglected or abused?

"Thank you for your time, Ms Foster." Neal said. After a pause, he added, "Contact us immediately if Simon gets in touch. We need to talk to him as soon as possible."

"I know," Anna whispered tearfully, "but you'll be wasting your time. Simon didn't kill Amy Hill." This time she did not reiterate her claim that Simon had been with her the night Amy died. Even Anna Foster must have realised that to repeat it would have sounded like desperation.

* * *

"What did you make of that?" Neal asked Ava as they walked back up the cobblestones towards the car park.

"I think she's lying about the alibi," Ava replied.

"A hunch?"

"You can call it that. But I think she'd say anything to protect Simon."

"It's a rare parent who can believe ill of their own child," Neal admitted. "My guess is she doesn't know what to think and she doesn't want to betray Simon by believing the worst. One thing's for sure, we need to speak to him. He might be the last person to see Amy alive, with the exception of her killer, of course."

"Looks bad for him, though, doesn't it, sir, the longer he stays missing?"

Neal didn't answer, and not just because the question was rhetorical; he hoped, for Anna Foster's sake, that Simon would turn up to help his mother with her stocktaking.

Chapter 5

"You're just in time," Maggie smiled, standing up to allow her brother to slide into the seat beside her in the spectator's gallery. Archie was competing in a swimming gala, and Neal was grateful to have a good view of the pool.

He kissed his sister on the cheek, "All down to Ava," he explained, a little embarrassed.

"Took some liberties with police privilege, did she?" Maggie said.

"Something like that," replied Neal, thinking of the hairy drive to the leisure centre, with Ava negotiating the rush hour traffic at breakneck speed, red light flashing, siren blaring. It really wasn't acceptable, but then again, he had told Archie he'd be there in time to see him compete in his heats.

"Look Jim, he's waving to you."

Neal looked in the direction Maggie was pointing and saw his son standing in the middle of a row of small boys shivering by the poolside. Archie was waving wildly, grinning all over his face. Neal waved back, commenting to Maggie, "He's too skinny."

Maggie shook her head. "Crap. He's just as he should be. Probably grow up long and lanky like his dad." She nodded towards the diving pool, and remarked; "Now that's what I call skinny."

A young girl was poised on the edge of the top diving board, arms stretched above her head, elongating her skeletal frame. She bent her knees then straightened, bouncing lightly on the board before launching into the air.

"She'll drift like a feather," Maggie said, watching as the girl turned a somersault before straightening her body to enter the water gracefully. Neal scarcely heard Maggie's remark. He had not taken his eyes off the girl as she executed her perfect dive, and he leaned forward in his seat watching as she resurfaced and swam to the edge of the diving pool in three long strokes. At that point, his interest deepened for she was helped out of the pool by a young man dressed in the yellow polo shirt and black shorts worn by the centre's lifeguards.

The young lifeguard slipped an arm around Becci Jones's wisp of a waist and kissed her. It was Gary Reed, one of Simon Foster's flatmates, whom he'd interviewed that morning. Neal raised an eyebrow. If Becci and Gary were an item, then how come Gary had claimed not to know Amy? Surely he would have known his girlfriend's best friend and flatmate by more than sight, as he claimed? Neal sat back in his seat, contemplating, his eyes on the row of coloured flags fluttering across the shallow end of the pool above the line-up of eager young boys poised to dive, one of whom was Archie. Then the race began and Neal put all other thoughts out of his head as he cheered himself hoarse throughout his son's heats.

* * *

The following morning, an excited Detective Sergeant Merry greeted Neal by thrusting a letter into his hand before he'd even removed his coat.

"What do you make of it?" she demanded before he'd even had a chance to finish perusing the contents.

"So who is this Professor Taylor?" Neal asked, confident that, even though the letter had just been received in that morning's post, Ava would have done her homework already.

"Christopher Taylor. Lecturer in English at the university. He's been there just over a year. Did his PhD on some poncy English Lit. topic that no one would have the slightest interest in reading. He's thirty-three years old. Did his first degree at Sheffield. Taught English as a second language whilst completing his doctorate.

"He's got a clean record, not so much as a parking ticket. It's not a criminal offence to have an affair with your student, though I doubt the uni encourages such relationships, particularly when the age difference is so marked. Probably regards it as unprofessional. Would be a bit like you going out with a sixth former."

Ava's enthusiasm seemed to be dissipating as she spoke, "Maybe it doesn't amount to much anyway. Probably just a spiteful letter from someone who was jealous of their relationship."

"Whoever wrote this letter thinks it important," Neal said, holding the sheet of paper in front of him, an anonymous note stating that Amy Hill had been having a relationship with her English professor.

"Let's see if forensics can tell us anything about it. And add Taylor to our list of interviewees," Neal answered.

"How did Archie get on last night?" Ava asked.

"He came third," Neal answered, no hint of disappointment in his voice. "He was gutted. Maggie and I were ecstatic, of course. "

He told Merry about Becci and Gary. "Gary claimed he didn't know Amy, yet she shared a flat with his girlfriend."

"It's possible he never visited Becci at Beech Road. Depends how long they've been together, I suppose." Ava remarked. "Did they seem like a well-established couple?

47

Neal stared at her. "Why would he lie?" Ava asked. "That's assuming he did lie, of course. Was it to dissociate himself from the whole affair, or to protect his girlfriend, perhaps?"

"What could Becci Jones need protecting from? Besides he must have known we'd already questioned her," Neal answered. "We'll need to speak to both of them again, as well as this Professor Taylor."

* * *

Life was looking rosy for Christopher Taylor. Still only in his early thirties, he had completed his PhD and gained an appointment at a university which, if not in the same class as the prestigious Russell Group, was rising steadily in the league tables. Not bad for a boy who had grown up without a book in the house and whose father had told him the only higher education he was ever likely to receive was in the University of Life.

It wasn't that his parents hadn't wished him to do well; it was simply that they did not see education as a priority. Christopher had had to fight long and hard to persuade them that he was not cut out for life as a plumber; one of the promises he made in return for the privilege of being allowed to stay on at school was that he would work in his father's business during the holidays, to earn his keep and learn a bit about the trade. Perhaps they thought learning a trade would stand him in good stead should he suddenly come to his senses and realise that university wasn't for the likes of him.

Putting in time as his dad's apprentice had been purgatory and a monumental waste, but at least he didn't have to spend a fortune in call-out charges whenever he had a leaking tap. He prided himself on being a man who could turn his hand to most jobs around the house.

Pride was one of Christopher Taylor's less agreeable attributes. He was proud of his achievements and proud of his appearance, and proud of the fact that women seemed to find him irresistible.

"'Ark at him," his mum used to say, "thinks 'e's God's gift," but Christopher could hear the pride in his mother's voice overriding her attempt at sarcasm. Most recently, he was proud of the publication of his first novel, which he did not doubt would propel him onto the bestseller list in no time.

Of course life had not always been a bed of roses. There was the bullying he had endured at school for instance, the price he had had to pay for having aspirations that were not in keeping with those of his peers. His left cheek still bore a scar from the wrong end of a broken bottle thrust into his face in a fight with a former 'best mate' who didn't appreciate that Chris Taylor was no longer one of the lads. He had left the lads far behind; nowadays the scar was embedded in designer stubble and, if anything, enhanced his sexual allure.

Then there had been the tedious English teaching he had done to support himself through his years of postgraduate study, mostly with Asian immigrants, in that grotty community centre in Sheffield. And that ugly business with the daughter of one of his students. No-one had been able to prove anything, of course, he had been much too careful for that, but it was something in his life he had less cause to be proud of, if only because it put his other achievements in jeopardy. He had been much more careful the next time.

He would have to be careful now, he thought, looking down from the window of his mews townhouse in the fashionable uphill area of town, five minutes' walk away from the cathedral, at the two police officers making their way towards him. His let his eyes linger on the woman. Who wouldn't? If he hadn't been expecting them he would never have taken her for a copper, though of course the only policewomen he could call to mind were the stern and sour PCs who had pulled him up for minor traffic violations. A mixture of good looks and charm had stood him in good stead then, but this woman might prove to be less susceptible.

She was limping, he noticed. He also noticed the way in which her companion walked close by her, close enough to steady her if she stumbled, and that told him a lot about the kind of man he was. The fact that she seemed unaware of this told him something about her too. Or did it tell him more about the relationship between them?

* * *

Neal and Ava were unaware that they were being appraised. Ava was concentrating on walking over the uneven road surface to the pavement. Her foot was throbbing from pressing on the foot pedals, but she had insisted on driving.

"Bloody road works," she moaned, "why can't they leave a flat surface and clear away more of those bloody pebbles?"

Neal didn't comment. He had given up suggesting that Ava see a proper doctor about her intermittent problems with her foot. She had claimed she had seen, 'a herbal bloke,' who worked wonders with sports injuries, but there was scant evidence that his wonders were working for Ava.

"Nice view," she remarked, turning back for a moment to check on the car, and give her foot a rest before tackling the stairs leading up to Taylor's house. Behind them, beyond the parking spaces, the ground sloped away in an expanse of grassy wasteland ending in a string of regimented allotments. The view that Merry was referring to lay in the middle and far distance: the newly named marina and the university buildings; the South Common swollen with pools of floodwater sprawling out to where the city ended abruptly, as small cities do, in the surrounding countryside.

Directly in front of them, a short slope up from the pavement, was Christopher Taylor's smart town house.

The main entrance was via a highly varnished maroon door to the left of the garage. Above the garage was a terrace featuring a cluster of empty, weathered terracotta pots behind newly painted white wrought iron railings. Patio doors overlooked the balcony, offering a glimpse of the room beyond.

Taylor answered his doorbell — an annoying rendition of the 'Charge of the Light Brigade' — promptly, and ushered them into a narrow hallway with an eye-tricking zig-zag Escher runner.

"We'll go upstairs," he said breezily, "there's only the kitchen and a cloakroom down here."

Ava gazed down at her foot and rolled her eyes.

"My apologies for the mess," Taylor said, as he opened the door into his spotless living area, "I've been working."

The light-filled room that he led them into was impeccably tidy, except for a scattering of papers and books around a computer table near the patio doors. Evidently, the professor liked to admire the view whilst working.

The room had a Mediterranean feel: pale blue walls and a tiled floor, white furnishings and rugs in sunny colours.

In summer, the pots on the balcony were probably bursting with geraniums. Christopher Taylor's heart obviously yearned for climes much further south, and Ava, appraising his blonde good looks and honed physique, had no trouble picturing him somewhere Greek and Olympian.

"To tell you the truth I was a little taken aback when you called and asked to interview me," Taylor said, addressing Ava. "I really don't see that I can be of much help. I was one of Amy Hill's lecturers, that's all."

"Is that right?" Ava said coolly, "we've heard differently."

"Really? From whom?"

Ava glanced at Neal. She could hardly cite an anonymous letter as her source.

"Sergeant?" Taylor prompted.

"That's not your concern. The point is your name has been connected with Amy Hill's." Neal's voice filled the awkward silence.

"In what way?" asked Taylor.

"You tell us," Ava replied.

Taylor removed the fine taupe cashmere sweater that had been draped around his shoulders and slung it casually over the back of the nearest chair. He was wearing a light blue chambray shirt and slim fit navy chinos that flattered his trim waist and long legs. For a moment he stood, hand on hip as if inviting them to admire his model good looks, oozing charm and elegance. It was all Ava could do to keep her mind on the job. But she guessed that his mind was turning somersaults, calculating, wondering how much they knew. How much he could get off without saying. The truth was, they had nothing on him.

"I was aware that Amy had a bit of a crush on me," Taylor said, "a lot of my female students do, you know. It's not something I encourage, of course."

I bet you don't, Ava thought cynically. "Meaning?" she asked politely.

"Meaning, Sergeant Merry, that I don't make a practice of becoming romantically involved with my students." He looked Ava up and down. "Besides, she wasn't my type."

It's a curse, Ava thought, that blushing is a reflex virtually impossible to control. In addition to colouring, she felt hot and prickly all over as though she were an animal whose hackles were rising in warning, or was it something else — a spark of sexual attraction? Was she really so shallow as to be flattered by the attentions of the demi-god that was Professor Christopher Taylor? Warning bells sounded; she couldn't afford to let him gain the upper hand by submitting so readily to his animal magnetism.

Before she could take control of the situation, Taylor said,

"I couldn't help noticing that you're limping, Sergeant. Why don't you sit down and take the weight off that foot? I suggest you prop your leg up on my coffee table." He gestured in the direction of a sumptuous leather sofa.

Ava was flustered. Is this how he had impressed Amy Hill, turning on the charm until she couldn't help but succumb?

The thought brought Ava rudely back to her senses, but before she could speak, she heard Neal say, in what was, even for him, a dry Scottish accent,

"Did anything happen between you and Amy?"

"She was a very persistent young woman, Inspector, and disingenuous. She came to me saying that her friends had made a bet that she wouldn't be able to persuade me to join them at their flat for dinner. To save her from losing face, I agreed, thinking there would be three other girls present. It wasn't a date."

"Amy invited me to dinner with the friends who had made the bet. At their flat. She said it was to be like some reality TV show, where a group of people entertain a celebrity for the evening."

"And that appealed to your vanity, did it?" Ava asked, released now, from the charm of Christopher Taylor's spell.

For the first time since their arrival, Taylor seemed ruffled. He gave every impression of being affronted.

"Hardly, Sergeant. The thought of spending an evening in the company of a bunch of not particularly bright undergraduates was less than appealing. As it turned out, it was a trick. She was alone when I arrived. I should have guessed. Amy had invented the whole story to lure me to her flat. It was most embarrassing. Amy answered the door dressed somewhat provocatively. I could tell immediately that there was no-one else at home."

"So you extricated yourself from the situation, leaving Amy in no doubt that you didn't approve of her attempt to seduce you? " Neal asked.

"Of course, Inspector. What else would I do?"

"May I ask what you were doing on the night of the twenty eighth of October, Professor?"

Taylor's answer was immediate. No doubt he had anticipated the question.

"I was at the theatre with a group of students. We'd travelled to London to see a production of King Lear at the Globe. We stayed overnight at a Premier Inn near King's Cross and returned to Stromford the following morning."

Taylor looked at his watch. "Was there anything else you wanted to ask me?" he said, looking at Neal, "only I have to give a lecture in forty minutes." Turning to Ava, he added, "On the Romantic poets."

"Never liked that lot," she said, dismissively, "all that crap about lonely clouds and daffodils sent me to sleep at school."

"Then you must have had a poor teacher, Sergeant."

Taylor gathered up some papers from his desk and zipped them into a leather folder. He accompanied them downstairs and out the door. His remote garage door opened up to reveal, predictably, a flashy red Porsche. The university was only ten minutes' walk away.

As Ava and Neal approached their modest Ford Escort, Ava veered in the direction of the driver's side, but Neal cut in front of her abruptly, saying, "I'll drive. You should keep your weight off that foot."

For once, Ava didn't object. As she bent to slip into the passenger seat, she caught Taylor's eye; he nodded at her and a lock of blonde hair fell over his forehead. He tucked it back slowly, seductively, never taking his eyes off her. Ava matched him stare for stare, managing, she hoped, to conceal the discomfort he aroused in her, with a look of professional detachment.

"Arrogant bastard," Neal said as he pulled out of the parking space.

"Good-looking arrogant bastard," Ava remarked.

"Not my type," Neal answered and they both laughed. Then, on a more serious note, he added, "Make sure his alibi checks out."

"I'm on it, boss."

Chapter 6

Richard Turner had been taken aback by Nancy Hill's sudden proposal. Considering the circumstances, he was not convinced that Nancy meant what she had said. She was in that state of mind that lay somewhere between shock and grief, and Richard was not the kind of man to take advantage of her vulnerability by allowing her to commit herself to a course of action she might later regret. He had permitted himself a moment's elation, before going on to reassure her kindly but firmly that he would be glad to accept her proposal, but not yet.

To his disappointment, Nancy had seemed to accept his reply with indifference; she seemed relieved almost, and he wondered whether he had just lost his one chance of marrying the woman he had loved for the better part of eight years.

To make matters worse, another thought nagged at Richard; it had occurred to him that Nancy's relief might have been because she had not meant to make the proposal at all, that she had been on the verge of making some other revelation and had blurted the words out as a kind of compensatory afterthought.

Richard had long suspected that there were secrets Nancy kept from him. It wasn't anything she said, but rather what she left out, as though her life before her arrival in Shelton had been lived in some other country. She was always particularly reticent about Amy's father.

In a literal sense, part of Nancy's past *had* been played out in another country. Amy's father was a backpacker, and Amy the product of a promiscuous period in Nancy's life, after she had left foster care and gone travelling 'to find herself.'

What she had found, upon her return, was that she was pregnant. For some reason, she had concealed her pregnancy and given birth alone, revealing Amy's existence only months afterwards when she realised she needed to register her daughter's birth.

Richard's attempts to uncover the finer details of the story were met with evasiveness, and even hostility, a clear warning not to pry any deeper. He had learned to accept this; otherwise he might have lost her.

Richard Turner knew very well what it was like to lose those you love. After fifteen years of marriage, his wife had left him for another man who had two children of his own, taking with her their son and daughter. Richard had felt their loss as a physical pain, and then his daughter Julia, on reaching the age of sixteen, had declared she'd had enough of her 'new family,' and returned to Shelton to live with him.

Richard couldn't claim to have been a father to Amy, and he acknowledged this with some regret. It was not that he couldn't love another man's child, nor was he fearful of displacing his own children by loving someone else's, for he possessed the strength of character and, perhaps more unusually for a man, enough sensitivity to deal with these kinds of emotional complexities.

If Richard had been prevented from being a father to Amy, it was for the same reason as his failure to be a husband to the woman he loved; Nancy's resistance. She kept him at a distance, never allowing him to be her equal in Amy's affections, as though she were afraid that including another person would eclipse her position at the centre of Amy's universe. Amy had once called him 'daddy,' only to be admonished by Nancy. He had accused her of denying Amy the father she so obviously needed and wanted.

To his surprise Nancy had agreed with him, and begged him to accept things as they were. So Richard had let it go. Their arguments were all now in the past, but as he held Nancy in her grief, sad too on his own account, Richard knew that Amy's death changed everything. However painful it might be for Nancy, he now needed to know the truth.

* * *

Amy Hill's funeral service was held at the fourteenth century church in the village that Nancy had brought her tiny daughter to seventeen years previously. Richard Turner had noted the presence of a number of young people, and was grateful, knowing that it would be a comfort to Nancy to know that her daughter's friends had come to pay their last respects, even if at that moment she was unaware of anything around her.

He was grateful too, for the presence of his son and daughter. Julia had cried when she heard the news of Amy's death. Whenever his children came to stay, usually during the school holidays, Julia and Amy had played together companionably enough, though never becoming, as he had once hoped, as close as sisters. Of the two, Julia was the more level-headed, the *kinder*, Richard believed, thinking of all the times when Amy had got Julia into trouble, or allowed Julia to take the blame for her misdeeds.

Bradley was another matter. He and Amy had been close as children, but Bradley's feelings for Amy had changed, and he had been unable to accept that they were not reciprocated. After that, the special relationship they had always enjoyed was irretrievably lost, so much so that on a recent visit to see his father, Bradley had not even bothered to look Amy up.

A smaller group escorted Amy's coffin down the sloping path of uneven flagstones, dangerously slippery with the soggy remains of lingering autumn leaves, to the spot where she was to be laid to rest. It lay on the other side of a beck that cut the graveyard in two, effectively separating old graves from new.

As the coffin was lowered into its black hole, Richard gave up all pretence of being strong for Nancy's sake and wept openly, matching his lover's grief, sob for racking sob.

When the gravediggers began shovelling earth onto Amy's coffin, Richard, stoic again after his lapse, led his family back up the path to the village pub where refreshments were waiting for those with the heart or stomach to eat.

* * *

That night, as he drew the curtains in Nancy's bedroom, he stood for a moment at the window and watched the rain battering against the glass, thinking of Amy's frail, broken body lying in the saturated ground of the south common. Sadly, he turned away and crossed the room to sit on the end of his lover's bed and began unbuttoning his shirt. He had already removed his black suit trousers and hung them in Nancy's wardrobe, the one he had made himself five or six years ago, saying he needed somewhere to hang the clothes he left at her house. Nancy had protested at first, no doubt concerned that he was trying to move in by the back door, even though the room already contained so many of his clothes.

The history of their relationship was peppered with such absurdities. Some weeks Richard would spend every night at Nancy's house, and then Nancy would insist that he go home for a couple of nights.

"My home is with you. We both know it," he told her often, and Nancy had never denied it. To please her he had gone home, slept alone for a couple of nights in his cottage that reminded him of his unhappy life with his ex-wife, and waited for Nancy to call. Amy had been dead for five days. Tonight was his sixth night in Nancy's cottage. She had not yet asked him to leave.

Richard removed his socks and joined Nancy in bed. He said, quietly,

"Bradley was very upset."

For a moment he thought that Nancy was asleep, for she made no comment, and no sound came from where she lay curled up under the patchwork quilt, one of many she had made herself. This particular one was a favourite of his, made from scraps of material in autumnal colours, shades of brown, russet, gold and ochre. "Nancy?" he whispered, "Love?"

"I'm alright," she answered.

"I was just saying . . ."

"I heard what you said."

"He loved her like a sister."

Nancy sat bolt upright in bed. Without her make-up she looked very similar to Richard. This was one of the things that he loved about her, her naturalness. But tonight there was something else about her features. It was not simply the red and swollen signs of prolonged crying that had transformed her face. There was a hardness that had not been there before, as though all the strength she had mustered to steel herself against her loss had robbed her of some part of her humanity. Richard hoped that this was a temporary change, that time and resignation would soften his lover's features and restore the face of the woman he loved.

"Don't ever use that word in connection with Bradley and my daughter again."

60

The vehemence in Nancy's tone took Richard by surprise. He wanted to stick up for his son, to protest that Bradley really had loved Amy, but Nancy's hostile look warned him off.

"Why doesn't she love me, Dad?" Richard had had no answer to give his seventeen-year-old son three years ago, when Bradley had pleaded with him to persuade Amy to take him seriously.

Try as he might, he could not convince Bradley that his pursuit of Amy was doomed to failure. Bradley had been smitten the previous summer, and could not be persuaded that she had no romantic feelings for him. He had experienced this as a kind of epiphany over the breakfast table one morning as he was tucking into a bowl of cornflakes.

Looking up sleepily from his cereal bowl, he had suddenly truly 'noticed' Amy for the first time. He watched her stir sugar slowly into her coffee cup and wipe a crumb of toast lazily from her bottom lip, the fullness of which he had been quite unaware of until that moment. He had been so smitten that his heart had quite literally missed a beat. Or so he claimed when he described the moment to his father.

If Richard could have foreseen the consequences of what became his son's obsession, he would have taken Bradley more seriously from the start. As it was, Bradley's behaviour had almost cost Richard his relationship with the woman he loved; he had defended his son at the time out of a sense of paternal loyalty, instead of facing the truth. Nancy's forgiveness had been hard won. Richard hoped fervently that the earlier unsavoury incident in the pub involving his son had not soured their relationship once more.

"I'm sorry," he whispered.

Nancy had settled down again and pulled the bedclothes over her head. Evidently she was not in a forgiving mood tonight.

* * *

In her chilly flat above the bookshop on the Long Hill, Anna Foster considered the events of the day. At the funeral service she had sat in the row behind Nancy, resisting the urge to lean forward and give her friend's shoulder a supportive squeeze. Nancy was sitting between Richard Turner and his daughter Julia, both of whom had slipped an arm around her waist. Without their presence, Nancy looked like she might have crumpled with the weight of her sorrow.

After the service, outside in the churchyard, Anna had lingered by Amy's graveside after the family had left, needing to distance herself for a moment from her friend's distress. She bent to read the sad farewells written on the cards on the wreaths laid out ready to be placed upon Amy's grave, wondering how Nancy could bear her loss. Not surprisingly, Simon was uppermost in her thoughts. He had been missing for five days now. What if something had happened to him too? She steered her thoughts away from the myriad possibilities because nearly all of them were unthinkable. Anna shuddered, looking around her, wondering where her son was, wishing he was with her.

"You alright love?" one of the gravediggers asked. It was an absurd, if well intentioned, question to ask a mourner by a graveside, but Anna smiled and replied that yes, she was fine, feeling guilty that the tears she was shedding were not for Amy.

She had been invited to a post-burial lunch at the village pub, The Black Horse. Hoping that Nancy might appreciate her presence there, she made her way out of the church grounds to the village green where the Black Horse door was propped open to welcome the funeral party. How long would it be before Nancy got to know that the police wanted Simon for questioning? Anna wondered, thinking that she should offer her friend comfort now, while it would still be accepted.

The old-fashioned interior of the seventeenth century inn felt momentarily warm and welcoming, before the subdued atmosphere hit Anna and became oppressive. The tall, dark detective and his attractive sergeant had attended the funeral and Anna spotted them sitting in an alcove near the bar. She slipped past them to the buffet where she concentrated on filling her plate and glancing unnoticed, she hoped, in their direction.

Inspector Neal was a handsome man, she thought, estimating him to be in his early thirties. He was tucking into a plate of sandwiches and a pint of beer. Beside him, Sergeant Merry was picking at a salad. Their heads were close together as they talked, but Anna could tell that they were watching the mourners closely, and she was careful not to catch their eye.

Nancy was sitting with her partner and his two children, Julia and Bradley. Anna recognised them from photographs Nancy had shown her of Julia's graduation the year before. She studied Bradley for a moment, noting how distressed he was. Hadn't Nancy told her that Bradley once had a crush on Amy? One that had bordered on the obsessive and had led to some unpleasantness? At least that's what Nancy had hinted. Anna had had the impression that there was more to it and, watching them now, she wondered again what Bradley had done for Nancy to seem so impervious to his grief.

A thought struck her suddenly; Bradley might actually qualify as a suspect. What if he had harboured feelings of rejection and loss that turned to rage? Was his grief genuine or did he have a terrible secret eating away at him, the expression of which had nothing at all to do with grief and everything to do with fear that he might be found out, particularly as the police were practically on top of him. Neal and the sergeant were eager to question Simon. Had they even considered that Amy's killer could be sitting not ten feet away from them at that very moment?

Anna was suddenly desperate to alert Inspector Neal to this possibility. She looked in his direction, but instead of catching Neal's eye, she attracted Julia Turner's. Anna reddened, fearing that Julia had somehow read her thoughts.

"Come and join us," Julia beckoned, sidling up closer to her father to make room for Anna.

"Thank you," Anna said, joining the solemn family group at their table. Nancy gave her a wan smile, Bradley was staring down at his half lager; Anna sensed an atmosphere.

"Thank you for coming," Nancy said, "You're a good friend."

For a few moments they talked in a desultory way about the turnout at the church service, the beautiful flowers, the impressive buffet, the weather, which was the same as it had been for weeks now, wet and miserable and becoming colder by the day. No one mentioned Amy.

Then, Nancy fell silent and Anna chatted with Julia, who seemed gentle and open, like her father. She was a pretty girl with waist-length strawberry blonde hair, pale, freckled skin and blue eyes which had a definitive limbic ring. Beautiful in an off-kilter way, as her nose was slightly too long, her lips not quite full enough, her face not perfectly shaped, but everything combined to create a look that was attractive and memorable. Sometimes, Anna thought, women who have faces that are too perfect are easily forgotten.

They began to talk about Amy, and Julia described how she and Amy had met as ten-year-olds, when Richard started seeing Nancy. It seemed to Anna that Julia was being circumspect, glancing at Nancy from time to time as she spoke, to see how her words were being received. As if she were holding back, Anna thought, trying not to speak ill of the dead. All the while, Bradley continued to stare morosely at his drink, contributing nothing. Once or twice

Anna thought she caught him flinching at the mention of Amy's name.

After a while, Bradley excused himself and went off to the 'gents'. He didn't return to their table, but joined a group of young people his own age, standing at the bar; Amy's friends, Anna surmised. Their voices had been getting increasingly loud, and every now and again there was a burst of laughter from their midst, followed by guilty shushing and subdued talking. Then the noise level would steadily rise again.

"Shall I ask them to leave, love?" Richard Turner asked Nancy, not noticing that his son had joined the group. Nancy shook her head.

"You'd think they'd know how to behave on an occasion like this," Julia remarked, "show some respect for Amy's family."

"They've had a skinful, I think," Anna observed. Glancing across at the group, she witnessed Bradley move closer to a plumpish young woman as if he meant to slip an arm around her ample waist. She hoped Nancy wouldn't see.

A moment or two later, a girl's shrill voice could be heard above the general chatter, "Get off me, you pervert!" All heads turned in time to see her fling the contents of her wine glass in Bradley's face.

"What the fuck? You little bitch!" a purple-faced Bradley gasped, stepping away from the girl and shaking wine out of his hair.

"He was touching me up!" the girl shrieked. Accusing eyes turned on Bradley who had pulled himself up to his full height and was now looming over the girl in a threatening manner.

A male member of the group stepped forward gallantly, with, "Take it easy, mate." Two more moved to support him, one of them grabbing Bradley's jacket by the lapels.

Anna moved out of the way quickly, as Richard Turner almost overturned their table in his haste to reach Bradley before his son had a chance to retaliate. He was beaten to the scene by Inspector Neal who quickly placed himself between the two lads, and the situation was speedily diffused. DS Merry led the girl away from the bar and spoke to her quietly, at a distance.

"What just happened here?" Neal asked, turning to Bradley.

"That little cow is crazy," Bradley responded, running his fingers through sticky wet hair and glaring at the girl.

"Bradley!" Richard Turner's voice seemed to freeze his son to the spot. It was very clearly a warning tone, and Bradley responded immediately, shrinking as if he had been struck by something much weightier than the sound of his name.

"I didn't touch her," he said in a low tone, "she's making it up, just like . . . just like . . ." his voice trailed off. Richard Turner glared at his son, and Bradley fell silent.

Jim Neal glanced across at his DS who was talking in quiet tones to the girl. Sergeant Merry looked back at him, shaking her head. Inspector Neal turned to Bradley and his father. Conversations gradually picked up where they had left off.

Anna heard DI Neal say to Richard, "Take your son home, Mr Turner. My colleague and I will be paying you a visit later to ask Bradley some questions."

Richard led Bradley to the door, pausing for a moment to apologise to Nancy for leaving so abruptly. Anna noticed the terrible loathing with which Nancy regarded the boy, and, glancing over at Inspector Neal, she saw that he too was observing Nancy intently, his brow furrowed in thought. There would be no need, after all, for her to give Neal or Sergeant Merry a nudge in Bradley's direction.

Not long afterwards the mourners began drifting away. Nancy refused Anna's offer to come home and sit with her, saying that Julia would stay for a while, so there was no real reason for Anna to insist. She returned to her shop, which, in Simon's absence, she had been obliged to close for the day, and spent the afternoon stocktaking.

* * *

Now it was gone midnight and she was chilled to the bone, as the store was without heating. Earlier in the week, her boiler had broken down and the repair service would not arrive until the following day. She made some hot chocolate and warmed her fingers on the cup as she drank, realising suddenly that she had had nothing to eat or drink since lunchtime at the Black Horse.

Whilst she waited for the kettle to boil for a second time to fill the hot water bottle that she meant to take to bed to warm her icy feet, Anna leaned over the sink to rub her condensed breath from the windowpane. Rain pattered against the glass, the sound now as familiar as her own breathing; and the night sky was still full of it.

A tear rolled down Anna's cheek. She longed to see Simon standing below on the pavement, fumbling in his pockets to find his keys. A sensation of dread, amounting to panic, threatened to overwhelm her. Ever since Simon had been handed into her care all those years ago, he had scarcely been out of her sight. How could she protect him now if she had no clue where he was?

With a stab of guilt, Anna acknowledged that rather than bear this uncertainty, she would even prefer to look down and see her son lying hurt on the pavement. At least then she could help him, the way she had helped him as a child when he came to her, damaged by his past. Sometimes, as he became more independent, she had entertained guilty fantasies about Simon becoming sick, or hurt, just enough to need her, enough to keep him safe from harm. Like an injured soldier, out of the fight for good.

In her bedroom, hugging her hot water bottle closely to her chest, Anna turned out her bedside light and lay awake in the darkness listening out for any sound that might mean that Simon had returned.

Chapter 7

"Nice place," Ava remarked to Neal as they pulled up outside Richard Turner's stone-built cottage on the outskirts of Shelton.

"Turner's a furniture-maker. Rents a unit with a small showroom attached in the industrial estate on the outskirts of the village. He's a craftsman — does bespoke pieces to order and restores old stuff for stately homes and the like. He's got a good reputation locally, and further afield, apparently."

Ava turned over the pages of her notebook. She had been researching Turner and his family, ahead of their visit.

"Both have clean records. Turner's ex-wife lives in Norfolk. They had joint custody of their children, Bradley and his sister, Julia, but for practical reasons, the kids spent most of their time with their mother until they were old enough to make up their own minds who to live with. Bradley's following in Dad's footsteps. Studying furniture design and restoration at a college in Sheffield; his sister's a trainee physiotherapist here in Stromford. Lived with Dad when she first moved here to do her training, but only for a few months, before moving into a place in town with her boyfriend who's a qualified physio at the county hospital. I've got someone in the Norfolk branch rooting around for information on Bradley's school record. Haven't got back to me with anything yet."

"Interesting that Turner and Nancy Hill don't live together. According to Anna Foster, they've been together for years," Neal said.

"Bit unusual," Ava agreed.

The front door of the cottage opened, and Richard Turner greeted them.

"Please come in, Officers. I'm sorry about that scene at the pub yesterday. Bradley had a bit too much to drink, I think, and lost control a bit. That, and he's upset about Amy, of course."

Neal nodded, "The girl isn't pressing charges," he said, watching Turner closely. The man's relief was as palpable as his surprise, causing Neal to suspect that Turner had expected a different outcome.

"She'd had a lot to drink and thought she might have been mistaken about Bradley groping her. She doesn't want to take it any further," Ava went on.

Richard Turner seemed like the sort of man who would have taught his children how to behave, Neal thought, but he also knew enough about criminal profiling never to make judgements when it came to parents and children. So far, his own son had not given him reason to worry, but who could tell what the future held? He'd seen it often enough — a much loved, well brought up child led astray by others or by their own nature. He was not naïve enough to think that good parenting alone was a safeguard against delinquent or aberrant behaviour.

Neal said, "We need to speak with Bradley, Mr Turner. On another matter, relating to Amy Hill."

"Bradley's in his room. I'll just fetch him for you. Please, bear in mind that Amy was like another sister to my son; he's been deeply affected by her murder, just like Julia and myself." He paused, as if uncertain whether to continue, "I sincerely hope you don't believe Bradley had anything to do with Amy's death, Officers?"

"We just need to ask him a few questions, Mr Turner," Neal repeated. Turner showed them into the lounge and closed the door behind him. They listened to the sound of his footsteps on the creaking stairs.

"Do you think he knows about Bradley making a nuisance of himself with Amy?" Ava asked. "He certainly seems sensitive about his son's behaviour. As though he's aware Bradley's no angel."

Bradley entered the room behind his father, looking sullen. He said, "Dad's already told me. I told you the little cow was lying," he said. Neal raised an eyebrow at Bradley's manners, and Richard Turner looked despairingly at his son. Neal imagined that he had given Bradley a pep talk before bringing him downstairs; evidently it had failed to penetrate.

"It's been brought to our attention that your feelings for Amy became more than brotherly," Neal said, a little provocatively. Predictably, Bradley became defensive.

Before he could reply, Turner interjected, "It's true that you had a bit of a crush on Amy, isn't it, Brad?" Turning to Neal and Merry, he added, "But that was a couple of years ago now and nothing ever came of it. Amy wasn't interested."

"Her loss," Bradley said, in a surly tone.

"Bradley, back in the pub, when you said that the young woman was, 'making it up,' you were about to say something else, but you were interrupted." Neal looked to Ava for confirmation, and she made a show of thumbing through her notebook.

"Here we go," she read, "you said, 'She's making it up, just like—'" Ava shrugged, "Just like who, Bradley?"

"I dunno," Bradley whined, "I don't even remember saying that."

"Was it Amy?" Neal asked, quietly, "Did Amy accuse you of behaving inappropriately towards her when you had a crush on her?"

"You what?" Bradley answered hotly, "Are you accusing me of murdering Amy, now?"

"Calm down, son, nobody's accusing you of anything," Neal said.

"I already told you, I don't remember what I said. I was . . . upset."

Angry, more like, Neal thought. He decided to change tack,

"I need to ask you both where you were the night Amy was murdered." At his words, Richard Turner sank down into a chair, looking like a man who'd just been kicked in the gut. "I'm sorry, Mr Turner. These are routine questions," Neal assured him gently. Turner made no reply. Either he was genuinely upset, or he was a very good actor. If he were to rely purely on instinct, Neal would have bet on the former, but he was well aware of all the unconscious prejudices and beliefs that could influence so-called intuition.

"Bradley?" Ava prompted.

"I was on a pub crawl with a mate, in Sheffield." Bradley muttered. "His name's Josh. He's my flatmate."

Ava nodded, jotting down the details.

"I didn't do it," Bradley said. "It wasn't me. And it wasn't Dad, either. You should stop wasting your time harassing innocent people and get on with catching whoever did kill Amy." His tone was petulant rather than hostile, but he also seemed nervous, as though he felt guilty about something. Glancing at Ava, Neal could see that she felt it too.

Richard Turner cleared his throat, "Brad. You might as well tell them about Amy. It's going to come out anyway." If looks could kill, Richard Turner's son would have been guilty of parricide at that moment.

"Bradley?" Neal said, "Care to elaborate?" Bradley, he could see, was seething. "Take a moment to gather your thoughts. As your dad says, if something happened between you and Amy, we'll find out one way or another, so you might as well come clean."

"There's nothing to tell. I fancied her; she wasn't interested, end of," Bradley muttered.

"How long did it take for you to get the message?" Neal asked, ignoring Bradley's scowl. "Were you pushy with her?" Bradley looked as though he was about to offer a vehement denial, but a nod from Richard Turner stopped him in his tracks. Perhaps, Neal reasoned, Bradley realised that if he didn't spill the beans, his father would.

"I might have been."

"How pushy? Did you stalk her? Did you make unwelcome advances?" Neal winced inwardly at the euphemism.

Bradley shrugged, "She might have thought I did."

"Ah," said Neal, "and you believe she was mistaken?"

Bradley looked at his father as if to ascertain how much he needed to reveal.

"I might have shoved her once," Bradley said in a low voice. Now they were getting somewhere.

"Because she wouldn't go out with you?" Ava asked.

Bradley glared at her, "Yes. And she made fun of me," he said.

There was silence for a few moments, filled by the sound of a grandfather clock chiming from the hallway. This elaborate piece, carved out of oak, had caught Neal's eye as they came in, because it reminded him of a clock in his grandparent's house when he was a boy; that always chimed the hour three minutes early. He resisted a sudden urge to check the time on his wristwatch.

The silence extended until after the last chime, as though the clock's deep, echoing sound had enchanted them all, forbidding speech. Neal broke the spell by asking how Amy had made fun of Bradley.

73

"She posted pictures of me on Facebook," Bradley said.

"I see," Neal said, thinking of Archie and the talks they had had about Internet safety. "I take it these pictures were not of a flattering nature?"

Bradley flushed crimson, telling him all he needed to know.

"When you said, 'I might have shoved her once,'" Ava quoted from her notebook again, "what exactly did you mean by that?" Another silence.

"Bradley?"

It was Richard Turner who answered. "He pushed her. Amy fell awkwardly and hit her head. She fractured her skull."

Bradley was staring at the carpet, an Axminster in a traditional design, which seemed to fascinate him so much he could not lift his eyes from it.

"I see," Neal said. "Were you a witness to this assault, Mr Turner?' Turner shook his head. "Did Amy report the assault?"

"Nancy wanted her to. I talked Amy out of it. She told the people at the hospital that she'd had an accident," Turner answered, "I was convinced that it was just that, a one-off, that Bradley hadn't really meant to hurt her." Neal wondered if Amy would have agreed.

"Did Nancy know you dissuaded Amy from pressing charges?" Ava asked.

"Not at the time," Turner said, "but she found out. Amy told her later. Nancy was so angry she nearly broke up with me."

"And was it a one off, Bradley? Did you ever hurt Amy again?"

"No. I didn't go near her. And it wasn't my fault she got hurt. Like Dad said, she fell awkwardly."

Neal could sense Richard Turner's discomfort at Bradley's lack of remorse. He thought of Amy's tiny body lying pressed into the muddy ground, where it had barely left an imprint. Bradley was easily six feet tall and heavyset. He wouldn't have needed to push very hard. Amy had sustained a serious injury, and Bradley's cowardly excuse that she had fallen awkwardly was repugnant. Richard Turner was hardly better, covering up for his son, making excuses. He was, perhaps, a good man, but a weak one.

A few more questions and they were done. Richard Turner had an alibi for the night of Amy's murder; he had been playing bridge with a group of friends, all of whom lived locally, so it would be easy enough to verify his claim.

"Thank you for your time," Neal said politely, as they left.

* * *

Outside it was drizzling, just for a change; a slice of washed out sunlight glowered behind the overhanging greyness of the afternoon sky, failing to make an impression.

"Bradley's a little shit." Ava commented, "Did you notice how reluctant he was to take any sort of responsibility for Amy's injury? He even went so far as to blame her for it."

"There's nothing little about him. He's twice Amy's size. Have his records at school and college checked out. I want to know if Amy really was a one-off. And while you're at it, have a look at Amy's Facebook page and see if you can find out what she put on there that incensed Bradley so much he felt obliged to 'push' her."

"Do you think he's capable of murder?" Ava asked. "Him, or Simon Foster, or Professor Taylor — who would you pick?"

"We don't pick and choose our suspects, Sergeant. We consider the evidence and make objective analyses based on facts."

"What about gut feelings, intuition? I know you have those."

"There's a theory that intuitions have their basis in experience or prior learning stored in our subconscious. I'd be worried about former experiences prejudicing present responses," Neal said. "Safer to stick to the facts. Do I take it that you've got a 'gut instinct' about this case?"

"My money would be on Christopher Taylor if it weren't for his perfect alibi. But, all things considered, I'll stick to the facts too, like you said."

* * *

Ava Merry left the station in the early evening, after a tedious afternoon spent chasing up Bradley's records. Academically, he had been an average student, behaviour-wise he had been no better or worse than his peers. His worst offence seemed to have been lifting up a girl's skirt at a school disco when he was fourteen, for which he had earned a two-week suspension. Not necessarily indicative of deviant sexual behaviour, but taken together with his treatment of Amy Hill, it might add up to something.

It was easy to see why the pictures Amy had placed on Facebook had enraged Bradley. They were, predictably, mildly obscene. Either Amy or someone she knew had a basic knowledge of Photoshop. Bradley had clearly been a victim of cyber-bullying. Looking at the images and reading their captions did nothing to give a positive impression of Amy's character, and reminded Ava of Anna Foster's negative comments about her treatment of Nancy. On the other hand, strangling someone in revenge for cyber-bullying was a wildly disproportionate response.

Ava's foot ached when she pressed down on the clutch on her drive home. She was relieved to pull into the drive leading to her rented stone cottage, one of a cluster of four that lay about three miles south of town. Set back from the road, a quarter of a mile down a country lane, and overshadowed by a small copse, it had been a tied cottage attached to a working farm that had once been large and prosperous, but was now a small, specialised business concerned with looking after a rare breed of sheep. Ava had had some reservations about moving out of town, particularly to such an isolated spot. Then she'd seen the property.

She had quite simply fallen in love with what the estate agent had described, with uncharacteristic restraint, as simply, 'a little gem.'

The property's littleness was, Ava supposed, what had brought it down to her price bracket, one of the two bedrooms being scarcely big enough to accommodate a single bed, and the second, the so-called 'master bedroom,' not much roomier. By the time Ava had fitted in her double divan and a small wardrobe, there wasn't much room left for anything else.

Downstairs was a bit more spacious, although there were only two rooms. The kitchen had been extended and was reached by an opening leading off her main living space, which was divided into a TV and comfort area on one side, and an office-come-dining area on the other. The strategic placing of her three-seater sofa effectively divided the room into a cosy and comfortable living space and a work/study area where Ava kept her computer, bookshelves and writing desk. Ikea and car boot sales had provided most of her furniture, and two colourful kilims ordered from a 'Fair Trade' catalogue added warmth to the grey flagstone floor. They had cost her practically a month's salary, but Ava considered that fair exchange for the years of pleasure looking at them would provide.

Outside, there was a long garden, fenced off from the woods at the bottom with a sturdy, plain wooden fence. Ava's nearest neighbour lived in another former tied cottage a quarter of a mile down the road. Her friends and colleagues had been surprised that she had chosen such an isolated home, but Ava, who had grown up in a big city, relished the peace and tranquillity of her rural retreat.

The cottage's owner was considering placing it on the market, and Ava was saving every penny to buy it when the time came.

The temptation to sit down and prop up her throbbing foot was almost irresistible, but first she microwaved a chicken tikka ready-meal, and poured herself a glass of sauvignon before collecting a bag of peas from the freezer and heading for the sofa.

She ate slowly, thinking that for the first time in her recent history, she had taken no exercise other than the amount of walking she did in a normal day's police work, and even that had, of necessity, been kept to a minimum.

'RICE,' colleagues had been saying to her all day, observing her limp, and at last she was heeding their advice.

It was a long time since she had felt so incapacitated, and she didn't like it. Ava wanted to be able to count on her body not to let her down in an emergency. That was one of the reasons why she so often pushed herself to the limit to stay in peak condition. She needed the reassurance of knowing that she could kick and fight her way out of danger, or failing that, make a decent run for it.

Ava found herself thinking of Christopher Taylor. In her head she went over the interview of the day before. She had not supposed that he had lied about his alibi, and he hadn't. Nevertheless, she couldn't shake the conviction that he was involved with Amy's case in some way. He had been uncomfortable when he talked about his relationship with Amy Hill. In police work, after a while you developed a kind of sixth sense that told you when people were hiding something, and Taylor had made Ava's detective hackles rise. If he wasn't guilty of killing Amy, there was something else he was hiding, she was certain.

In Ava's experience, people with nothing to hide talked too much. Most people enjoyed being the focus of the police's attention. They would elaborate without prompting, their words rolling out unguarded. They were unselfconscious, since they weren't afraid that their words might betray them. Taylor had been none of these things. He had been charming and forthcoming enough with his answers to their questions, but he had also been guarded, deliberate in his replies. No chance of Taylor letting anything slip out by mistake.

Ava sighed. The bag of peas on her foot was already starting to defrost in the warmth of the room but she was reluctant to move. Her laptop sat on the coffee table in front of her; it was an effort to stretch forward to pull it towards her. She googled Taylor's name and read his profile on the university's English department staff list. A brief biography stated that he had obtained his BA at Sheffield University, and had stayed on to complete an MA and PhD in record time. He had published numerous papers on the Romantic poets and he was working on a book.

Ava stared at the accompanying photograph; it was flattering, even for him. It wasn't at all difficult to imagine Amy Hill — or any other undergraduate — lusting after him. Her eyes lingered on the picture, taking in the blonde hair, ice-cool blue eyes and oh so charming smile; the bastard even had dimples. She thought of the way his eyes had lingered on her, his chivalrous concern for her injured foot, and found herself idly entertaining a few fantasies of her own about the handsome professor.

She was attracted to him, she admitted grudgingly, and she knew he had been attracted to her in the way most men were. Yet there was something about him that set her alarm bells ringing. Had she been wrong to speak of her gut feeling about Taylor to Jim Neal? She remembered his caveat about gut feelings arising from past experiences. For a moment she considered the possibility that Neal knew something about her that he couldn't possibly know. Ava shuddered. Nobody knew, and that's the way it had to stay.

Her thoughts were beginning to stray into dangerous territory and as a distraction, she lifted the now dripping bag of peas off her foot and returned it to the freezer and poured herself another glass of wine. Christopher Taylor's alibi was watertight. Even so, she would root around in his life and see what she could dig up. Maybe nothing; maybe he was as unblemished morally as he was physically, but she didn't think so.

Chapter 8

Feeling achy with the beginnings of a cold, Anna Foster made her way to the shop's entrance to close up for the day, even though she'd been open for less than an hour. Her heart just wasn't in it, and now it looked like she was going to be feeling physically below par as well.

On the mat inside the front door she noticed a folded sheet of paper and bent to pick it up. Probably a flyer of some sort. Before she could unfold it, she caught sight of Nancy's Hill's strained face at the window. Fearing a confrontation, she braced herself.

On the day of Amy's funeral, Anna had been welcomed as one of the family. Nancy had wept on her shoulder and asked if Anna knew what it was like to lose someone you loved. Having lost a husband, Anna considered she was in a good position to empathise, but in the pecking order of grief, Nancy clearly considered the loss of a child paramount, and who was Anna to argue?

Thinking about Nancy's behaviour over the course of the day, Anna had been puzzled; in particular, some of her utterances had sounded odd. Though she had her own worries about Simon's disappearance, Anna had lain awake on the night of the funeral wondering about Nancy's words and what they might mean. Over and over Nancy had wailed that her sacrifice had been in vain, that it had all been for nothing, that she should have left Amy to her fate; that she was responsible for Amy's death as surely as if she had killed her herself. Odd words, but a mother so recently bereaved of her only child was entitled to be irrational.

Richard Turner's grief had also worried Anna. He had wept uncontrollably at Amy's graveside, but afterwards he had been a pillar of strength for Nancy, perhaps understanding that his grief must necessarily take second place to hers. But anyone could see the man was distraught. And the boy, his son Bradley, had been upset, and Anna had been aware of a tension in the air whenever Bradley and Nancy came too close. She had wondered what was at the bottom of that.

Of them all, Richard Turner's daughter Julia had been the calmest. It was plain that there was no special closeness between her and Nancy, no bond. There was no real reason why they should be close; they were not mother and daughter, after all. But it seemed to Anna that an opportunity had been lost somewhere in this 'family's' history. For Julia was a lovely girl, attentive to the father she had probably not seen enough of in her teenage years, and respectful, if not overtly affectionate, towards Nancy.

Anna had found herself comparing Julia to Amy; Richard Turner's daughter appeared to have none of Amy's pretentiousness or self-centredness. They were physically very different. Julia was curvy and healthy, with a tangled mane of titian hair. Anna regretted that she had had so little time to talk to her. It would have been interesting to hear this girl's impressions of Amy, of Nancy; to have learned something more about the family dynamics.

And now, here was Nancy, banging against the window, purple with rage and looking dangerous. The sight of her set Anna's nerves on edge and she wished she'd locked up earlier.

"It's open," she mouthed, surprised that Nancy had not thought to check.

Perhaps the doorknob was refusing to budge. It was always a little awkward, and a sign on the door indicated which way to turn, but even so, sometimes people assumed that the shop was closed and walked away before they could be admitted.

There was no way Nancy was going away. She rattled the knob noisily and as Anna opened the door inwards, a startled Nancy was propelled over the threshold in a manner that lent her little dignity. On another occasion it might have been funny. Today it simply fuelled her anger.

"I thought you were my friend," she seethed.

"Nancy, calm down."

"You know where he is, don't you?" She pushed past, giving Anna no time to answer.

"He's here, isn't he? These old buildings are riddled with secret hiding places. I bet you had him hidden away when the police came round."

"Nancy that's ludicrous. Simon isn't here. I only wish he were. That way he could tell you he had nothing to do with Amy's death."

There, she had said it. For the first time since her row with Simon on the night he'd disappeared, she believed it herself, and along with the realisation came a wash of guilt and enormous relief.

"Then why has he disappeared? If he's got nothing to hide, why isn't he here?"

"He's angry with me, that's all. We had a row; I said some hurtful things to him. He's punishing me." Anna felt herself choke, "He knows I can't bear to have him out of my sight." Nancy stared at her. For a second the two women connected on a level that they both understood, then Nancy's anger kicked in again.

"What things did you say to him? That he's a murderer? That he dragged Amy across the common that night and strangled her? No wonder your poor little boy's feelings were hurt. He knew mummy was telling the truth."

Something snapped inside Anna's head. Now that she had accepted how absurd it had been of her to suspect Simon of that heinous crime, it appalled her to hear someone else accuse her son of such brutality.

"That's not true! Get out! Get out of my shop!" she said as her own anger mounted.

Nancy stood, defiant, looking as though she wanted to spit. Or strike out. For several moments, both women glared at each other, neither willing to back down.

Then, suddenly, Anna felt ashamed; she was afraid of losing what she loved most. Nancy already had. In a kinder tone, she said, "Please. Just leave. Simon isn't here." Her eyes met Nancy's and registered only anger. Then Nancy turned her back and stumbled out the door.

Tears blurred Nancy's departure. Anna locked the door behind her and bent to straighten the mat. At that moment she remembered the flyer that she had picked up earlier and pulled it, crumpled, from her pocket. It was not a flyer. It was from Simon.

* * *

Minutes after her row with Anna Foster, Nancy Hill was stricken with regret. She had stumbled angrily out of the shop and onto the pavement, turning instinctively in the direction of her own shop, a little way up the Long hill. Richard had left a sign on the door saying, 'closed due to family bereavement,' and Nancy stared at it numbly before remembering that she was the one bereaved.

The shop's gloomy interior absorbed her misery. The heating had been off for days, and an aching cold seemed to seep out of the walls into Nancy's bones. Without turning on the lights, or taking much note of the tidy little shop she had been so proud of, Nancy made straight for her 'office' at the back, where she sat down and howled, safe in the knowledge that no one could hear her.

Anna Foster was her friend. Her son was missing, a murder suspect. If the victim had been anyone else but Amy, Nancy would have been consoling her friend, taking her side, supporting her, refusing to believe that Simon could be guilty of such a terrible crime. But the victim had been Amy. Her child; and that was the reason Simon had vanished, or so it seemed. Nancy moaned aloud; she wanted so badly to have someone to blame.

* * *

The following morning, Nancy pretended to be asleep until she heard the garage door creak shut, followed by the sound of Richard's car revving up and pulling out of her drive. Just before he left the house, he'd come upstairs and crept over to the bed to kiss her lightly on the forehead and whisper goodbye. Perhaps he really had believed she was still asleep, but she didn't think so.

They had rowed again last night. Round and round in a circle of denial and disappointment, Richard asking her to open up to him, she insisting that she had nothing to conceal, until they were both too exhausted to care.

Perhaps later she would call at his workshop and watch him work. It was relaxing to watch him smooth a piece of timber lovingly with his hand plane. Richard had large, calloused, craftsman's hands that were capable of creating objects of great beauty. For ethical reasons, he eschewed the use of tropical hardwoods, nowadays working mainly with sustainable, recycled or reclaimed materials. For her fortieth birthday, he'd presented Nancy with an exquisite, sweet-smelling rosewood jewellery box, which had taken her breath away. She hadn't dared to ask whether he had compromised his ethical standards in obtaining the wood — it frightened her to think he could love her that much.

Thinking of Richard's workshop, reminded her again of her own business; her shop which had been closed for a week now. Nancy felt no inclination to return to work, and wondered whether she would ever feel that there was any point to anything ever again. In the days since Amy's death, she had felt inert and heavy, sluggish and unmotivated. The slightest movement required an effort that was beyond her.

She had been awake long before Richard this morning, but was unable to move. Richard, stirring beside her when the alarm went off, throwing his arm about her and pulling her close, had shocked her with his effortless movements and easy affection. Nothing in Nancy's own heart moved in response, and, more shockingly, even when she thought of Amy, nothing stirred. The absence of emotion was alarming but it was also liberating, freeing her from the need to feel pain. Music blared suddenly from the clock radio as if mocking her — 'Everybody Hurts,' by REM.

Richard must have reset the alarm when he came in to kiss her goodbye. Last night, he'd suggested that going into work might take her mind off things. She glanced at the clock; there was still time to open the shop at ten, only half an hour later than normal, but her mood weighted her to the bed and any hope for the day ahead was buried deep under the duvet.

"*Hold on . . .*" droned Michael Stipe, but Nancy was adrift. Motherhood had anchored her to her life and now that it was gone, nothing made sense any more, nothing mattered. The next song was one that had been everywhere the summer she first moved to London. Nancy struck out with her arm and hit the off button on the radio, but, stirred by the familiar music, the malevolent worm of her past began burrowing under the covers to torment her.

* * *

Life had dealt her some cruel blows. Nancy's childhood had been overshadowed by the loss of her parents. As a teenager, she had endured four years of living with foster parents who did their duty by her without love; more often than not, she had been bullied — or worse — by the other children in their care. When Amy came into her life, Nancy swore her daughter would always be loved. What if she had gone a little over the top, if in her eagerness to be a loving parent, she had spoiled Amy in other ways too?

At little more than Amy's age, Nancy had arrived in London with a backpack containing everything she owned in the world; it didn't amount to much. Her final foster home had been crowded and chaotic and there had been no money for extras. At sixteen, leaving care with an unfinished education and no prospects, she had moved into a flat-share with three other young people and started work in a Costcutter. In the evenings, she attended a local further education college and took some GCSEs and A Levels and, on reaching twenty-one, she had at last gained access to her parents' estate and planned to use the money to move to London and apply for a place on an art and design course.

Her home in London was a basement flat in a converted Victorian house on a street lined with tall London plane trees leading up to the gates of Victoria Park. It had been sublet to her by a girl she'd befriended whilst working part-time in a bar on Fleet Street, who had gone off travelling for a year. A stroke of luck at last.

One day, walking in the park, she had met Debbie Clarke. A small boy had run out in front of her, near the lake, chasing the Canada geese at the water's edge, and Nancy had looked around for his mother, concerned that he might end up in the water. A thin young woman was sitting on a bench staring in the other direction, one hand on the handle of a buggy, pushing it backwards and forwards. Nancy was aware of two things; the little boy's potential danger and the distressed cries of a very young baby coming from the buggy.

The boy's danger was the more immediate. She caught the hood of his jacket as he shooed an indignant duck into the lake, pulling him gently out of harm's way. It was a risk, touching someone else's child. Nancy looked around nervously, half expecting the young mother to scream that her son was being kidnapped or molested, but the woman was still looking the other way, rocking the pram, more for her own comfort, it seemed than for the infant's, whose wailing she continued to ignore.

The boy looked up at Nancy in alarm, tugging at his sleeve to loosen her grip.

"Hey, little man. What's your name?"

"Peter," he'd answered, squirming to free himself.

"It's not safe to play so near to the water, Peter. What if you fell in?" He stared at her as if she were mad. "Let's go get your mum." Together, they walked to the park bench.

"Are you Peter's mum?" Nancy asked the young woman, who seemed oblivious to their presence. Peter leaned into the pram, making shushing noises and the baby's wailing calmed to a fretful whining.

"Yeah. What's it to you? Been doing something naughty, has he?"

"Oh no. He just seemed to be getting a bit near to the water, got carried away chasing the ducks, probably."

"Yeah, probably. He likes ducks," the woman said, unconcerned. She looked younger than Nancy, too young to be the mother of two children. Was she too young also to appreciate that her son might have been in danger?

One of Nancy's foster mothers had suffered from post-natal depression; she had been out of it a lot of the time, distant, let the kids in her care do pretty much as they liked, which had often amounted to bullying Nancy. Something about this young woman's behaviour and attitude reminded Nancy of her foster mother's disinterested detachment.

"I'm Nancy. I live on one of the streets leading to the park. Do you live nearby?"

"Over there," the woman said, waving her arm loosely. Through the skeletal branches of a barrier of late autumn trees fringing the park's west side, Nancy made out the skulking, jaundiced blocks of a run-down council estate. It was one she had been warned to avoid because of its reputation for having a high crime rate.

"We're practically neighbours," she said, "Look; I know it must be hard having two young kids to look after. Is there anything I can do to help?"

"How do you know it's hard? Got kids, have you?"

Nancy's words seemed to have roused the young woman from her passivity.

"I grew up in foster homes. One of my foster mothers suffered from depression. I used to look out for the younger kids."

"Yeah, well it's hardly the same, is it?"

"No, I suppose not." The baby's screaming had ceased. Peter was leaning into the pram, waving a soft toy, a caterpillar with purple spots and fuzzy red feet, at his baby sister.

"I meant what I said, you know. I'd really like to help."

The young woman took out a cigarette and lit it, looking the other way. There was a hissing sound from her lips as she drew the smoke in between her teeth. She seemed to hold her breath for a long time. When at last she exhaled, she breathed a cloud of fuggy smoke over the buggy.

"Look, I could come home with you for a bit, if you like? I'm not at work until this evening. I could feed and change the baby, play with Peter for a little while. You could have a rest, or have some time to yourself," Nancy urged.

"I could have a sleep," Debbie said and Nancy could see how tired she was, how dark the rings were under the girl's seemingly emotionless eyes.

Debbie Clarke lived in a ground floor flat in what struck Nancy as one of the worst blocks on the estate. A seeping waste pipe outside her kitchen window told a story of neglect and failure on the part of the Council, but it was the sight of moss thriving on the damp brickwork behind it that drove the message home. No one had cared about conditions on this estate for a long time.

"What happened to your door?" Nancy asked, seeing the chipped and splintered wood around the frame near the lock.

"Wade kicked it in couple of nights ago. Couldn't find his key."

"Who's Wade? Is he your husband?"

"He's Em and Peter's dad. We ain't married. He stays here sometimes. Got his own place in Mile End. You coming in, or what?"

Nancy realised she was hesitating outside the open door, already reconsidering her offer of help. A small, sticky hand curled around hers, and she stepped inside.

Inside, the flat smelled of stale cigarette smoke and prolonged neglect. It was furnished minimally with a shabby imitation leather three-piece suite of the standard seen on pavements outside those second hand furniture stores that accepted DSS cheques. The only other piece of furniture in the living room was a glass-topped coffee table, on the surface of which lay an overflowing ash-tray and a couple of empty beer cans. In a corner of the room was a large television set, around which were piled up an assortment of children's videos. Even before she took her coat off, Debbie was popping one in for Peter to watch.

"Was it Wade who gave you that black eye?" Nancy asked quietly when Peter was engrossed in the cartoon that had been put on for his entertainment.

"Yeah. He was here Saturday night. I had to let him in. 'E was kicking the door in. I've asked the Council for a move but they ain't found me nothing yet. But something's got to be done. I know he'll be back."

Nancy made Debbie a cup of tea and changed and fed the baby. Emily was a beautiful child. Cradled on Nancy's arm, she sucked contentedly on her bottle of warmed formula milk, big, round eyes staring into Nancy's. Nancy was overwhelmed suddenly with a feeling of profound love that startled her with its intensity. By the time the bottle was empty, Nancy knew every soft curve of Emily's face, every gesture the baby made as she sucked hungrily at the teat — from the way her ears wiggled to the way her eyebrows rose and fell as her jaws worked hungrily, to the way her cheeks burned with rosy contentment as she burped up milk which dribbled down her chin and drifted off to sleep.

As Emily's lids closed, Nancy realised with a start that, feeding the infant, she had been in another more sublime place, and she looked around the room, as if expecting to be admonished for partaking of a guilty pleasure. Debbie was dragging on a cigarette, her eyes staring unseeingly at the television, and Peter was playing happily with some toy action figures, glancing up at the action on the screen from time to time.

It was with reluctance that Nancy placed Emily in the shabby straw Moses basket that Debbie had left beside the chair in anticipation of the child's falling asleep after her feed.

"I can come back, if you like," Nancy said to Debbie, worrying that she was outstaying her welcome. "Do a bit of baby-sitting, give you a chance to get out a bit."

"I'm on the social. I can't afford to pay you."

"I don't want any payment. I just want to help." At that, Debbie had shrugged, which Nancy took to mean she didn't care one way or the other.

When she left Debbie's flat, Nancy called in at the housing office to report the leaking soil stack. There, she spoke with the officer responsible for managing the estate. Far from ignoring Debbie's plight, it appeared that the Council had moved her twice in the last fifteen months, both times to escape her abusive partner. No one was sure if he had tracked her down or if she had invited him back.

Women like Debbie, explained the weary young housing officer, fell into patterns of abuse.

Nancy knew from her foster homes that there were women who became caught up in a cycle of abusive relationships. Debbie was known to Social Services and her two children were on the 'at risk,' register because of her aggressive partner. But she had admitted Wade Bolan to her flat willingly on two occasions after restraining orders had been put in place to deter him from bothering her.

"So you see," the young man at the housing office had assured Nancy, "giving Debbie a transfer to yet another flat isn't the answer. She'd only let Bolan know where to find her." It was hard to disagree.

A few days later, whilst browsing a market stall on Bethnal Green Road, Nancy came across Debbie again. Nancy was picking out some apples when she felt a tugging on her coat and, looking down, she saw Peter's shy, grubby face smiling up at her.

"Nancy," he'd said in his babyish voice and his mother had turned at the sound. She looked at Nancy, frowning, as though she sort of recognised her, before saying, disinterestedly, "Oh, it's you." Nancy noticed that she didn't smile and looked neither pleased nor displeased to see her. Debbie seemed to have no emotions at all.

"Where's Emily?" Nancy asked, looking around for a buggy. Debbie didn't answer, didn't even seem to hear. Concerned, Nancy turned to Peter,

"Where's Emily, Peter?"

"Emmie home," Peter answered in his sweet little voice.

"Debbie! Have you left the baby at home alone?" Nancy asked in alarm. No response. "Debbie?"

"So what if I 'ave? She was asleep. She won't wake up until it's nearly time for her next feed."

"What if something happened? What if she wakes up and chokes or . . . or something?" Debbie's expression signified that she thought Nancy completely crazy.

"You don't have to leave her or Peter alone, Debbie. I meant it when I said I could look after them for you. Promise me you'll call me next time."

"Yeah. Okay," Debbie answered. Nancy had a sudden idea.

"Why don't you give me your key? I could go to your flat and make sure she's alright. I could take Peter with me, if you like. If he'll come." To herself, she thought, s*he's only met me once. I could be anyone. How does she know she can trust me?* But she could see immediately that Debbie was game; for the first time a spark of life seemed to shine in her eyes.

"I suppose I could go and 'ave me nails done."

"Yes. You do that. I'll take care of the children. We'll be fine, won't we Peter?" Nancy looked down at the small boy and saw the uncertainty in his expression that had been absent from his mother's, but when she offered him her hand he took it.

Debbie rummaged around in her handbag for her house keys. To Peter she said, "You be good for . . ." She hesitated over the name.

"Nancy."

"Be good for Nancy." Turning to her, she said, "Put a video on for him. That'll keep him quiet. He won't be no bother."

Nancy made a call to another girl who worked at the pub, asking if she would cover her shift. It meant losing money, but she could not leave the children until Debbie returned. They walked through Bethnal Green gardens hand in hand and, as they passed the library, Nancy asked Peter if he liked stories, resolving to return with him and his sister.

They found Emily as Debbie predicted, asleep and oblivious to her mother's neglect. Nancy could have sobbed with relief. She woke the infant up, changed and fed her and dressed her in a grubby white snowsuit before tucking her into her buggy. Peter stepped on to the standing platform and they set off for the library.

Peter loved being read to. He sat on Nancy's knee and listened to story after story without stirring. After an hour and a half, Nancy reluctantly returned the books to the shelves and prepared to go.

On their way out, the woman on the desk spoke to Peter, commenting on how good he had been, how much he seemed to enjoy his story time.

"Next time you come, ask your mum to bring something with your address on and we can see about getting you a library card so you can take some books home," she said.

"I'm not his mum," Nancy said, "I'm just looking after Peter and his sister for the afternoon, but I'll tell his mum to bring him along." She had little faith that Debbie would bother. Peter was a bright little boy, she was sure, but with no books at home, and TV cartoons providing most of his entertainment, what chance would he have to develop?

She thought of her own early childhood, growing up with loving and attentive parents who had given her every encouragement to learn and flourish. Her life had been rich until the accident that had so cruelly removed them from her young life.

When they arrived back at Debbie's flat, Nancy searched the kitchen cupboards and the fridge for something for Peter to eat. There were no vegetables to be found, only tinned and packet food. In the end, she heated some beans and made some toast, and Peter ate these happily while she warmed up another bottle for Emily. Then, she played with Peter as Emily dozed again.

The hours ticked by. Nancy began to worry.

"Where's mummy?" Peter asked, when it was beginning to grow dark outside and there was still no sign of Debbie.

"She'll be home soon," Nancy reassured him, but Debbie did not return until well past midnight, and she was drunk. Moreover, she was not alone.

"Where have you been?" Nancy asked, "I've had to call work and say I couldn't come in." It was a lie but she wanted Debbie to feel bad.

"Who's this?" The man with Debbie asked.

"Just the babysitter," Debbie said, in a slurred voice as she staggered over the threshold. Nancy felt anger welling up.

"It's gone midnight. What were you thinking? I put the children to bed hours ago. Peter wanted to know where you were."

"I was out having some fun. What's so terrible about that? You say you'll look after the kids anytime and the minute I take you up on your offer, you change your mind. I might have known you didn't really mean it."

"I haven't changed my mind. I just thought . . ." What had she just thought? That Debbie would have had the decency to let her know she would be late? That she cared for her children enough to be there for them; that she was mature enough to understand that they were her responsibility? What right did Nancy have to take such things for granted? She had no idea what it was like to be a single parent in Debbie's situation. Suddenly, she found herself apologising.

The man whose voice she'd heard was following Debbie into the kitchen. He sneaked up behind her and grabbed her backside and Debbie turned around, giggling. One of the man's hands slid up her skirt, the other squeezed a breast and Debbie moved lasciviously against him. Nancy turned away, embarrassed. Were they about to do it right in front of her?

She coughed loudly, saying, "I'll see myself out," making for the door. In two strides, the man was beside her, Debbie pulled along with him. A hand rammed roughly between Nancy's legs and a feeling of intense, sick shock riveted her to the floor.

"Why don't you stick around? We like a threesome, don't we, Debs?" Shocked, Nancy struck out at him; pain bolted through her right arm before she'd even realised he'd grabbed it and twisted it behind her back.

"Leave her alone, Wade," Debbie said, sounding bored, "she wouldn't be no fun anyway."

Wade released her. Nancy staggered backwards out the door and ran without looking back. She ran across the estate, feeling violated, her vulnerability exposed cruelly in the brilliance of the halogen floodlights. The harsh unnatural light seemed to transform the estate into a vast 'film noir' set, filled with sharp angles and long shadows, and dark, impenetrable areas where danger lurked. Nancy kept running until she was clear of the estate and her lungs burned for air.

Over the next few days, from the safety of her basement flat, she revisited Debbie's home in her head, reliving the shock of Wade's assault. Behind her shock and burgeoning anger lurked something more disturbing; a deep sense of shame at having abandoned the two innocents inside. And something else stirred too, something she'd tried hard to forget; the memory of her thirteenth birthday and Johnny Duke's weight pinning her to the bed in her foster mother's room.

She thought of alerting the police, but what had Wade done, except flirt with his partner and touch her friend inappropriately, which would be hard to prove in any case? It wasn't as if Debbie would back her up. As for the children, they were already known to social services and Wade hadn't laid a finger on them.

Despite her concerns for the children, for a couple of weeks Nancy avoided any place she might bump into Debbie Clarke. Then, one morning, she saw Debbie cross the street and head straight for her. A new bruise on the girl's cheek stirred Nancy to pity. At once, her resolve to have nothing more to do with Debbie and her kids evaporated.

"Where are the kids?" For days, she'd been picturing Peter and Emily in a box, like Schrödinger's cat, their fate undetermined as long as the lid stayed on. She could not be sure that they were safe, but neither could she be sure that they were not. There was a lot to be said for a state of unknowing.

"They're with my friend, Nina. She owed me one since I tipped her off about the cops . . ." Debbie checked herself, "since I helped her out a couple of weeks ago."

"And Wade?"

"He ain't been round for a bit. Left me this," she said, touching the bruised and tender-looking skin around her left eye, "'spect he'll be back when he wants some." It was said in a matter of fact way, as though it were something over which Debbie had no control.

"Why do you let him?" Nancy asked.

"He ain't all bad. He puts some cash my way sometimes." Debbie said, defensively.

"Why do you want the Council to move you if he's only going to find you again? If you keep telling him where you are?"

"Because maybe next time, I won't tell him." Debbie said, unconvincingly. "Will you watch the kids for me Tuesday?" she asked.

"Yes," Nancy sighed, feeling a sense of inevitability about the elements of her life that had brought her to this moment and this choice. She could have just walked away, but she did not.

"I'm sorry about the other week," Debbie said, "We was both drunk. Nothing would have happened, honest. Wade's bark's worse than his bite."

But not his fist, Nancy thought, bleakly, looking at Debbie's black eye.

The next day Debbie turned up at Nancy's door with her kids in tow, which surprised Nancy, as Debbie had never visited her before.

They drank tea together at Nancy's drop-leaf kitchen table. Emily was asleep in her buggy and Peter was playing on the floor with his box of beloved toy animals.

"Men like Wade are bad news," Nancy said, tentatively, "I know he's the father of your children and that even though he treats you badly, you still have feelings for him. I won't pretend I approve or even understand that. But if you promise to keep him away from me, I'll watch the kids for you whenever I can."

It was against her better judgement, but Nancy wanted, like her mother and father, so distant to her already by then, to be and to do good. She could not erase the years of unhappiness since their death almost half her lifetime ago, but through doing good for someone else, perhaps she could restore the feeling she had carried inside when they were still alive.

"You won't see him again," Debbie assured her. At that precise moment, Peter looked up from his toy animals and smiled at Nancy. In his unsteady hand, he held out a small, grubby panda from his tin of animals.

"Bless him," Debbie said, then in her next breath, "I'm just nipping out for a fag."

Nancy scooped Peter up and sat him on her knee, admiring his treasure.

"Favourite," Peter said in his small voice, holding a tiger out for her to keep, "Nancy keep him safe from daddy." Nancy choked back a tear.

Over the next few weeks, Nancy saw as much of the children as their mother did. Debs would turn up on her doorstep unannounced saying she had to go here or there; sometimes she just turned up and left them with Nancy because, 'they was driving me crazy and I just need to get away.' Nancy didn't mind; it meant the children were safe with her, and not left alone in that depressing flat to where, at any moment, their father might return.

One night, Nancy had awakened sometime after midnight to the sound of urgent knocking on her door. Warily, she made her way through her small living room to the kitchen where her door opened onto some steps leading up to the pavement. Through a gap in the curtains, plainly visible in the light of the streetlamp spilling down from above, she could see Debbie hovering halfway up or down the stairs, poised between staying and going.

Had Nancy stepped away from the window and slipped unseen back into the dark interior of her kitchen, Debbie would no doubt have continued on her way up, but in Nancy's moment of indecision, Debbie saw, or sensed, that she was there and came running back down the steps to the door.

"Nancy!" she'd cried in a voice edged with panic, "Let me in, quick." A couple of seconds later, she was standing in Nancy's kitchen, yanking the curtains tightly together.

"Debbie! What's going on? What are you doing here at this time of night? Is that blood?" Nancy looked in horror at a trickle of blood running from Debbie's mouth down her chin.

"Bastard knocked one of my teeth out."

"Are you saying Wade did this?" Nancy asked, pulling Debbie into the living room where she saw that Debbie's whole face was a mess.

"Where are the children?" she asked, in a panic.

"It's alright. They're with my friend, Chantelle. I took them over this afternoon when Wade phoned and said he'd be round later. Nancy was shaky with fear and relief. She also wondered why Debbie hadn't brought the children to her instead, and then remembered she had been at work.

"Sit down," she ordered, taking control. "I'll get a cloth or something for your face. And some paracetamol. And a cup of tea."

"I'll have something stronger if you've got it," Debbie said. Nancy didn't drink much but there was a bottle of brandy that she'd discovered in a kitchen cupboard; no one would miss a little of that.

She bathed Debbie's face with cooled, boiled water and cotton wool and gave her a cold, damp cloth to hold against her eye. They sipped their brandies, leaving the tea untouched.

"I'm sorry I woke you up," Debbie said.

"It's alright. I'm glad you did. Was Wade following you?" Nancy said, remembering how Debbie had rearranged the curtains.

"He came running after me, but he was too drunk to catch up. I was just being careful with the curtains. He doesn't know where you live."

Nancy was grateful for that, at least.

"Does it hurt a lot?"

"Painkillers are helping. I'm more bothered about losing my tooth," Debbie replied, a finger probing the inside of her mouth.

"We can go to the dentist in the morning. They might be able to do something about it," Nancy suggested.

"Yeah, maybe," Debbie yawned, "Does that mean I can stay here tonight?"

"Yes," Nancy sighed.

In less than half an hour, Debbie was curled up asleep on the sofa. Nancy covered her with a spare duvet before going back to bed, but she lay awake for a long time afterwards, listening for any sound that might be Wade, and even when it began to grow light outside, she slept only lightly.

In the morning, Debbie let slip that she'd left the children at home, not, as she had told Nancy the night before, at her friend Chantelle's. Nancy stared at her, mouth agape, anger replacing pity for the young woman in front of her.

"Wade wouldn't hurt them. State he was in, he probably went straight to bed after he punched me one. Only kicked off like that 'cos he was pissed. The kids was asleep through it all, honest. Nothing wakes them once they go off." She moved to the door, cigarette in hand.

When Nancy did not respond but only kept staring at her with mounting contempt, Debbie added, "If you tell the social, you ain't seeing them kids again. Just so's you know."

* * *

Nancy pulled the duvet tighter around her, all thoughts about opening up the shop abandoned. There had been a moment, not so long ago when, looking at her beautiful, independent, eighteen-year-old daughter, she had felt absolved of the wrongdoings of her past. Right from the start, Nancy had realised that if she were to live with the conflict within her, she would have to find ways to justify what she had done. Loving Amy, keeping her safe and giving her a good life, had been the way forward. But Amy's death had changed everything, and had left Nancy in a moral black hole from which she feared she would not emerge intact.

Chapter 9

It was easy to find an excuse to bump into Christopher Taylor. She merely hung around the university campus at ten o'clock on a Tuesday morning, when the good professor made his way back to his department after giving a lecture.

Ava had perused Taylor's timetable the evening before, having requested information on his schedule from one of the English department administrators.

"He usually stops at the Coffee Bean counter in the Oasis for a coffee on his way back," the woman she spoke to on the phone had said, helpfully, allowing Ava to be at the cash till paying for her skinny latte, just as Taylor joined the queue. The Oasis was the university's main eating area, a large open air space with different outlets selling a variety of foods. Most of the world's cuisine seemed to be represented.

Heads turned as Ava sashayed across the floor of the cafeteria in her killer heels. There was a pair of trainers in her bag and her ankle was aching, but it was worth the temporary discomfort, for a glance out of the corner of her eye confirmed that Christopher Taylor's head was turning along with the rest.

"May I join you?" he asked, arriving at her table hot on her heels. Ava tossed her blonde hair over her shoulders and flashed him one of her most alluring smiles, hoping she didn't have a frothy milk moustache.

"Haven't seen you in my neck of the woods before," Taylor said, "But I must say, you're a very pleasing addition to the usual clientele."

"I'm here on business," Ava said, after acknowledging the compliment with an elusive smile. "Friend of mine's doing a PhD in forensic psychology. I was asking her advice on a case."

"The Amy Hill murder again? Or aren't you allowed to discuss that with a mere member of the public and a suspect to boot?"

"I can't discuss the specifics, of course, but it was a matter pertaining to that case, yes."

"Am I allowed to ask how the investigation is progressing?"

"You can ask, but I'm afraid my answer would be so general as to leave you none the wiser."

"Something along the lines of, 'we're exploring every avenue, leaving no stone unturned in our search for the killer?'" Taylor said.

"See, you can read my mind."

Taylor leaned towards her and dropped his voice, "Bet you can read mine, too. What am I thinking, Ava?" His manner and expression left little room for doubt. In a lesser man, it would have been sleazy, but Christopher Taylor was a charmer and he looked like an Adonis.

"You're wondering what I look like naked?"

A slow smile spread across Taylor's chiselled, designer-stubbled face.

"I'm an open book, but then again, I think every heterosexual male in the room was wondering the same thing as you walked from the counter." His tone was low, without a hint of irony. It made Ava nervous, and she wasn't sure why. That, and the fact that he had locked eyes with her, and it was she who had to look away first, like some kind of submissive pack animal yielding to the alpha male. Predatory. That's what his eyes were. Not just his eyes but his whole demeanour. Predatory — and sexier than any man had a right to be.

All part of the plan, Ava reminded herself, to make him desire her, so why did she feel that she was the one being lured into a trap? She felt uncharacteristically disarmed

"We can't speak plainly about your work, Ava, but there's no need to be coy about other matters. We're both adults. You were attracted to me that morning at my flat. I was attracted to you. The question is, are we going to do anything about it? Or am I still a suspect and as such, out of bounds to you?"

"Your alibi was good," Ava answered.

"Then have dinner with me. Thursday evening?"

"You're a hard person to say no to."

"So I've been told."

Ava raised an eyebrow. Charming and humorous. Irresistible to an impressionable young girl, no doubt.

"Professor Taylor?" Two young female students stood blushing by the side of their table. Taylor beamed at them.

"Hannah! Eloise! May I present two of my most diligent students, Ava?" Ava inclined her head, but the girls weren't looking at her.

"We were wondering if we could come and see you about this morning's lecture, Professor Taylor," the one named Hannah ventured, "only all that stuff about the metaphysical poets and conceits was like way over our heads." More blushing, and some self-conscious giggling.

"Maybe we could come to your room and go over it?" suggested Eloise. Taylor affected a look of regret, "I'm afraid I won't be able to fit you in before your tutor group tomorrow, ladies. We'll go over it again then. I'm sure if you two excellent scholars had difficulties, other members of the group must have struggled too."

Hanna and Eloise exchanged disappointed glances, having failed in their unsubtle effort to secure the professor to themselves for an hour. Another beaming smile from Taylor sent them on their way, still giggling. God, how could he fail to love himself? thought Ava.

"Pair of groupies?" she asked.

"I have to fight them off all the time."

"Must be tough. Amy Hill was obviously not the only student carrying a torch for you." To his credit, Taylor didn't flinch. "It can't always be easy maintaining a professional distance," Ava added, struggling to sound less accusatory, I get it too, you know, even in my line of work. Young lads thinking they can chat me up while I'm questioning them."

"The curse of being attractive." Taylor seemed to relax.

"You mentioned dinner," Ava prompted. Now his whole demeanour suggested that he was back in his comfort zone.

"I'll pick you up at eight. Where do you live?"

"Out of town. I'll meet you."

"How do I know you won't stand me up?"

"How do I know you won't?"

Taylor's eyes travelled over Ava's body, causing her to blush like one of his undergraduate students. "I can assure you, Ms Merry, that there is absolutely no chance of that."

They arranged to meet at an Italian restaurant they were both familiar with, and then Ava looked at her watch and apologised for leaving so soon, saying she had to report back to Neal. She felt Taylor's eyes lingering on her as she walked across the floor of the cafeteria towards the exit. It bothered her a bit that she was not only concentrating on the job at hand. Part of her was enjoying the experience of being admired by a man like Taylor.

And what sort of man was that? Ava acknowledged that her feelings for Taylor were ambivalent. There was no mistaking the undercurrent of sexual magnetism between them, but at the same time, Ava was aware of a tension that had nothing at all to do with sex and more to do with fear.

Taylor was arrogant and no doubt, vain. His manner of dealing with the two love-struck students had been professional, but, she felt, insincere. There had been a dichotomy between what he had said and the way he had said it, as though he were playing with them. She had seen him appraising them even as he dismissed them, how his gaze had lingered, just that bit too long, as they walked away. Wouldn't any man have done the same, she asked herself, and again the word 'predator' came to mind. Of course other men would have looked, but there was something about Taylor's cool appraisal of the young women that troubled her, as if he were not just appreciating or desiring, but wanting to dominate and control.

From her handbag blared the opening bars of Beethoven's ninth — her younger brother had changed her ringtone again — how he managed to get hold of her mobile without her realising, was a mystery. It was Neal asking her to meet him at Nancy Hill's flat to question Becci Jones again.

"Our friend Gary's going to be there too," he said, "it'll be interesting to see if he still denies knowing Amy."

* * *

They met outside Becci's flat. Neal asked how Ava had fared at the dentist and she felt a pang of guilt for lying about her whereabouts for the past hour and a half.

"Filling," she muttered, feeling even guiltier as Neal winced in sympathy.

"Reid's just got here."

Ava followed his nod and saw a slouching Gary Reid, face semi-concealed by a maroon hoodie, waiting to be let in. He was looking up and down the street in a furtive way.

"Now what's he so nervous about?" Ava said.

"Probably wondering why he'd been stupid enough to deny knowing Amy."

It was Reid who opened the door to them when they knocked; grunting an incoherent welcome, face still lost in his hood.

Becci seemed even thinner and paler and more nervous than before, if that were possible. She didn't rise from her armchair when they entered the room. Neal turned immediately to Reid, with:

"You told us you didn't know Amy Hill, Gary, yet your girlfriend was her friend and flatmate. Care to explain?"

"I didn't know her very well," Gary said, "she was Becci's friend, not mine."

"Becci, how long have you and Gary here been an item?" Neal asked.

"Six months," she answered, sullenly.

"And does he stay over sometimes?"

Ava thought of the narrow bed in Gary's room at the university, and guessed that even the skeletal Becci would be balancing on the edge if she had to share it with Gary, who was at least six one and bulky to boot.

"Sometimes," Becci answered, sulkily.

"So he would have met your flatmate?" Again, Becci's eyes flickered to Gary's face.

"Yes, but like he said, he didn't know her very well. Amy was out a lot and we tended to spend a lot of time in my bedroom when he was here." At this, Becci blushed bright scarlet.

"Still," Neal persisted, ignoring her embarrassment, "Their paths must have crossed from time to time, surely?"

"I s'pose," Becci mumbled.

Gary butted in, "What difference does it make whether I knew her or not?"

"The difference is, that it makes hardened police officers like myself and Detective Sergeant Merry wonder

107

what else you might have lied about," answered Neal sharply.

"Not to mention making us wonder why you lied at all," Ava added, raising an eyebrow. Usually when two people colluded in a lie, they looked to each other for support, and Becci and Gary had exchanged a lot of looks. "So, why did you?" asked Neal.

"It's like Becci said, I didn't know Amy that well. She didn't really speak to me."

"Did you like her?"

The question fazed him momentarily.

"Not much. She was a bit stuck up, and she didn't like me staying over."

"Why not?" Ava asked.

"She was always going on about this being a pricey place and if I wanted to stay here I should pay something towards the rent." He shrugged, "It's not as if I was here all the time."

"Did you row about it?" asked Ava, looking from Gary to Becci.

"Not really. It just meant there was a bit of an atmosphere whenever I spent the night here."

"Did Amy ever have overnight visitors?" Neal asked, looking at Becci.

"Sometimes, but like I said before, she didn't have a regular boyfriend."

"She never confided in you about guys she was seeing? You were BFs, right?" Ava said.

"Amy could be secretive. When we were younger she was always sneaking off into town and asking me to cover for her."

"You mean sneaking off to meet a man? "

"I think so," Becci replied, "She wouldn't tell anything about him but I got the impression he was older than her. They broke up ages ago, though. Probably as long ago as Year Eleven, I think."

Ava and Neal exchanged looks.

"What made you think he was older than her?" asked Ava.

"He wasn't a student and he must have been pretty well off. He was always buying her stuff."

Amy had been wearing designer clothes when she was found, and an expensive watch, which Nancy Hill had not recognised when it was returned to her along with her daughter's other possessions. Not the sort of gear your typical student sported, not unless Mum and Dad's bank was super solvent; Nancy Hill was comfortable but not wealthy.

The watch had thrown up no leads; Ava had had a constable try to trace its purchase but it hadn't been bought locally and was a make sold widely in many different outlets.

"Year Eleven, that would make Amy how old — Fifteen? Sixteen?"

"Amy was the youngest in our year group so about fifteen, yeah."

"And how long had they been seeing each other for, do you remember?" Neal asked.

"Dunno exactly. 'Bout a year, I think."

A question was on the tip of Ava's tongue but she knew better than to ask it. Instead she said, "I know you said you thought this boyfriend was older than Amy because he bought her expensive presents. Did Amy ever let on how much older?"

Becci shrugged, but Gary caught on. He asked, "Do you reckon she was seeing one of those paedos, then?"

Becci's jaw dropped open, her eyes widening in horror. "But she hadn't seen him for years; it couldn't have been him who killed her?" She looked imploringly from Neal to Ava. Neither responded.

"Becci, do you still have my contact details?" Ava asked, and the girl nodded, "I'd like you to think very carefully about this person Amy was seeing, and about her recent behaviour. If you remember anything, however insignificant it might seem, call me straightaway."

Ava wasn't expecting to hear from Becci Jones any time soon. They left her visibly upset, being comforted by a more than willing Gary.

Outside, Neal asked Ava, "What did you make of that, Sergeant?"

"I was desperate to ask Becci if she thought Amy was having sex with this 'older boyfriend,' but I think we can take that as a given. Why else would he shower her with expensive gifts?"

Neal agreed, "I reckon there's something that pair aren't telling us, but I'm damned if I know what it is. Bloody kids; wasting police time." He sighed, "We'll need to check out their fucking backgrounds, which'll no doubt tell us nothing."

"Are you okay?" Ava asked. She'd seldom heard Neal swear, "Archie okay?"

"Archie's fine. Where were you this morning? I know you weren't at the dentist."

How did he know that, Ava wondered? Sometimes, she thought Jim Neal was psychic. She murmured an apology, saying she had some personal business to attend to, hoping he wouldn't ask her what it was.

"Don't lie to me next time, that's all," Neal said.

"There won't be a next time, sir," Ava assured him. She did not tell him about her meeting with Christopher Taylor, or about her plans to see the professor again. Nor did it occur to her that omitting to tell him might be another form of deceit.

Chapter 10

"Your mobile's ringing, Dad."

Jim Neal looked up from his crouched position on the garage floor, removing his hands from the bucket of water through which he had been passing the inner tube of his ten-year-old son's front bicycle wheel, searching for the tell-tale bubbles that would lead him to the elusive puncture.

Wiping his hands on his jeans, he took the phone from his son and put it to his ear. Archie knelt down and took over the search. Neal took a few steps outside the garage, removing himself from Archie's earshot. When he stepped back inside, he saw his son looking up at him, clearly trying to hide his disappointment.

"Sorry, pal, I've got to go out," Neal said, apologetically. It went without saying that he didn't know how long he would be. Archie gave him a cheerful grin, "It's okay, Dad, I can fix the puncture myself."

Sometimes Neal wished Archie were less understanding; perhaps then he would feel less guilty every time he let his son down.

Maggie poked her head round the door leading from the garage to the kitchen.

"Going out?" Maggie was Neal's younger sister. She had taken up residence with them following the breakup of her romance with a much older, married man, something Neal had predicted from the start. To his credit, he had refrained from pronouncing, 'I told you so,' when she turned up on his doorstep with all her worldly goods. Maggie didn't take kindly to advice from her older sibling. What was his advice worth anyway, with his own failed relationship, and no long-term relationships to speak of since?

From the start, Neal had insisted that he would not treat Maggie as a convenient live-in child minder, but she was family and Neal wasn't charging her rent, and she was more than happy to spend time with the nephew she had doted on since the day he was born. Their arrangement had been in place for six months now, and benefited all concerned. Neal didn't have to worry about childcare; Maggie had a roof over her head and Archie adored being with his Auntie Maggie. It was an unconventional household, but it worked, and how many 'normal' families were there nowadays, anyway? Of course it was a temporary arrangement. Maggie wouldn't stick around forever, but Neal had learned not to look too far ahead, and he was pretty sure his sister wouldn't be in a rush to move in with the next man she fell in love with.

"It's Anna Foster," he said. "She says she has something she wants to tell me."

"On a Sunday?" Maggie asked.

"She may have information about her son's whereabouts," Neal answered.

"Better go then. Archie and I will be alright, won't we?" she said, smiling at her nephew, who had just found the puncture and was holding the bicycle tube aloft in triumph.

* * *

Even though it was a Sunday morning, Anna Foster's bookstore was open for business, a fact that seemed to have escaped the attention of the shoppers in the Long Hill area, most of whom walked past with hardly a glance at her window display. The allure of the many tearooms and cafes in the area might have been partly to blame, but Neal knew that in these days of Internet shopping, anyone opening a bookshop had to be an optimist. Across the street from Anna's doorway, a young, rosy-cheeked woman with a round, pretty face, dressed in a long black peasant skirt, a cheerful headscarf tied around her hair was calling, "Beeg Eessue!" in some indeterminate Eastern European accent, most probably Romanian.

"Beeg Eessue," she called out to Neal, holding up a copy of the magazine, optimistically. He had already bought one earlier in the week from the homeless man who stood in the draughty alcove outside Smith's, and so he shook his head.

Despite the apparent lack of trade, Anna Foster had help in her shop, a teenage Goth, who introduced herself as Maya. Neal wondered if the girl's slightly scary appearance frightened the customers away — she had glossy blue-black waist-length hair and looked like she bought her jewellery and accessories in a pet shop, judging by her leather collar and assorted, spiky wrist bands. Neal didn't judge her. In his profession, you judged no-one at first sight.

"Anna's taking a break. She's upstairs. She's expecting you."

Neal let himself through the gate leading to the stairs. Anna Foster was waiting for him at the top.

"I've just made coffee. Would you like some?"

Normally, he would have declined the offer, but he could tell that Anna was nervous; she needed an icebreaker, and fixing coffee would do the job.

He followed her into a small kitchen, where she busied herself for a few minutes looking for mugs and pouring their drinks. Then they proceeded into the living room, which had two slender windows overlooking the Long Hill.

"Interesting view," Neal commented, looking down at the quiet street below. Anna was hovering near him, clutching her coffee cup, also looking out of the window, but her eyes kept flitting to a piece of paper weighted down by a squat tortoise ornament on the coffee table in front of the sofa. "There was something you wanted to tell me," Neal said.

"I found this yesterday morning when I was about to close up," Anna said, crossing to the table and picking up the folded piece of paper, "it's from Simon." She handed it to him and Neal unfolded it carefully, noting the contents. The note was brief, telling Anna not to worry, that he was safe, but he was worried that if she thought he had something to do with Amy's death, perhaps the police would too. He was going away for a while to give them an opportunity to catch the real killer.

"I know running makes him look guilty," Anna began, "he's scared and he's not thinking straight."

"Ms Foster, do you have any idea where Simon might be? Any idea at all?" Anna Foster shook her head, "I've already told you I don't. That's why I called you. I thought you might be able to find out from his note. I know your forensics people can look for things we'd miss with our eyes. Inspector, I want him found more than you. I need to know he's alright."

"I know," Neal said gently, thinking of Archie.

"Simon's special," Anna said, turning back to the window. At first Neal dismissed her comment. Archie was special too. All children were special to their parents. Then — curious — he asked, "How so?" Anna had already told them that her son was adopted. What else did she have to say?

"My husband and I couldn't have children of our own. Not long after we were married, I was diagnosed with cancer. The treatment left me infertile. When a potentially fatal disease threatens your life Inspector, you learn to appreciate what you have. I had been granted my life; it seemed greedy to want more and so I accepted that I would never be a mother. And, for a time, it was enough simply to be alive, recovering my strength, simply existing. It was a long time before I started thinking beyond the present moment. I can't say precisely when I started wanting more. Maybe it was when I was finally given the all clear. Bit by bit I began making plans again, daring to have hopes for the future." She paused and sat down, inviting Neal to sit as well.

"You must understand; I hadn't longed for a child before my illness, hadn't particularly cared about becoming a mother. Why would I long for one now? Martin kept on and on about it, telling me to go for counselling, or consider adoption. So like a man to think a woman couldn't be complete without a child, I thought. Do you know, I was so wrapped up in myself, that it wasn't until much later that I realised that Martin was grieving as well, that he too had lost the chance of completeness?"

"Simon made your lives complete?" Neal asked, quietly, Archie's face flashing in his mind. "That's why he was special?"

"No," Anna said, "that's not it at all." She began to tell Neal about her early days with her son. The truth was, Simon had not made her life complete; he had made it hell. She had not been entirely honest with Inspector Neal on their first meeting when she had dismissed his questions about Simon's troubled childhood so lightly. It was true that he had been a remarkable child, replete with intelligence and a buoyant resilience that belied the terrible trauma in his young life, but there had been another side to his behaviour.

Anna closed her eyes and pressed her fists to her eyelids, as she recounted the tantrums, the nightmares, the bed-wetting, the mood swings and rages, the tears.

An army of professionals had been on hand to proffer advice. Social workers and health visitors, child psychologists, behavioural therapists and teachers. But it was not Simon's behavioural anomalies that distressed Anna. It was his almost total rejection of any demonstration of love on her part; his isolation and aloofness. The total detachment. After his mother's murder and his sister's disappearance he regressed. For almost a year, he hardly spoke, and his behaviour was challenging in the extreme.

"He doesn't have any concept of how to behave with other people."

"He needs to learn that he can trust you first. Trust first. Love later."

"He's learning to re-evaluate everything he's learnt about adults."

"There's never been any consistency in his life."

"He's afraid you're suddenly going to turn into his father."

This last piece of advice, directed at Martin, had ricocheted round in Anna's exhausted brain with the barrage of other gems of wisdom proffered by various professionals.

In the end it had been Simon himself who built the first bridge. Anna had been rushing down the stairs to answer the telephone one morning when she'd missed the last step and landed awkwardly, twisting her ankle. The sudden sharp pain caused her to cry out, and brought tears to her eyes.

She had raised her arm to wipe her face with her sleeve and when she lowered it, Simon was standing before her, staring at her with a confused expression on his face. Instead of smiling to reassure him, Anna had sniffed and pretended to cry even more, curious to see what effect her distress might have on him.

"Does it hurt?" he had asked, looking at her ankle, which she was cradling in her hands. Swallowing her astonishment at hearing his voice, Anna nodded and to her disappointment Simon had merely turned away and returned to the lounge where he had been playing with his animals. Then, a moment later he had returned holding Buddy, his favourite teddy bear, the one he always turned to for comfort.

"Would you like to hug Buddy?" How Anna had resented that bear, which Simon had seemed to prefer to the comfort of her arms. Now she nodded as though only Buddy could comfort her, too. Hugging Buddy, suddenly inspired, she had whispered, "You know what? Buddy's not helping."

Simon had stared at her in puzzlement. Buddy had never failed him after all.

"Do you know what might do the trick?" she asked and when Simon shook his head, she said, "It might help if you give me a cuddle."

He hesitated for just a moment. Suddenly, they were holding tightly to each other, Anna fighting back tears of joy. She was a mother at last.

"That's why he's special," Anna said, wiping away a tear, "he came back to me, the little boy I used to read to in the library; he came back."

Neal felt a lump in his throat, remembering the loving toddler Archie had been. Their love had been reciprocal; he could not imagine how he would have felt if his son had transferred his love to a cuddly toy, or rejected his embraces.

"We'll do what we can to find your son, Ms Foster," he said, tucking the note carefully in an evidence bag in his inside pocket.

"In the meantime, please contact me if he reaches out to you again."

"Thank you, Inspector." She didn't say the words but he saw them in her eyes, *my son is innocent*. He wished he could reassure her, but he had seen too many mothers come to grief over their sons to offer what might turn out to be hollow comfort.

On his way home, Neal dropped the note off for analysis, though he didn't hold out much hope that such a slight lead would lead to finding Anna's son. Simon's words had been written on a sheet of lined A4 paper torn from a ring-bound notebook, a type often used by students. He had probably just torn a page out of one of his notebooks, scribbled a few words to Anna and stuck it through the letterbox in the night. He might even have given it to someone else to post. Anna had let a couple of days go by before contacting him — time enough for Simon to disappear.

Neal thought suddenly of the Romanian woman selling the Big Issue, and made a mental note to have her questioned to see if she'd seen Simon posting the note, not that that would tell them much more than they already knew. He sighed. The case was progressing too slowly.

Neal parked his car in the drive. It was still early enough to take Archie somewhere for a treat. He found his sister and his son so engaged in a game of Wii tennis that they obviously hadn't heard the car pull into the drive, or the door close.

Then Archie looked over at the door and caught sight of his father. Neal's heart lurched with emotion as he witnessed the joy on his son's face. It was moments like these that made parenthood worthwhile. Small wonder that Anna Foster had thought Simon special for sharing his love with her.

"Thank goodness you're back," Maggie said, "I'm really rubbish at this. Want to take over?" Neal smiled. There were plenty of other things he could be doing, but they could wait.

"Want to go for pizza later?" he asked Archie, ruffling his son's hair and smiling at Archie's enthusiastic response.

* * *

At around the time when she was arranging her blonde hair in a French pleat, Ava Merry started to have second thoughts about her date with Christopher Taylor. It was seven thirty — too late to cancel. In fact, if she didn't get a wiggle on there was a good chance she'd be late at the restaurant she'd picked out, a popular Italian at the top end of the Long Hill.

She tried telling herself that her motivation for seeing Taylor was sound; he was a good-looking, intelligent guy and he was clearly attracted to her. So far, so normal. What wasn't so normal was the ambivalence of her feelings for him. On the one hand, she felt physically attracted to him; on the other, she felt repulsed by him; moreover, agreeing to meet him was not entirely without ulterior motive.

Acknowledging that she was attracted to him was preferable to admitting that she had a 'gut feeling,' about the guy. She tried telling herself this was based on knowledge accumulated from past experience, rather than prejudice. Was it possible to think someone was creepy and still be attracted to them? Next thing, she'd be writing to convicted murderers expressing her undying love.

Ava unpinned the elaborate pleat and shook out her hair. On both of the previous occasions that she'd met Taylor, she'd had it tied up or back. Let him believe she wasn't on duty this evening.

* * *

"You look gorgeous," Taylor said, pecking Ava on the cheek when they met outside the restaurant an hour later. A pretty waitress with a sexy Italian accent showed them to their seats. Taylor whistled admiringly as Ava removed her jacket, his eyes all over her. She'd chosen to wear a short, floaty silk dress in inky blue, with a plunging neckline.

"You really are a very beautiful girl, Ava."

"I prefer 'woman,' but thank you all the same." She allowed her eyes to linger on him a moment, "You're not so bad yourself, Professor." Taylor's slightly wavy hair was slicked back and curled over his shirt collar at the back; his skin was smooth and unlined and his aftershave brand was familiar and chic. Ava visualised the expensive male grooming products jostling for space in his bathroom cabinet.

Taylor ordered a bottle of champagne. "Are we celebrating?" Ava asked.

"Being in the company of a beautiful *woman* is cause enough for celebration, but as a matter of fact I do have something else to be happy about. I heard from my publisher a couple of days ago; it seems that my book is the subject of a bidding war."

"You've written a book?" Ava had read about this on Taylor's Facebook page.

"What's it about? Metawhatsit poets?"

Taylor smiled, "I've written a number of scholarly articles on the metaphysical poets but no, it's a novel." He looked so ridiculously puffed up and pleased that Ava had to stifle a laugh.

"So, what's it about?" she asked.

"I suppose the overarching theme is love and betrayal," Taylor said, a patronising edge creeping into his tone, "but I suspect you want to know about the plot?"

"Well, duh!" Ava said, "Don't most people like a book with a good story?"

"Well, actually, like a lot of literary fiction, it's rather loosely plotted. My protagonist is an attractive, intellectual man in his thirties who . . ."

". . . So, it's kind of autobiographical?" Ava interrupted. The question was playful but it seemed to annoy Taylor.

"I'm a writer, Ava. All writers bring influences and experiences from their lives to their work, but my novel is first and foremost a work of fiction."

The champagne arrived and Ava graciously toasted Taylor's success as a man of letters. She studied him as he dealt with the waitress, who was clearly captivated by his manners and charm — that word again — it tripped off the lips with such ease where Taylor was concerned.

Ava took a sip of champagne, holding it in her mouth before swallowing, enjoying the delightful sensation of creamy bubbles exploding on the roof of her mouth, making her feel light-headed with anticipation. Without realising it, she had closed her eyes and when she opened them, Taylor was looking at her with amusement.

"What?" she said, embarrassed, "I don't often drink champagne. Got to make the most of it."

"You are a very sensual woman, Ava," he said, circling the back of her hand with the tip of his elegant finger, "seeing how sipping champagne can send you into such raptures makes me wonder how you would respond to a lover's caresses."

"Keep wondering," Ava snorted. She was trying her best to seem unflustered, but the truth was, Taylor's caresses were sending little bolts of electricity all through her body. From his slow, satisfied smile, she could tell he was enjoying her discomfort.

The waitress arrived with their hors d'oeuvres and they ate and talked, the soft candlelight flickering warmly between them, creating a sense of intimacy, which was enhanced by the effect of the champagne. To her surprise, Ava found herself beginning to relax in Taylor's company, to the extent that she admitted googling his biography. Maybe not such a bad move, as he was obviously flattered that she had done so.

"So, you know all about me, do you?" he asked.

"Not at all. A few paragraphs about your academic credentials reveals nothing about the man," Ava said. "Tell me something about the real Christopher Taylor."

"Well, I was almost a plumber."

"You're kidding me."

"My old man's got his own plumbing and heating business. Wanted me to learn the trade, join the business. Unfortunately for my father, I didn't want to spend my life with my head stuck down a toilet." He looked at Ava, "Your turn. Tell me something I don't know about you."

"Not a lot to tell. My parents divorced when I was quite young. Wanted to be a vet when I was a kid. Did A levels, went to university, gave it up after a year and became a cop."

"Why did you give up after a year?"

"Personal reasons."

"Boyfriend trouble?"

"Something like that. That's all you're going to get," Ava added, surprised that she'd even alluded to her disastrous university experience. Alcohol loosened her tongue; she seldom drank in company and she needed to be more circumspect, especially with this man, who it seemed was capable of making her confide things she seldom talked about.

At the end of the meal, Taylor requested the bill and Ava offered to pay her share, hoping he'd decline — which he did, to her relief when she saw how much the champagne alone had cost. Even tipping the waitress would have left her short.

"How about coffee at my place? It's only five minutes' walk away," Taylor asked as they left the Bistro. Ava considered his offer. She was still feeling tipsy from the champagne and the excellent wine Taylor had selected to accompany their meal. Driving home was out of the question, and the prospect of spending the night with the charming professor was too tempting to resist, it seemed, for she found herself agreeing without thinking much about the implications.

He slipped his arm around her waist as they strolled down the long hill, pulling her close until they were joined at the hip. As if in anticipation of the pleasure ahead, they began walking faster and there was no doubt that their minds were occupied with a single thought.

As soon as they reached his front door, Taylor pulled Ava into the hall of his townhouse and slammed the door behind them. It was built on three levels, and Ava wondered if they would make it to the bedroom, so urgent was their desire.

On the first level, Taylor pushed her into the lounge where he'd received her and Neal a few days earlier, and pinned her against the wall, kissing her and sliding his hand inside her dress to caress her breasts. Ava moaned with pleasure. Then, just as she thought they were about to do it right there against the wall, Taylor scooped her into his arms and carried her effortlessly upstairs to his bedroom.

"I've been imagining this all evening," Taylor said, as he unzipped the silk dress and let it slip from her shoulders.

"And I thought we were connecting on an intellectual level; all you wanted was my body."

"From the minute I saw you walking towards my house with that dour Scots DI, I've wanted nothing else." For a fleeting second, Jim Neal's face flashed into Ava's mind, inducing a peculiarly displaced feeling of guilt. Then it was gone, dismissed by Taylor's kisses and caresses and her own overwhelming urge to devour and enjoy his body as he was enjoying hers.

* * *

The next morning, Ava awoke suddenly, startled by the unfamiliar softness of the bed and the presence of another body in a warm, heavy sleep by her side. A bolt of pain shot through her head as she turned to see whose bed it was that she was sharing. Taylor was lying on his front, face squashed against the mattress, snoring softly. One long leg was wrapped around the cover, pulling it down, exposing his long, lean naked body all the way down his left side. Lust and repulsion vied for dominance in Ava's alcohol-befuddled brain. The events of the night before rushed into her thoughts: the dinner, the champagne, the sex. How could she have let things get so out of control?

Quiet as a cat, she slipped out of bed and gathered her clothes. In Taylor's en-suite bathroom, she splashed her face, cleaned her teeth with her fingers and some borrowed toothpaste, gargled some mouthwash and crept back into the bedroom, holding her breath lest she should awaken Taylor and be tempted back into his bed.

Downstairs, Ava toyed with the idea of snooping round a little. Taylor had appeared to be fast asleep, and she was sure she would hear him stirring in time, but she was also anxious to be out of his house as quickly as possible.

She hovered a moment outside the lounge, then slipped inside.

Taylor's laptop was lying on a chair, but there hardly seemed any point even taking a look since it was bound to be password protected. Ava turned it on anyway. When asked for a password, she typed in some random letters, hoping for a forgotten password prompt that would be as easy to decipher as her own. To her astonishment, it was. Taylor's prompt was, 'poetry' and she typed 'metaphysical' in the box.

Hardly believing her luck, she searched through a number of files, finding nothing but information on various aspects of English literature — clearly this was the laptop Taylor used for work. There were also a number of files that were obviously related to research for his novel, and drafts of the novel itself. Ava stifled a yawn as she read through the first paragraph, quickly deciding it wasn't likely to be her sort of book.

The power light started to flash a warning. A charger lay on the desk beside a black scarab paperweight, but Ava had seen all she needed to see. If Taylor had anything to hide, he knew better than to leave clues on a laptop that offered such easy access to its content.

Taylor's elegant eighteenth century writing desk was the next obvious place to search. Ava pulled out drawers and rifled through them with a trained eye, turning over papers and flicking through notebooks, being careful to return everything exactly as she'd found it.

Next, she searched Taylor's writing bureau. He was an organised man, she noted, everything filed away in cardboard wallets with the contents clearly written on the cover. One was labelled, 'photographs,' but it was quite slim and in fact contained only one picture. Curious, Ava held it up to the light. It was an image from a newspaper showing a smiling Taylor surrounded by Asian women. The caption had been cut off but it was clear that he was their teacher and Ava had already done enough fishing around in Taylor's background to know that he had taught English as a foreign language in some sort of community centre in Sheffield.

She was about to return the picture to its wallet, when she was struck by the smiling face of a lovely young girl, clearly the daughter of the woman beside her, who was also attractive but not as stunning. Ava turned the picture over to see a single name on the back: 'Rohina.' For some reason, Ava felt her detective senses tingle. She toyed with the idea of pocketing the photograph, but that was far too risky. Instead she used her phone to take a picture and returned the photo to its wallet and back into the drawer. With a last furtive look upstairs, Ava stepped outside into the waiting morning.

The road sloped steeply away from Taylor's townhouse, and though she longed to run, Ava was forced to walk slowly and carefully in her high heels. It was after seven now and there was a chill in the autumn air that hinted at frosty mornings to come, but Ava scarcely noticed the cold. As she walked the empty early morning streets, conscious that she looked like she had spent the night in someone else's bed, she was too wrapped up in thoughts about Christopher Taylor, the mysterious photograph and concerns about her own conscience to bemoan the lack of a warmer coat.

Chapter 11

"Bradley Turner's school record doesn't show anything particularly out of the ordinary behaviour-wise," Ava said to Neal as she plonked a mug of steaming coffee on the smiley face coaster on his desk, a present from Archie. Under her arm was the report from the investigating officer, which she'd read through, preparing to brief Neal.

"His behaviour gave no cause for concern. Described by most of his teachers as a quiet lad who wasn't particularly academic, but had an aptitude for art and design. Used to helping his dad out in his workshop, knew he wanted to design and make furniture from early on and obtained the qualifications he needed to get him on the right course. He's currently in his second year of a furniture design course at a college in Sheffield."

"Any issues at college?" Neal asked.

"He shares a flat with another lad, also a student. Other students on his course didn't have a lot to say about him except that he tends to keep himself to himself, but no one expressed dislike of him. No inappropriate behaviour towards girls, but . . ." Ava paused a moment for effect, "his flatmate said Bradley told him he was going out with a girl from home."

"Amy Hill?"

"That's right."

"Well, his love certainly wasn't reciprocated. To Amy, Bradley was just someone she had to put up with because of her mother's relationship with his father," Neal commented. "And we know he was aggressive towards her on at least one occasion."

"She mocked and ridiculed him both privately and publicly. Did his love turn to hate?" Ava mused.

"Forensics haven't come up with anything that would place him at the scene of the crime. And I can't help feeling that a spurned lover would want his victim to see his face as he killed her. Amy's killer was efficient and quick, almost in the manner of an executioner who cared nothing for his victim."

"Like a hit man. He just wanted the job done quickly," Ava agreed.

"Exactly," answered Neal, "there's also Simon Foster. As far as we're aware, Amy and Simon didn't know each other well, despite the fact their mothers were friends. But we know that Simon was probably stalking Amy, and that for some reason Amy regarded his presence as non-threatening, protective even. Was that a misconception on her part or did she have a genuine reason for trusting him? And if so, what was it?"

"She already knew him and decided he wasn't a threat to her?" suggested Ava.

"Maybe," said Neal, "Simon's disappearance certainly makes him appear guilty, despite Anna Foster's insistence that he was with her on the night of the murder. And, he had a trauma in his childhood that may have skewed his moral development."

Ava nodded, "His mother described him as being gentle and kind, naïve almost in his trust of other people's goodness. She's obviously biased, but the same words keep coming up when we question other people about him."

"Well, if our training and experience as police officers tells us anything, it's to be alert to the hidden lives people often lead, that no one in their immediate circle would guess at."

Neal was referring to Simon Foster, but Ava couldn't help thinking of Christopher Taylor.

"We need to find him," she said, stating the obvious. "Do you think Anna Foster knows where her son is?"

"No. I think she's as desperate as we are to know where he's gone," answered Neal. "She's very protective of him, probably because of his past."

"What about his father?" Ava asked.

"What about him? He has the soundest alibi of anyone," Neal said, sounding surprised.

"I don't mean as the killer," Ava said. "That's way out of the box. What I meant was, he's been in prison all these years; maybe he's used the time to reflect on his past misdeeds, wanted to make amends. Perhaps he contacted Simon recently without Anna's knowledge and asked to see him. Simon could have gone to London to visit him."

Ava saw Neal's lips ruck up, but he didn't immediately dismiss her idea. That was one of the things she had learned to appreciate about her boss; he listened and was never too quick to dismiss another person's contribution.

"Anna Foster certainly didn't mention that Simon had heard from his father, and I suspect it would distress her to know he'd been in touch. It's the sort of thing Simon would hide from her, for obvious reasons. I'll arrange for one of the local people to pay the father a call, find out if he's a reformed character seeking redemption or forgiveness, or whatever crap these rehabilitated murderers come out with. It's hard to see how he could hope for Simon to forgive him for his mother's — and sister's — murder. That'd be a tall order, even for someone as allegedly compassionate as Simon. In the meantime—" Neal was interrupted by a call on his mobile. It wasn't Archie or Maggie; Ava was familiar with their ringtones.

Besides, Neal was nodding gravely and looking at Ava as if eager to share the news with her.

"Come on," he said, as he returned his mobile to his inside jacket pocket.

"Where are we going?" Ava asked.

"Amy Hill's flat. Two bodies have been discovered there."

* * *

Nancy lay on her bed on top of her crumpled white bedspread, the one she had painstakingly embroidered by hand with hundreds of tiny pink roses. It had taken her months to complete and every stitch had been a labour of love, for it was an exact replica of her grandmother's bedspread torn up for rags, of which only one small square remained.

Richard had spent the night with her as he had every night since Amy's death. They had rowed again the previous evening and she had told him to go home for a while, which she regretted now; in a way she found his prolonged presence in her home reassuring, not suffocating as she sometimes had.

She could still hear his words buzzing around in her befuddled brain. "Tell me what it is you've been keeping from me all these years, Nancy. Let me share your worries. Let me help."

"Leave me if you can't live with my so-called secret past," she had yelled at him, unkindly, then, relenting, "for a few days at least. I just need some time."

Richard had been rooting around in her head for a long time, bleating about how she could trust him with whatever baggage she had brought from her past. It had been tempting to blurt it all out, to relieve herself of the burden of carrying her secret alone. But telling him would change everything between them; like admitting to an affair, it would fester between them, poisoning any hope of a happy future.

He would try to accept what she had done — and she knew he would try quite hard, for Richard was at heart a weak man, desperate for love. However much he tried, one day, sooner or later, the words would tumble out, "You're not the woman I thought you were." Nancy was tired of keeping her secret. She longed for someone impartial to guide her through the moral uncertainty that had beset her throughout all the years since Amy had come into her life. She wanted someone to tell her, once and for all, that she had been right — or wrong; for she was ready to be judged, even harshly, in return for some moral clarity.

Nancy closed her eyes and kneaded her forehead with her knuckles. It was still early in the day but she had awoken with a dull headache that was sucking away any promise the day might hold. The clock on her bedside table glowed distractingly. Eleven thirty. She had risen at five, unable to sleep, and sat in the living room watching the news. She found the repetition of the same stories over and over again oddly comforting, even though she could not concentrate on the content.

At six, when Richard came downstairs, she had pretended to be asleep. He kissed her lightly on the cheek and crept from the room, leaving the TV on. To her surprise, he had not returned to kiss her again before leaving for work. She had hoped he wouldn't, because she didn't like deceiving him, yet she couldn't help her prick of disappointment.

In the kitchen, she found a note saying that he would stay at his own house for a couple of days to give her some space. Tears stung Nancy's eyes at the thought of the pain she was causing this kind-hearted man whose love she didn't deserve.

Now, lying on her bed in a mid-morning slump, she wondered whether she would bother to move before he returned. In two days' time would he find her still lying there, weighted to the mattress by grief and self-pity?

Someone was knocking on her front door. Nancy stood up, a sudden cramp knotting her calf and she rubbed the back of her leg vigorously for a few moments, growing irritated when the sound persisted. She made it to her bedroom window in time to see a deliveryman retreating down the garden path, a long rectangular box tucked under his arm. Flowers. From Richard, no doubt. She watched guiltily as the man took the package next door, wishing she'd gone downstairs in time to catch him. Now her nosey neighbour Maureen would have another excuse to come knocking and prying.

The light from the window made her eyes ache and the pain in her head was getting worse. She took a couple of painkillers and lay down again, hoping to sleep but, underneath the pain, her mind was intent on remembering.

The last time Nancy had seen Amy alive, her daughter had come to 'In Stitches,' to meet her for afternoon tea; they'd gone to the new patisserie and, as always, Amy had ordered the most expensive items on the menu. Nancy didn't care; she was happy to see Amy, happy to pay to spend time in her company.

Amy had been wearing a smart designer dress and an expensive-looking gold and coral necklace which she claimed was a gift from a boy she had dated a couple of times. She didn't reveal much about him, except to say that he was a student in her year and that he had wealthy parents who gave him a generous allowance. They had only dated two or three times before Amy called it a day.

Nancy hadn't commented, except to admire the necklace, but she had wondered about it; however generous the boy's parents were, buying such an expensive gift must have left him out of pocket. Nor was it was the sort of gift you gave someone after a couple of dates.

Amy had been wearing the necklace the night she was killed. For the time being, it was in the possession of the police in a plastic evidence bag along with the other items that her daughter had been wearing that night. Eventually it would be returned to Nancy, which was not right; Amy was supposed to inherit Nancy's riches, not the other way around.

At last the mildly analgesic effect of the painkillers began to kick in, and Nancy felt a faint, chemically-induced glow of well-being numb the edges of her depression. Sleep would come now, deep enough, she hoped, to obliterate all sense of pain, past and present.

Perversely, she lay awake, obsessing over the past. Since Amy's murder, she kept experiencing her past like a victim of post-traumatic stress disorder, in random flashes that shocked her with their intensity. It was like the nightmares she had suffered when she first moved to Shelton, which had lessened with time, as her carefully constructed story about the past began to seem real to her. She thought again of the night Debbie had turned up at her door, bruised and beaten, and the aggressive way Debbie had warned her off contacting social services. Knowing the care system as she did, that would be the last thing Nancy would do. She knew that the only way she could keep Peter and Emily safe was to continue to be involved in their lives, acting as a safety net between their inadequate parents and the pitfalls of state care.

After that night, and Debbie's revelation that she had abandoned her children to the violent Wade, Nancy looked upon Debbie's estate as a moral void, a place where you could act according to your own sense of right and wrong. Nancy was only twenty; her moral sense was inchoate. She grew to believe that, in her case at least, the ends justified the means. Now Amy's death had resurrected all the old doubts and thrown her moral compass out of kilter.

"I'm sorry," Nancy whispered — to Amy, to Debbie Clark's ghost, to the girl she had been, but most of all, to Richard, for she now knew what she had to do to put things right.

* * *

A small crowd had gathered on the pavement where the emergency services were parked outside the entrance to the house where Becci and Amy had shared a home. Ava looked up at the first floor window, flinching at the sight of Nancy's pretty handmade curtains, the thought of all those lovingly stitched cushions, the carefully chosen rugs. The house had absorbed so much tragedy in such a short time, and yet it looked so cared for. The path leading up to the door was weed and clutter free, the door itself recently painted a fresh sky blue, the brass fittings polished to a sheen.

Neal parked his car in front of the house next door, behind the gaping doors of a waiting ambulance. A paramedic greeted them with a sombre expression as they stepped out of the vehicle. Two uniformed officers standing sentinel at the gate, shuffled out of the way to let them through.

"What happened here?" Neal asked.

"Cleaner found two bodies in the back bedroom when she came by to clean the flat, sir. One male, one female, believed to be Rebecca Jones and Gary Reid. She's inside having a cup of tea with PC Dale. Says she didn't touch anything, just saw them on the bed and knew they were dead so she phoned 999 straightaway. Dale got here first but by then Mrs Pringle, the cleaner, had attracted the attention of a couple of neighbours. None of them's been inside, sir, so the scene hasn't been compromised."

Neal nodded approvingly. "Good work."

Inside the house, someone, probably Dale or one of the other officers had cordoned off the stairs with crisscrossed tape. Neal and Ava ducked under the tape and took the steps to the bedroom two at a time. No doubt one of the constables would already have made notes, but Ava was jotting down her own observations.

The most obvious detail was the absence of violence. Nothing in the room appeared to have been disturbed. There was no sign that anyone but Gary and Becci had been in the room. The couple lay intertwined on the bed, Gary's hand clasped around the TV remote control, but the set had been turned off — not with the remote, or it would have been on stand-by.

"Someone turned the TV off," Ava remarked. "The cleaner? These two look like they were watching it and fell asleep." It wasn't quite true, then, that the scene was uncompromised.

"Cause of death," Neal said, walking over to the gas fire, an out-dated, utilitarian-looking model placed in front of an original tiled fireplace. "Carbon monoxide poisoning? Judging from their appearance." He checked the switch on the fire; it was turned to the off position; a window sash had been thrown open to admit fresh air.

They found PC Dale and Mrs Pringle drinking tea in the kitchen. Mrs Pringle was pale and quiet; not the sort of woman who made a fuss, it seemed. She answered Neal and Ava's questions calmly and without drama. Yes, she had turned the TV off. Ditto the gas fire 'on account of the smell of gas.' She had also opened the window. No, she hadn't touched anything else; no she hadn't noticed anything out of place. How did she know that Becci and Gary were dead? asked Neal. She replied that she, 'just knew,' which was as good an answer as any. That, and the fact that they hadn't responded to her wake up calls.

"Was this an accident?" Ava asked, when she and Neal were safely out of earshot across the hallway. "The fire could have been tampered with. Maybe someone had a reason for wanting to shut these two up. The same someone who murdered Amy."

Neal looked sceptical, "They're not necessarily connected. We have to explore all the possibilities, Merry. Including the one that suggests these deaths, even if not accidental, have nothing to do with Amy's case."

"Becci and Gary were hiding something from us that day we interviewed them."

"We can't be sure of that, either," Neal said, "and even if they were, it wasn't necessarily anything to do with Amy. People are often nervous around the police."

"Bit of a coincidence, though, isn't it, sir? Even you have to admit that one."

"Even me?" Neal answered, sounding amused.

Before Ava could make an embarrassed apology, he cut her off. "You're wrong if you think I lack imagination Sergeant. I'm not a pedant. I've just learned by experience to rein in my initial responses — which may be the same as yours, by the way. Only difference is, I'm far too aware of all the instances of cases crashing because somewhere along the line, someone closed their mind to other possibilities."

Ava tried not to let her frustration show in her face, but she was not good at dissembling. From her point of view, she had been doing exactly what Neal was saying; opening her mind to all the possibilities. As if reading her thoughts, or, perhaps, her damaged ego, Neal added,

"Of course the cases may be related. You're right to bring it up. Look, I just want to be sure that you don't become one of those detectives who single-mindedly pursues an idea to a disappointing end up a one-way street. There are enough of those types on the force already, and you're so much better than that."

Coming from Neal, this was a sort of compliment and Ava accepted it as such. She didn't look for praise from her DS and she knew he didn't dispense it for its own sake. If there was a connection between the deaths, they'd find it. If not, then, she'd have other theories at the ready.

They were distracted by a sudden banging on the door, and the pathologist walked briskly into the hallway, dressed, casually for him, in a pair of jeans and a zip-up hooded fleece.

"What have you got for me this time?" Ashley Hunt asked, in his usual high spirits, which deflated within seconds of catching sight of the victims through the half open bedroom door.

"Aw guys, not more kids?"

"We don't select your clients, Ash." Neal said, dryly. They waited while he made a preliminary examination of the couple.

"I think there's little doubt we're looking at carbon monoxide poisoning," he concluded after only a couple of minutes. "Look at those rosy cheeks — dead giveaway, if you'll excuse the pun. Victims always look like they're glowing with health." He glanced over at the windows, "I see someone's already taken sensible measures."

"Thanks, Ash. I appreciate your arriving so promptly. I know you were on a day off."

"I wasn't far away," Hunt answered. "My favourite coffee shop is just around the corner and I had my bag in the car. Only too glad to help, if it means you catch the bastard who's preying on all these young kids."

Ava glanced at Neal. Seemed like Ashley Hunt was drawing the same conclusions she had about the killer. Neal didn't correct him. They watched as Hunt departed, pausing for a friendly word with one of the constables guarding the door, who apparently was his wife's friend's son. Hunt was one of those affable people who seem to know everyone.

"Let's treat these deaths as suspicious until we have confirmation one way or the other," Neal said briskly.

They spent the next half hour searching through the house. Becci's room was freakishly tidy. Books were arranged on shelves in alphabetical order, nothing lay on the carpet except a pair of fluffy pink slippers, which had been placed side by side near the bed; it held no clutter, and no personal touches. It was a Spartan room that seemed to scream its lack of personality.

"No knickknacks or photographs, not even any make up lying about. Becci's tidiness borders on the obsessive," Ava observed."

Neal walked over to Becci's wardrobe.

"Take a look at this," he said, whistling. Inside, the rail was crammed with designer clothes and shoes.

"Wow," Ava said, pulling out coat hangers at random. "She didn't buy these in Primark — Prada, Gucci, Stella McCartney. Who'd have thought our little mouse Becci had such expensive taste in clothes? And look at this, the majority of them are BNWT."

Seeing Neal's look of puzzlement, she clarified, "Brand New With Tags."

"Are all these Becci's?" Neal said, a look of incredulity on his face.

"I'm guessing they were Amy's," Ava answered, holding a Nicole Farhi dress up and posing in front of a long mirror on the back of the wardrobe door.

"Suits you," Neal remarked. Ava made a face and returned the dress to the rail.

"What makes you think they were Amy's?"

"Remember how Amy was dressed when we found her? Think how Becci was dressed when we interviewed her the day after Amy's death — this is more Amy's style than Becci's."

She went on, "Do you reckon Nancy Hill gave permission for Becci to have these? I reckon she didn't even know her daughter had such a well-stocked wardrobe of designer gear. I bet Becci cleared Amy's wardrobe out before Nancy even had a chance to look. Probably just after we turned up to interview her that day — remember she said Amy's bedroom door was locked and we didn't bother to check?

She probably kept what she liked and put the rest on eBay. Maybe that's what she and Gary were uneasy about the day we interviewed them. Should be easy enough for our tech guys to check if she's been selling stuff, by looking on her laptop."

Neal nodded. "Expensive jewellery, expensive clothes. Nancy's business is doing well, but she's hardly a FTSE

100 contender. So where was Amy getting the money from to finance her designer lifestyle? Who or what was she involved with?"

There was a name on the tip of Ava's tongue, but she wasn't about to say it aloud. Christopher Taylor had a sound alibi for the night of Amy's death.

"I'll have Becci and Gary's bank account details checked out, sir."

"Amy's has already been scrutinised. There was no sign of any deposits other than an allowance from Nancy, which was generous but not enough to pay for all of this," Neal said, running a hand along the line of garments on the clothes rail.

"Looks like she was spending it as fast as she got it," Ava remarked. On an impulse, she crossed to Becci's bed and stuck a hand under the mattress. Her arm disappeared up to her elbow as she slid it along the bed.

"Eureka!" she cried, tugging a creased manila envelope out and waving it in the air. The contents spilled out across the bed, a flurry of different coloured notes.

"There must be a grand here if not more. No wonder Becci and Gary were uneasy about having a couple of cops in the house. This was Amy's money, I'll bet, along with the clothes. I'm beginning to wonder if Becci's concern when Amy went missing was motivated by self-interest. She was certainly quick to capitalise on her friend's death."

"Was Amy involved with someone other than Professor Taylor?" Neal asked, "A sugar daddy?" Ava wrinkled her nose in distaste at the term, but it was a possibility. Then a thought occurred to her.

"Do you think it's possible she was blackmailing someone, sir?"

Neal pursed his lips.

"The obvious candidate would be Taylor but on what grounds? If they were in a sexual relationship, Taylor wasn't breaking any laws; they were both consenting adults. At most it would have been an abuse of his position of power and may have been a disciplinary offence, depending on what view the university takes of such affairs. It's a moot point, anyway. Taylor has a cast-iron alibi for the night of Amy's murder."

Back to that, Ava thought, unhappily. She said, "Supposing Becci knew Amy was blackmailing someone and she decided to carry it on after Amy's death? If the person Amy was blackmailing killed her, why would he stop at Amy?"

Neal didn't dismiss her theory. Instead, he reminded her that they didn't even know whether Becci and Gary had died as a result of a faulty appliance or deliberate tampering. In her mind, Ava was convinced it wasn't the former, but she reined in her impulse to rush to a conclusion without proof. As Neal had reminded her, the worst thing a detective could do was close her mind to other possibilities. Things were not always as they seemed.

* * *

That evening, in the quietness of her secluded cottage, Ava sipped a second glass of wine and ruminated on the events of the day — and on the nature of her relationship with Christopher Taylor. There were five messages from him on her smartphone, asking when he could see her again. So far, she had been stalling him, saying that she was busy with the investigation and had no free time, hoping that he would work it out eventually. God knows, he was smart enough in every other sense, surely even someone with an ego as massive as his would click eventually that she wasn't interested.

Except, it wasn't that simple, was it? Ava's mind returned to the night she had spent in Taylor's bed. However much she disliked the man, there was no doubt that he pushed all her buttons sexually, damn him. Even as her reason told her he was not a good bet, her body was betraying her with subtle feelings of arousal as she pictured the way she had last seen him, his long lean body wrapped in his exquisite Egyptian cotton sheet.

"Why am I so convinced he's a rat?" she asked her fat cat, Camden, who was curled up beside her on the sofa, purring hypnotically. As always, when she consulted him on any matter, urgent or trivial, he stared at her with the same bored expression, as if to say, "Why should I care?"

"I mean, it's not as if I know he's guilty of anything; it's just a bloody *feeling*, for goodness sake. The man could be a saint for all I know." Camden yawned and turned away.

"Jim doesn't like him," Ava said to Camden, wondering why that mattered, but it did. She said Neal's first name aloud again, enjoying the sound of it on her lips.

"I think I need another glass, Camden," she said to the cat, who meowed in protest when she rose from the sofa to pour a refill. After the third glass, Ava fell asleep, waking well past midnight from dreams in which the things she did with Christopher Taylor and her boss in turn made her blush with shame, regretful that her only male companion was of the feline variety.

Chapter 12

The following morning, Neal greeted Ava with a train ticket.

"Don't take your coat off. I picked this up for you earlier this morning. If you move yourself, you can make the eight thirty-five." Ava took the ticket and glanced down at her destination: Sheffield.

"Bradley?" she asked.

"I want you to question him again. Find out about his obsession with Amy; get a list of the dates when he was in Stromford recently. Even if he's innocent of any wrong-doing himself, he may have information that can help in the investigation. Focus on who he saw Amy with, where she went, you know the kind of thing."

Ava cast a regretful look at the coffee machine before making for the door. She had just fifteen minutes to make it to the station and decided to make a run for it rather than take her car and get stuck in the morning traffic.

She made it with three minutes to spare but her dodgy ankle throbbed with pain as she sank, breathless, into a backwards-facing window seat, looking once more with regret, at a coffee kiosk on the station platform that she'd had no time to visit.

As soon as the train pulled out of the station, she went in search of the buffet car. Five minutes later, large black americano in hand, she settled into her seat and gazed out of the window at the receding view of a flat, harvested wheat field overhung by a rain-swollen sky and a low autumn sun that made the shadows between the ridges of golden stubble look as though they were smudged with charcoal.

It had been a while since she'd been out of town and even longer since she'd visited a decent sized city. Stromford was more of a large town, despite its pretensions and its resplendent cathedral perched on just about the only hill in the county. The shopping could be better, Ava had thought on first arriving in Stromford, bemoaning the lack of fashionable chain stores on the high street. But new retail developments were underway that would bring the town up to date, including the imaginative adaptive reuse of a number of nineteenth century commercial buildings that had fallen into disuse, as shops, cafes and restaurants.

The journey would take about an hour and a half and though the seat next to Ava was empty, she didn't want to risk having a passenger getting on at the next stop sit next to her and attempt to engage her in banal conversation, so she put her headphones on, closed her eyes and made the world go away in a blast of sound.

This wouldn't be Jim Neal's music of choice, she thought absently, her head nodding to the beat. He was a classical music man, particularly fond of Bach and the Baroque period, but lately she had heard him humming modern stuff that Archie liked. The thought made her smile. Neal wasn't exactly dour, but he was a tad on the serious side and it was as well that he had a young son — and a light-hearted sister — to keep him from becoming a fossil.

A man in a pinstripe suit got on at the next stop and settled into the seat beside Ava's. Not the chatty type, thank goodness, Ava thought, watching him extract a tablet computer from his briefcase and turn it on. Within seconds he was immersed in reading The Times online. Ava stared out of the window, mentally reviewing the case. She had turned her music off — it was too distracting, but kept the headphones on to deflect any conversation.

She deliberately avoided thinking about Taylor. This morning, she needed to focus on Bradley and his part in Amy's tragedy. He had grown up with her these past seven or eight years. They had been children together, then teenagers, even though Bradley had lived with his mother and only seen Amy when he was staying with his father on occasional weekends and holidays. They had never actually shared a house, where a true brother and sister relationship might have developed. It was quite natural, then, that Bradley should develop un-brotherly feelings towards Amy.

According to various sources, Amy had no such feelings for Bradley. Far from it; she seemed to have treated him badly. She had mocked his feelings and belittled him, and Bradley had clearly suffered a blow to his self-esteem.

It was the kind of thing that often happened to teenagers, especially in these days of social networking. Most got over the humiliation and moved on, but for some, resentment might fester until it found an outlet. Had Amy's ill-treatment pushed Bradley over the edge? It was already established that he could be aggressive; his behaviour at Amy's funeral had proved that he did not have himself entirely under control.

* * *

The journey passed quickly and Ava was surprised when the shantytown façade of the famous — or infamous

— Park Hill flats loomed into view, signalling that she had arrived at her destination.

She took a cab to Bradley's address; he'd been contacted first thing in the morning and given the choice of talking to a police officer at home, or going down to the station to answer some questions. Bradley had chosen the former. When he answered the door to Ava, he was still in his pyjamas.

"You're an early riser, I see," Ava remarked dryly.

"I got wakened up at the crack of dawn by you lot phoning me. No point getting up early when I wasn't going to be in class this morning."

Ava didn't bother to point out that he did have an interview to get up for. Obviously, talking to the police wasn't an activity he deemed worthy of getting out of bed for.

"May I come in?" Ava asked.

"Give me five minutes to put some clothes on," Bradley said, inviting her inside. He disappeared off upstairs after showing her into a kitchen diner. Ava looked around in some surprise. Bradley rented his accommodation with another male student, she knew. She also knew that it was sexist of her to assume that the place would be a mess. In fact it was clean and tidy to the point of obsession. Either these guys were not your typical students or one of them was suffering from OCD.

Bradley returned, dressed in a pair of jeans and a red T-shirt with a caption saying, 'Keep calm and build a cabinet,' on the front. Ava declined his offer of a coffee, then changed her mind when, to her surprise, she spied a state of the art coffee maker. It wouldn't hurt to be a little informal. As they waited for the coffee to perk, she spoke with him about his course, hoping to break the ice.

"You're learning to design and make furniture, I hear," she said, "Do you need to be good at art for that?"

"It helps," Bradley answered, "Art and design was my best subject at school. I was pretty crap at everything else."

"Are you hoping to go into business with your dad?"

"Maybe. Dad taught me everything he knew, but it's still good to get a qualification under your belt. My course includes modules on how to run a business and I've got big plans." Bradley puffed up with self-importance, perhaps seeing himself as Alan Sugar's next apprentice entrepreneur.

Ava noticed that Bradley spilt some coffee on the worktop and that he left the teaspoon he'd stirred his cup with lying on the side of the sink; not the one, then.

"You've come about Amy, haven't you? Not to talk about me."

"Yes," answered Ava.

"I've already told you everything I know."

"I just want to ask a few questions, that's all. It's possible that you may have information that will be of use to us, without even knowing it."

"I didn't kill her," Bradley said, sullenly.

"But you did like her?" Ava said, not unkindly.

"I used to. You know that already. She wasn't interested. End of. Like I said."

"Not exactly. We know you were following Amy, possibly stalking her. You told your flatmate — and other friends at uni that you were going out with her. Why did you tell them that, Bradley?"

Bradley shrugged, "I thought she'd come to her senses eventually and go out with me."

Bradley wasn't bad looking. He was tall enough and looked as though he worked out. He could stand to lose a couple of pounds, but it wasn't a stretch of the imagination to see girls his age fancying him, Ava thought. On the downside, Bradley had an unfortunate manner, aggressive and rather domineering. This might appeal to some girls, but apparently it hadn't won him over to Amy.

"Look, I cared about Amy. Okay, I was a bit obsessed with her, but I would never have hurt her, even though she was a bitch to me."

But you did hurt her once, didn't you, Ava thought, convinced Bradley was in deep denial, "Do you think every girl who isn't attracted to you is a bitch?"

"No, you're twisting my words — I meant she behaved like a bitch towards me — made fun of me in front of her friends, put stuff on Facebook about me. Told them all I was a pervert. She wasn't above borrowing money from me, though."

Ava's senses were alerted,

"Amy borrowed money from you? How much? How often?" Bradley shrugged. No doubt he was ashamed of being so in thrall to Amy that he had actually lent her money even though she had made it clear she despised him.

"Not much. I'm a student, remember? I make a bit of money selling stuff I've made — jewellery boxes, animals carved out of wood. Amy always seemed to know when I had money in my pocket. She was nice enough to me when she wanted to borrow some."

"How much?" Ava asked again.

"The odd tenner here and there."

Not enough to pay for the kind of clothes Amy had hanging in her wardrobe, thought Ava. Whoever had financed her expensive tastes, it wasn't Bradley. She had probably just extracted money from him for fun, because he was such easy bait.

"When you were following Amy, did you ever see her with anyone else?"

"What, blokes, you mean? I saw her with a smooth-looking git once or twice. Looked quite a bit older than her. And with Simon Foster."

"Simon?" Ava asked, tingling with interest, "Amy knew Simon Foster? You saw them together?"

"Not exactly," Bradley answered, "I wouldn't say they were together. I think Simon was following Amy too." Ava shuddered at the idea of a double stalking. What was it about Amy Hill that turned men into predators?

146

"Why did you think that?" she asked

"When I was . . . following Amy, I used to see him hanging around, watching her. I think she knew he was there but didn't mind. I think she pretended she wasn't aware of him. She didn't seem threatened or annoyed by him."

Just like Becci had said, Ava remembered. Very likely, Simon was Amy's benign stalker; the one she believed was looking out for her.

"What about you? Did she know you were stalking her?"

"I'm not a weirdo, you know. I only followed her a couple of times. After that time when I . . . when she fell over, I gave it up, decided she was a waste of time. I didn't mean to hurt her, you know. It was an accident."

"Yeah, right," Ava said, thinking again of Bradley's behaviour on the day of Amy's funeral.

"Am I a suspect?" he asked, "I've got an alibi, you know. My flatmate can vouch for me."

It was true, Bradley's claim about going on a drunken pub crawl with his flatmate had checked out.

Ava finished her coffee, feeling a little uncomfortable about having enjoyed it so much. It didn't seem polite to accept a person's hospitality, and then insinuate that you suspected them of murder.

"And that girl in the pub? If Inspector Neal and your father hadn't stopped you, you'd have given her a black eye at the very least."

Bradley gave her a dirty look, "I've got a temper, right? Sometimes I can't stop myself, but I never meant to hurt her."

Any twinge of pity that Ava had felt on seeing the Facebook pictures of the drunken, naked, overweight Bradley in a series of unflattering poses was quickly evaporating. She decided to try a different line of questioning.

"Would it surprise you to learn that Becci and her boyfriend were found dead yesterday at Becci's flat?"

It was evident that Bradley was shocked by the news. The colour drained from his face and he stared at Ava in disbelief.

"You're not trying to nail me for that as well, are you? Because I've been in Sheffield for the past two weeks — ask anyone."

"We will," Ava answered. "Bradley, do you have any idea why someone might have wanted either of them dead?"

"I didn't know Gary that well. He was a bit of a clown and he didn't seem that bright to me, considering he was at uni. Becci was a bitch but she didn't deserve to die. Was she strangled like Amy?"

Ava wasn't surprised to hear Bradley describe Amy's best friend as a bitch. Probably tried it on with her too.

"No. Carbon monoxide poisoning."

"In her flat?" He sounded surprised.

"Yes. I already told you that."

"They had an alarm," Bradley said, "I remember my dad telling Nancy to make sure they had one when Amy moved in. And he gave me one when I moved in here. Look." Bradley got up and crossed to a bookshelf, and pointed to a round white monitor with a green light that flashed intermittently.

Ava nodded. She had one herself. The piercing signal it emitted had startled her out of a deep sleep one morning; a warning that the battery power was low. She had taken the batteries out . . . had she replaced them? Ava made a mental note to check at the earliest opportunity. They had searched Amy and Becci's flat for a monitor, and found one which had dead batteries, but she didn't reveal this to Bradley.

"If there's anything else you remember that might help with the investigation, I hope you'll contact me," Ava said.

Bradley nodded but she wasn't convinced she'd be hearing from him any time soon.

Out on the doorstep, she asked him, as an afterthought, how well he knew Simon Foster. She was puzzled by his flustered, stuttering denial of ever having spoken to Simon. Nancy wasn't Bradley's stepmother or anything like that, but she was Anna Foster's friend, and it wasn't too much of a stretch to assume that Simon and Bradley might have known each other.

"I never spoke to him," Bradley repeated unnecessarily, giving Ava just the opposite impression. She left Bradley's place feeling that she had learned nothing new, and with an intense feeling of frustration.

Ava suspected Bradley of lying about Simon, and wondered suddenly if he were protecting him. Did he know where Simon was? It might be worth having someone watch Bradley's place for a while, and follow him to see if he might lead them to Simon.

* * *

Her business with Bradley concluded for the time being, Ava should have had no reason to linger in Sheffield, but the next through train to Stromford wasn't for a couple of hours, and she had wanted to take a trip to Sheffield in any case, to carry out a bit of her own research on Christopher Taylor. After finding the picture of the Asian women in his bureau, she had carried out some off-the-record checks into Taylor's background, in particular his time teaching English to recent immigrants at a community centre in Sheffield, while he had been completing his doctorate. It had not taken great powers of detection to discover where this was.

To save time, Ava took a cab, and within twenty minutes of leaving Bradley's flat, she was standing outside the door of a community centre in eastern Sheffield — an area with a sizeable Asian population.

A slight, pretty, Pakistani woman greeted her at the reception desk.

"How may I help you?" she asked Ava.

"I was wondering if you or any of your colleagues might recall working with a man by the name of Christopher Taylor. He taught English here a few years back so it's quite likely he would still be remembered, or that you have records of his time here."

"May I ask why you are looking for this man?" the woman asked.

"I'm afraid that's confidential," Ava answered, reluctantly producing her badge. The woman checked the records on her computer, having tilted the screen so that Ava couldn't see what she was doing.

"Yes, I can confirm Mr Taylor worked here."

"Would it be possible for me to obtain a list of names of the women he taught?" Ava asked.

"I'm sorry. Data Protection Act forbids me from supplying that information without their permission." It was the answer she had expected, but still Ava was disappointed. It was frustrating to be so close to information on Taylor and yet so far from obtaining it. It wasn't as if she could go through the legal route; there was no valid reason for checking into Taylor's past given his watertight alibi.

"It seems that Mr Taylor left very suddenly," the young woman added, shaking her head. Reading off the screen, she said. "It says here that one of his classes did exceptionally well, and they were interviewed for a feature in the local paper. There was a picture of the group with their tutor," she said, directing a meaningful look at Ava.

"Thank you," Ava said, smiling back, already planning a detour to the newspaper office.

In less than an hour, on the pretext of being a sociology PhD student researching the impact of learning English on recent immigrants' chances of finding employment, Ava had a copy of the photograph and the names of all the women pictured with a smiling Christopher Taylor.

Locating them would be easy, as they all lived in one or other of the estates serviced by the community centre. Stopping only for a takeaway coffee and croissant in a Costa near the newspaper office, Ava made tracks for the centre, armed with a copy of the picture.

The community centre was housed in a former primary school building of Victorian origin. Carved in stone above the two doors, you could still see the separate signs for boys' and girls' entrances and the date — 1862 — when the school had been built. There was nothing dreary about the place, for all that it was utilitarian in purpose and over one hundred and fifty years old. The doors were painted a cheerful glossy red and the windows were UPVC and brilliant white.

The old school playground at the side of the building had modern play equipment, a wooden tower with a twisty slide, swings and tunnels and climbing frames in bright primary colours. On the other side there was a garden landscaped with shrubs and wooden seats. It was a multi-cultural, multi-purpose centre intended to cater for the needs of the local community, both educational and recreational, like hundreds of others across the country. It wasn't the sort of place Ava could imagine the suave Taylor fitting in. She was in no doubt that his volunteering there had been a means to an end, had ticked some boxes on his career path, or maybe he just needed the money.

Ava stepped inside, pausing at a notice board that displayed signs about clubs, events and classes being held at the Centre. ESOL, or English as a Second Language classes were held on Mondays and Wednesdays in the afternoon. Ava jotted down the contact details for the class and then followed a sign directing visitors to the information desk. The young woman she had seen earlier was nowhere in sight. The information desk was in a small classroom that a couple of paid community workers and volunteers used as an office.

As soon as she walked through the door, Ava was greeted warmly by a middle-aged woman in an emerald green sari. On her way to the Centre, Ava had embellished her background story. She was a social sciences student, researching the experiences of women from other cultures learning English, and was interested in interviewing the women to find out how the lessons had benefited them in the years since their qualification. She had been given a copy of the photograph of Christopher Taylor's former class by the professor himself, she said, as well as the names of some former students of his who might be willing to talk to her.

It all sounded a bit implausible to Ava, but the woman in the makeshift office seemed genuinely pleased to help and — amazingly — contacted three of the women there and then to see if they were available for interview.

* * *

That was how, only twenty minutes later, Ava came to be sipping warm, milky tea in the flat of one of the women, while they waited for more members of the group to arrive, her enthusiastic hostess having made calls to several of the others.

As she sipped, Ava began feverishly putting together a list of questions to ask the women, feeling a twinge of guilt at exploiting their willingness to help.

Six members of the group turned up within ten minutes of Ava's arrival. They were all complimentary about Taylor, saying what a fine teacher he had been and so handsome and charming. Clearly, he had made an impression. Of the ten members of the class, four were missing. Two were at work, one was visiting relatives and the last, pictured with her arm around a beautiful young girl, had moved away.

As they looked at the photograph, and were reminiscing, one of the women pointed at the missing group member, prompting a discussion about her sudden departure from the estate, soon after the photograph was taken. It was the last time the group had been together. Mr Taylor had departed soon afterwards and his students were split up, most of them going to a class run by his replacement, a retired female schoolteacher, very dull by comparison.

From their hushed voices as they discussed the woman's departure, Ava could tell that something was amiss.

"Why did she leave the group?" Ava asked, noting the way they all looked at each other, unwilling to talk.

"She was transferred to another estate. It all happened very quickly, within a couple of days," one of them volunteered.

"Is that unusual?" Ava asked. Her question sparked a heated debate about how long most people waited for the Council to transfer them, even in circumstances of severe overcrowding. Even though she had been their friend, the woman had apparently left without a word of explanation. For a few minutes they chattered in their own language, but from their lowered tones and furtive glances, Ava could tell they were gossiping.

"Was there some kind of emergency?" she asked, eager to know more. She directed her question at the group, but let her eyes linger a little longer on one woman, whom she believed to be the lead gossip. At first it seemed that no one was willing to answer, and then the woman she had singled out confirmed Ava's suspicions.

"We don't really know, but we think there must have been some scandal involving the family," she said. "For a family to move so quickly, it must be something of that nature." It was clear to Ava, that this implied some kind of sexual scandal, though she was certain the woman would never say so.

On a sudden impulse she asked, "Who is the young girl with her? Is it her daughter?"

"Yes, that's Rohina, her daughter. She sometimes came with her mother to the evening class. Very pretty girl. Only fourteen when picture taken." The others looked at her as though in warning. There was a silence. A couple of the women looked down. No one spoke but the atmosphere had changed suddenly. Ava felt less welcome than before.

"Is it alright if I ask you some questions relating to my research?" she asked hurriedly in a bid to repair the situation. For the next half hour she played the part of academic researcher. The women were cooperative and answered her questions fully and honestly, but they were a different group now, guarded, closed, wary of the outsider in their midst.

Back at the information desk, Ava spoke with the woman in the green sari, whose name was Rukhsana, this time revealing her true purpose in visiting the estate. At first Rukhsana was angry at being deceived, but she also seemed a little in awe of Ava's badge, and her rank of Detective Sergeant. Before she said good-bye to Rukhsana, Ava had elicited a promise from her to find out what she could about Rohina and her family, and pass on what she knew to Ava.

It was mid-afternoon by the time Ava left the estate with a notebook full of notes for an imaginary thesis. She had also made other, more relevant notes, and in particular, about the coincidence of Taylor's sudden departure from the class at roughly the same time as Rohina and her mother's disappearance from the estate.

Chapter 13

A little before eight the following morning, Ava slipped into Neal's office, coffee cup in hand, and made a beeline for her boss's black leather chair, that he had brought in personally when a trapped nerve in his spine had made it impossible for him to sit comfortably in anything else. Every time she sat in it (and that wasn't often) Ava too felt spoiled for any other chair.

There was a lot of paperwork on the desk in front of her. Jim Neal was normally a neat person, but this morning his desk was strewn with the detritus of a late night: an empty coffee cup, a pizza box sitting atop a pile of untidy files, mail left where he'd opened it the previous day.

Ava felt no urge to tidy up. Instead, she picked up the framed photo of Neal and his son, Archie, that always sat by the phone. She found her gaze lingering on the father's face, taking in the dark hair and the blue eyes that could only be described by resort to cliché — in other words, they were piercing. His eyelids were slightly hooded, giving him a permanently seductive look.

Suddenly embarrassed by the direction in which her thoughts were nudging her, Ava hurriedly returned the photo to its spot on Neal's desk. She couldn't afford to permit herself to see her boss as anything other than a colleague — possibly a friend, but no more. She suspected he worked to a similar code. Most men seemed to be attracted to her, but if Jim Neal appreciated her natural charms, he was doing a good job of not letting it show.

She remembered how flustered he had been when she had teased him about Anna Foster, and wondered if he preferred older women? There was no doubt that Anna was attractive, but she had about her an air of sadness that spoke of small tragedies in her life. Physically, she was fragile and unthreatening. Perhaps she aroused Neal's male protective instinct, unlike Ava who was hale and athletic, her body honed and ready. Ready for what? One of her ex-boyfriends had suggested she was perpetually ready for flight. Ava preferred to think that she was ready for its corollary; a body prepped for flight was also one ready to kick ass.

"Hands off, he's mine."

Ava looked up to see Polly Jenkins, or 'PJ' as she was better known, standing in the doorway, a big grin on her face. PJ was a police constable and she and Ava had hit it off at a drinking session at the White Hart, the station's favourite watering hole, after Ava's long first day on the job. Having been invited to come along and toast another colleague's birthday, Ava had walked into the pub in her running gear intending only to stay for a polite fruit juice. But she and PJ had got talking and discovered they had a lot in common. It had been raining outside, and the lure of good conversation as well as the opportunity to make a new friend had persuaded Ava to stay on, and she'd never regretted that decision. On that first evening, an inebriated PJ had confessed that she had a major crush on Jim Neal.

"You know I only go for good-looking men," Ava joked.

"That's why I'm worried. The man's a babe magnet and he doesn't even know it, which makes him all the more desirable, of course." Though attractive, PJ could in no way be described as a 'babe.' She was on the short side and was a little heavy for her small frame. But she had a pretty face and perfect hair, dark brown and wildly wavy in its natural state, though today she had it straightened within an inch of its life, and that suited her too. PJ was also funny and good-natured, and a great favourite with the men at the station, particularly Steve Bryce, a DS who was often assigned to Neal. PJ continued to pine for Jim Neal rather than accept the sad reality that her love for him was doomed. And she was blind to Steve's adulation.

"Where is he?" Ava asked, taking a sip of her coffee and planting her dodgy foot on the edge of her boss's desk, "it's not like him to be late." PJ gave a loud, exaggerated cough, and Ava looked up to see Jim Neal looming in the doorway, his eyes on her raised foot. She dropped her leg to the floor and stood up, coffee splashing over her mug onto the desk.

"He's here," Neal said, amusement in his eyes.

"Can I do anything for you, sir? A coffee maybe?" PJ asked sweetly.

"Thank you, constable; that would be welcome."

"Milk, no sugar?" Did she really have to ask, Ava wondered. There wasn't much about Neal's likes and dislikes that PJ didn't already know. Ava had once caught her scrabbling around in his waste bin looking for clues to his preferences.

Neal settled into his chair with a grunt. Too late, Ava remembered that she'd adjusted the height slightly and her heart sank. As Neal fiddled with the lever, she plonked herself down in the regulation chair on the other side of the desk.

"Sorry, sir."

"Trying it out for size were you, Sergeant?" Ava flushed, catching his meaning.

"Oh no, sir. It's just so comfy and my ankle was playing up a bit."

"Have you seen anyone about that yet?"

157

"I borrowed my mum's foot massager last time I was down there. Haven't tried it out yet. Maybe I'll have a go this evening." Ava was glad Neal didn't comment; he'd made clear his opinion on the subject of alternative remedies on a number of occasions.

Ava had spoken with Neal after she'd returned from Sheffield the previous day. She could tell he was dissatisfied with the lack of progress on the case, not least because their DCI, George Lowe, was making noises, never a good omen.

"Archie okay?" she asked, wondering if Neal had been held up by some family crisis.

"Archie's fine." Okay, that's the niceties dispensed with, Ava thought, catching the hint of impatience in Neal's tone.

"It's been confirmed that the cause of death for both Becci and Gary was carbon monoxide poisoning. However, there's no evidence to suggest that the gas fire in Becci's room had been tampered with. It looks like an unfortunate accident resulting from a fault that would probably have been picked up on in its next service, which was due next month."

"What about the carbon monoxide detector?" Ava had already reported what Bradley had said about Nancy making sure there had been a functioning carbon monoxide detector installed in Amy's flat. He'd also mentioned that the device had been checked at the beginning of term.

"Batteries were dead."

"Someone could have replaced the batteries Nancy put in with duds."

Neal looked sceptical, "The report is quite clear. The fault with the fire wasn't a common one but it could have occurred at any time, given the age of the appliance. Moreover, the girls had cancelled an appointment made by the landlord for a safety check to be carried out, and failed to inform him so that he could rearrange it. If the scheduled service and safety check had gone ahead as planned, this tragedy might have been averted. Ava, your instinct to connect the deaths is sound, but we have to adhere to the facts, and right now they're telling us it's unlikely the fire was deliberately tampered with."

"Unlikely, but not impossible," Ava mumbled. "How many people had access to the flat?"

"The girls left a spare key under a loose slab by the door," Neal replied.

Ava shook her head in disbelief, then thought ruefully of the spare key she had hidden under a terracotta jardinière in her back garden. At least it wasn't in full view of the street.

"Anyone could have seen them use it. You can see the front door of the flat from the café across the street where we went after we interviewed Becci."

Neal's look of frustration mirrored Ava's feelings.

"I'm afraid the verdict is going to be accidental death. There's no reason for us to pursue any other line of inquiry on this one." Neal's voice carried a note of finality. He said, "I want you to go back to the girls' flat and take another look round. See if you can determine whether any of those designer clothes were purchased locally. Then get Jenkins to show Amy's picture around the stores and see if anyone remembers her. I have a meeting with Lowe this morning."

Ava threw Neal a sympathetic look. As a chief, George Lowe was tolerable as long as a case was moving along at a jaunty pace. All he seemed to care about was how his stats looked to the people further up the line. Legend had it that he could bellow, "Get me results!" in a voice that shattered glasses in the White Hart across the street. Neal was probably nervous about the interview. That's why he'd stayed late last night, why he was a little later than usual this morning; he was likely to be as well prepared as a newly qualified teacher facing the scariest class in school.

"Yes, sir," Ava said as she limped towards the door.

* * *

Outside, the sky was overcast, but for the third day now it wasn't raining. Ava drove to Amy and Becci's place and found a parking space two doors along. She flashed her badge at the young police constable standing sentinel outside the house.

"Go grab a coffee if you like," Ava said to her, nodding in the direction of the café opposite. "I'll be here for at least half an hour." For a split second, the young officer hesitated, before relaxing and expressing her thanks. Ava had guarded properties countless times in her career and she appreciated what a monotonous job it could be, not to mention the ache in your legs from standing still for hours on end.

Inside, the house was already beginning to smell fusty. Mrs Pringle had evidently been instructed not to come in and clean. Ava spent some time in the other rooms before revisiting Amy's bedroom. It too smelled stale and unlived in. The curtains were drawn tightly against nosy thrill seekers, admitting only a laser beam of dust-speckled light. First things first, Ava thought, pulling the green velour drapes apart. The morning was too dull for the room to be flooded with light, but at least she would be able to see what she was looking at.

For a teenager's room, it was surprisingly neat and tidy, especially the drawers and wardrobes, which were practically empty. The scant garments that were folded away in the drawers, or hanging on the rails in the wooden wardrobe, were arranged neatly by colour. They looked down-market compared to the garments Becci had helped herself to after Amy's death.

Ava frowned, recalling Becci's crowded wardrobe full of shiny new clothes. It was rather a mean thing to have done, but Ava didn't feel genuine disgust at Becci's behaviour. The cut and feel of some of the clothes hanging next door had brought out covetous instincts in her too. Who wouldn't be tempted by some of those labels?

Forgetting the clothes for a moment, Ava scanned the room, taking in the neatly ordered bookshelves. A framed photograph on the bedside table caught her eye. She picked it up to take a closer look, frowning at the image. It was a picture of Becci and Gary standing outside the cathedral. With a start, Ava looked around the room again, taking in the faint traces of Blu-Tack on the walls where posters had been recently removed, the shabby cushions and the faded throw on the bed, the stained rug on the floor, the titles of the books on the bookshelf.

"Something's not right," she said aloud. For a couple of moments she stood in the room, staring around her in puzzlement. Then, suddenly, it clicked.

She crossed the corridor to the room where Becci and Gary had been found. A shiver of excitement coursed through Ava as she stared at the gas fire, now covered in 'condemned' stickers. She'd had a revelation that could be very significant, but she needed to talk to Nancy Hill before she allowed herself to become carried away.

The PC she'd sent to the coffee shop started at the sight of Ava heading towards her, about ten minutes sooner than she'd probably been expecting her. She hurriedly covered a pastry on her plate with a napkin, but the tell-tale crumbs were on her lips. As if Ava could care less what she had been eating.

"I'm sorry. Took a bit less time than I thought and I really have to be somewhere right now. I'm afraid you'll have to finish up." The PC nodded, gulped down the last of her coffee and stood up.

"Take a doggie bag," Ava said, deftly picking up the Danish and rolling the napkin around it at the same time, "I know you're on duty but nobody's going to notice if you nip in the hallway of the house and finish it off. It's not as if there's crowds passing by every couple of minutes." The PC's smile was all the thanks she needed.

* * *

161

Ava wasn't expecting Nancy Hill to be anywhere but at home, but she phoned ahead anyway, and within half an hour, was tapping on the door.

Nancy took a long time to answer, and when she did, Ava was shocked by the woman's appearance. Nancy had looked bad enough at her daughter's funeral, but then she had been dressed for the occasion, and made up so that she appeared presentable. Now she looked as though she had just dragged herself out of bed. In fact, Ava was pretty sure that was the case, even though it was gone eleven o'clock.

"I'm sorry to bother you, Ms Hill, but there are some questions I'd like to ask you. May I come in?"

Nancy shrugged. She was wearing one of those soft fluffy dressing gowns in a shade of brown that reminded Ava of one of her childhood teddy bears. Nancy looked like she could use a bear hug. She was pale, and her formerly sleek hair was dull and lifeless. As Ava followed the large woman down the hallway of her house, she caught a whiff of body odour. Nancy wasn't even bothering to shower. Would she have even got up this morning if she hadn't been disturbed by Ava's visit?

"Is it about Amy? Have you found the man who killed her?" Nancy asked, flatly. She led Ava into the kitchen but didn't offer her a drink. Instead she sank into a chair at the kitchen table and looked up at Ava with heavy-lidded eyes. Sedated, Ava thought, recognising the look from other victims of violent crime she had encountered. She felt a sudden rush of anger at the man she suspected had brought such misery upon the woman before her. An image of his face flashed briefly in Ava's mind before she suppressed it. Its owner had a watertight alibi.

"I'm sorry. There's no more news. Can I make you a coffee?" Ava offered. Nancy didn't say yes, didn't say no, so Ava moved towards the kettle. With what seemed like a gargantuan effort, Nancy heaved herself to her feet to show Ava where to find what she needed.

"When did you last eat?" Ava asked.

"I don't know. I'm not hungry. Don't look so concerned, I'm not in any danger of fading away." Good, an attempt at humour, Ava thought, but she also knew that it was forced. At least Nancy took sugar in her coffee, she thought, watching her heap two spoonfuls into her mug.

"Ms Hill—"

"Nancy."

"Nancy, did you visit Amy at her flat in town?"

"Not once term started, but I did go round before she moved in to see if I could help make the place a little more comfortable. You know, cushions, rugs, the odd bit of furniture. The landlord only provided the basics."

"So you knew which of the bedrooms was Amy's?"

"Of course, it was the larger one at the back with the alcove bookshelves. Her flatmate, Becci, had the one at the front above the bay window. There is another tiny room, barely large enough to accommodate a single bed. It's a wonder the landlord didn't let that out, too. We stored some of the shabbier furniture in there when I bought Amy some new pieces." Ava nodded, suppressing an exclamation of satisfaction and excitement at being proved right about her theory.

"Ms Hill, did Amy have a part-time job, or did you give her an allowance?"

"I gave her what I could afford, but it wasn't a great deal. She had a student loan, like most kids nowadays."

"Would you say she was extravagant?" Nancy paused,

"She definitely had a liking for the finer things in life, but I like to think I taught her to cut her coat according to her cloth."

Ava told Nancy about the clothes.

"She definitely wouldn't have been able to afford clothes like that on her budget," Nancy said, frowning. "Do you have a theory that might explain how she acquired these things, Sergeant?" At last, a spark. Nancy's eyes had shown nothing but dullness until then.

"It's possible that they were given to her as a gift, or that Amy bought them with cash from a boyfriend," Ava said.

"I've told you before that Amy mentioned having a boyfriend who gave her an expensive necklace, but she only went out with him two or three times. I'm sure she'd have told me if there was someone special. She didn't have much time for boyfriends, Sergeant. Before she went to university, she was studying for A levels and doing a part time job. She didn't earn much — not enough to pay for the kind of clothes you say she had."

Ava nodded. The boyfriend had been checked out. He'd been a foreign student who was not even in the country at the time of Amy's death. "Where did she work?" Ava asked, interested.

"She was a waitress at the pizzeria on Gold Street. Sometimes she worked Sundays as well, stayed overnight at a friend's house in town to save me having to come and collect her after a late shift." Ava was instantly suspicious; such an arrangement would have given Amy the perfect opportunity to stay overnight with Taylor.

Nancy was a single parent, Ava knew. She said that she'd had a series of one-night stands with men while travelling in France, resulting in a pregnancy. She didn't know which of them was the father, and claimed she hadn't known their surnames.

She had concealed the pregnancy and had not registered Amy's birth for a year after her daughter was born because she was young and afraid of being censured. Nancy also claimed to have given birth at home, alone. It was an unusual story, particularly as Nancy didn't strike Ava as being either a promiscuous or a risk-taking type. Whatever Amy's origins had been, there was little doubt that she had been loved.

"Thank you, Nancy. I won't trouble you any longer," Ava said.

"Why did you ask about Amy's room? Have you found something?"

"I just wanted to be sure, that's all."

"Sure of what?"

Nancy's question caused Ava to hesitate. If Nancy were spending most of her time in bed, drugged to the eyeballs, it was more than probable that she didn't know that Becci and Gary were dead.

For a moment, Ava hovered by the door to Nancy's house, wondering if she should tell the unfortunate woman about the latest tragedy.

In the end, she bottled out. "Just a detail I'm looking into. I'm afraid I can't say much more at the moment." She glanced at Nancy, and saw that the spark had gone out. Ava wished she could offer some words of comfort, but she knew there were no words that could heal Nancy Hill's anguish.

* * *

Leaving Nancy standing on her doorstep, Ava walked to her car and reversed down the drive. Driving back to town, she wondered how significant it was that after Amy's death, Becci had moved into her dead friend's bedroom, bringing only some of her clothes in anticipation of the crammed wardrobe of designer outfits that awaited her in Amy's room.

There was no doubting the significance for Becci and Gary. They had wound up dead. But was it enough to prove that the faulty gas fire had been intended to kill Amy, as Ava suspected? Had the killer grown impatient waiting for Amy to use the fire in her room, and decided to deal with her more swiftly? Had he (in Ava's mind the killer was a very specific 'he') simply not cared that the faulty fire might cause other deaths? If Ava's theory was correct, and the gas leak had been intended to kill Amy, then the deaths of Gary and Becci could indeed be linked to Amy's. Ava suspected she would have a hard time convincing Neal that this might be the case.

* * *

For several minutes after Detective Sergeant Merry's car had disappeared, Nancy Hill stood on her doorstep, inhaling the first fresh air she'd breathed in days.

Richard had been trying to encourage her to go outside since the funeral but she couldn't seem to get beyond the doorstep and anyway, she had no desire to do so. Now, standing on the threshold, Nancy was surprised to feel nothing much at all, no accelerated heartbeat or sweating palms, no sense of impending disaster, no urge to slam the door shut and hide away inside for the rest of her life.

Nor did she feel tempted to step across the threshold; that was too far for now. It was the pills the doctor had prescribed for her kicking in. For a couple of days now, her pain and anxiety had been floating away from her on a cloud formed of anti-depressant cotton—wool.

But she wasn't yet empty of all feeling. Even as she greeted the outside world for the first time in days, she felt her whole body begin to tremble with guilt and self-doubt.

Never before had she doubted the rightness of becoming Amy's mother. Protecting Amy and providing for her had redeemed the anger and pain caused by the death of her own parents. The love that had gone from her life the day they died had been restored to her the moment she first held Amy in her arms; the joy and love coursing through her at that moment had cancelled out any doubts.

Now that she had failed to keep Amy safe from harm, she feared she had done something terribly wrong, and was being punished. More than that, the means of her punishment lay in her own hands.

Chapter 14

Jim Neal looked up, startled, as Ava burst into his office, giant red Costa cup in each hand.

"Your caffeine intake belies your healthy lifestyle," he remarked, accepting her offering, "how many lengths did you clock up this morning?"

"I didn't count. Never do less than sixty-four; that's a mile. Probably about eighty this morning."

Ava Merry was a fitness fanatic. Neal survived on two or three half hour workouts a week that he did at home in his mini gym in the garage, and the occasional run. Walking and climbing were his sports of choice, preferably in Scotland in the company of his boyhood friend, James, 'Jock' McAllister, now a consultant cardiologist at the Royal Infirmary in Edinburgh. They both led busy lives and it wasn't always easy to schedule time away, but a couple of weekends every year they would head off to bag another Munro and catch up on each other's lives.

Neal was looking forward to the day when Archie would join them on their expeditions. As soon as his son could walk any distance, Neal had introduced him to the great outdoors. Every October holiday they'd headed for the Lake District and roamed the hills. Last year Archie had scaled Helvellyn. Though his heart had been in his mouth all the length of Striding Edge, Neal had found the same organ swelling with pride when they reached the summit. A few more years, he'd thought, and Archie would be bagging his first Munro.

Ava was pacing the room, he noticed, obviously bursting to tell him something. Neal was immediately attentive.

He listened as Ava rattled through her theory about Becci switching to Amy's room immediately after her friend's death.

". . . so it's entirely credible that the deaths are linked after all, sir," his sergeant concluded in a high pitched voice that betrayed her excitement. She cleared her throat, embarrassed.

Neal was reluctant to rein her in. She had done good work in finding out that Becci had swapped rooms with her friend, but he wasn't as willing as Ava to attach any particular significance to this. He began by congratulating her on her deduction, adding, "It's also entirely possible that the fire might just have been faulty, and Becci and Gary were simply unlucky," he said watching Ava's face crumple.

"If it was the killer's intention to poison Amy with carbon monoxide fumes, why the sudden change of method? And after he'd killed Amy, why leave the fire as it was; a risk to someone else?"

Ava shrugged, "Maybe he decided he couldn't wait for her to spend an evening in her room; maybe something happened to make her death more imperative?"

"That's a fair enough assumption, although the methods are very different — strangling involves closer contact with the victim; it might be consistent with a killer who felt a heightened sense of urgency. Both Bradley and Simon may have been stalking Amy. We know that stalking can escalate to violence against the victim, but carbon monoxide poisoning isn't really consistent with that kind of killer. It's premeditated, calculating.

There is a type of stalker who thinks he's protecting his victim. Simon would fit that mould; we know Amy didn't feel threatened by him. Bradley was obsessed with her, but he was allegedly getting over it." Neal paused to gauge Ava's reaction to his words. She was obviously ruffled that her idea had failed to captivate him.

"I'm sorry, Ava. I'm not entirely convinced."

"But what if Amy had been seeing someone who was generous with his money?" Ava persisted. "They could have split up. Amy could have had something on him that she could use to blackmail him, something that would give her killer an increasing sense of urgency."

Not wanting to dampen her enthusiasm, Neal did not point out how unlikely he thought this scenario was. Then again, what else did they have to go on?

"It might be worth following up," he said, and was rewarded by a grin that would have put a Cheshire cat to shame. Then, he moved on.

"Anna Foster's holding something back," he said. "I'd like to interview her again, this time with you present, see if you can find a way in — get her to open up. I want to know if she'd noticed any change in Simon's behaviour recently, what might have prompted it. That kind of thing. We'll pay her a visit this afternoon. Tomorrow you and I are taking a trip to London."

"London, sir?"

"We're going to pay Simon Foster's father a visit."

Neal picked up his coffee. He preferred to drink from a proper cup, but years on the job had taught him to enjoy the contents and ignore the vessel. Costa was just across the road and the drink was still piping hot. He sipped and nodded at Ava to show his appreciation. He glanced at his watch. "Meet me in the car park in fifteen minutes," he said, needing a few minutes to himself.

169

When Ava had gone, Neal noticed that the photograph on his desk had been moved. He pushed it back a little, tilting it to the left until he had the correct angle. This way, from his normal sitting position, he could look up from his work and see his son's face smiling directly at him. Archie was a good-looking boy, he thought, not for the first time. Everyone told him so; he wasn't just a besotted parent. He heard Maggie's voice in his head telling him Archie was handsome, just like his dad.

It was true, there seemed to be little of Myrna in the boy as far as looks and personality were concerned, but he had her talent for music and Neal didn't begrudge the amount he paid out each week on Archie's piano, cello, and most recently guitar lessons. Even if Archie's future career took him in an entirely different direction, Neal felt obligated to nurture this talent. He wanted Archie to have choices. Neal had not intended to become a police officer; he'd wanted to go to university and study law, but Myrna's pregnancy had meant that he had to put aside his ambitions, and, by the time he'd advanced sufficiently in the job, Neal found that by serendipity or pragmatic thinking, he'd stumbled into the perfect career; one which satisfied both his temperament and his insistent intellectual curiosity.

Myrna had never wanted Archie. She would have ended the pregnancy had Neal not pleaded with her to bring the child to term, absolving her of any commitment or responsibility towards the baby after it was born. Myrna had been at a key point in her career, and a child had not been part of her plans. She'd agreed, reluctantly, to give birth to their son, as long as she could walk out the door afterwards and never see either of them again.

He couldn't avoid noticing the ever-soaring arc of her career as an opera singer, although the Myrna who stared out at him from the covers of international glossy magazines was barely recognisable as the girl he'd thought he loved back then. She had worked her way through a string of lovers since leaving Neal and Archie, the latest being a director who had filmed her in a version of 'Aida' that had flopped spectacularly — much to Maggie's delight.

Looking at her photograph, and reading about the extravagant life she lived, Neal could scarcely believe he had ever known her. Whenever he thought of Myrna — and then of Archie — he could only pity her for what she had lost.

Neal had not hidden Myrna's identity from Archie, and he knew that his son had a box under his bed containing newspaper and magazine clippings about Myrna's successes. Once or twice Archie had even written to his mother, but she had never replied. Neal never blamed her for her decision. She hadn't wanted to become pregnant; a damaged condom had been to blame. Myrna had desired only to nurture her talent. Neal had reasoned that if he was going to be a dad one day anyway, why wait? In his opinion, they had both got what they wanted; although Neal was convinced he'd got the better part of the deal.

* * *

On the drive to Long Hill, Neal asked Ava a question that had been provoking him since their interview with Professor Christopher Taylor.

"This Professor Taylor," he said casually, "Are you seeing him?" As soon as the words were out, he wished he'd kept his mouth shut; he was certain he'd crossed some kind of line. Then again, they were colleagues. Colleagues were meant to talk to each other, weren't they? If he were a woman, a conversation like this wouldn't be embarrassing at all. Ava, he noticed, was turning a deep shade of crimson. He fully expected to be told to mind his business.

"We've been out on a date. Just the one. I'm not sure if we'll be seeing each other again." From her colour, Neal could tell that it had been much more than a simple date.

171

He could also tell — and he was proud of this, because weren't men supposed to be bad at that sort of thing — that Ava's feelings about Taylor were ambivalent. His own feelings about the professor were crystal clear — he disliked the man intensely.

"Sorry, it's none of my business."

"No, it's alright. He contacted me almost immediately after we interviewed him. I suppose there was a kind of mutual spark when we met."

"Well, be careful, Sergeant. He struck me as a bit of a 'smoothie.'"

"A smoothie?" Sergeant Merry's face was a picture of delight, "Did you just say 'smoothie?' I thought that word went out with the ark. And what's with the fatherly tone? You're not that much older than I am." It was Neal's turn to be embarrassed, and Ava wasn't about to let him off lightly either.

"While we're on the subject, what about you and Anna Foster? I saw the way you were looking at her. Beware of cougars, sir."

"Cougars?"

"You know, predatory older women."

"My interest in Anna Foster is purely professional, Sergeant. Her son is a suspect in a murder case."

"Yeah, right," Ava teased.

Anna Foster was at least ten years older than him, but Neal was attracted to her. He would deny this to Ava until he was blue in the face, but he had to be honest with himself. Ava's talk of predatory women was wide of the mark; there was nothing remotely predatory about Anna Foster. She was reserved to the point of shyness, petite and vulnerable. Neal cringed at his own description. He didn't want to be a stereotypical male looking for a little woman to protect. Maggie would have had a lot to say about that.

At this time of the afternoon the Long Hill area was uncharacteristically quiet. The rain had started up again with a vengeance, keeping all but the most steadfast shoppers away. In this sort of weather, the crowds tended to flock to the centre of town with its big stores and heated shopping centre offering shelter.

As Neal and Ava crossed the slippery cobblestones towards Anna Foster's bookshop, a particularly heavy shower battered on their umbrellas. The word, 'dreich,' rose to Neal's lips, though even that Scottish adjective fell short of summing up the miserable weather. The rain, he noted, still in Scottish mode, was 'stottin' off the ground,' and he was glad to step over the threshold of 'Books Now,' after shaking the excess water off his brolly. Across the street, sheltering in another doorway near her habitual spot, was the Big Issue seller he had seen on his last visit to Anna's shop. She gave Neal a shy wave, which he returned.

Ava stepped inside first. Anna Foster was sitting at her desk near the doorway, tapping away on a laptop. She looked up as the doorbell sounded, her fingers still darting over the keyboard. The customer-ready smile on her face waned when she saw who her visitors were.

"Good afternoon, Sergeant Merry, Inspector Neal," she said, her tone neutral. "Do you have some news for me or are you looking for a second hand copy of 'The Virgin and the Vampire,' like most of my customers today?" The novel had just been released as a movie, starring one of those young actors who had made his name playing vampires — or was it werewolves? "We just have a few questions, Ms Foster," Ava said. Anna Foster sighed, but she didn't repeat that she had already told them everything she knew about Simon's whereabouts.

"I'm sorry," Ava said, "This won't take long."

"Let me just call Maya down to take over here. She's upstairs unpacking some boxes of books I picked up at a house contents sale."

The young 'goth' woman appeared within seconds. Recognising Neal, she said, 'hi,' then turned to look at Ava.

"Maya, this is Detective Sergeant Ava Merry. Inspector Neal you've met before." Maya and Ava stared at each other, each possibly seeing her mirror opposite. Ava's blonde hair tumbled loose over her shoulders and she was wearing a pretty yellow blouse under a beige Mac. She looked healthy and her make-up was subtle and understated. Maya's dyed jet-black hair was arranged in an untidy coif; her face was pale, powdered nearly white and her clothes were black and lacy. But both women had ruby red lips, and they smiled at each other as if in mutual admiration.

"Cool. I was a Goth for a bit," Ava said, "God I miss the scene sometimes."

"Now look at you, totally mainstream!" Maya said, but there was no hostility in her voice.

Anna led them upstairs and into her flat. She offered to make them a drink, but even Ava had had enough caffeine to last her quite a while.

"Ms Foster," Ava began, conscious that Anna had been looking in Neal's direction, expecting him to take the lead. Now she turned her big, sad eyes to Ava.

"I know you feel that you've told us all you can about Simon, but I'd just like to take you back to the weeks before his disappearance." She tactfully avoided any mention of Amy's death.

"Did you notice any change in Simon's behaviour? Did he seem quieter or more agitated?"

"He was a little distracted," Nancy admitted. "Not his usual self."

"Can you relate that to anything he'd been doing, any incident in his life, however unimportant or irrelevant it might seem?"

Anna seemed to have given up being defensive about her son, Neal thought. Perhaps she had rid herself of any lingering doubts about his innocence, and no longer felt the need to reassure herself as well as others.

"Simon did act a little strangely the first time he met my friend, Nancy Hill," she said at last. "It was at my book group meeting, here in this room a couple of months ago. I can let you know the exact date if you think it's important."

Ava nodded and Anna reached for a notebook on a bureau by her chair. "It would have been a Wednesday evening at eight o' clock, first Wednesday of the month. Yes, here it is, Wednesday the second of September. Simon doesn't always attend the group, but he was at that one because he particularly liked the choice of book: 'The Master of Ballantrae' by a writer who is probably dear to your own heart, Inspector: Robert Louis Stevenson." She smiled wanly at Neal, a smile that touched her lips but left her eyes unmoved. Neal responded with a faint nod.

"Can you tell us what happened at the meeting?" Ava asked.

"It was just that Simon seemed to keep staring at Nancy, as though he knew her from somewhere."

"Could he have recognised her as someone from his past, do you think? Someone he knew before he was adopted? Before his father murdered his mother?" Neal flinched at Ava's bluntness, but he would have asked the same question.

"No. Nancy told me she never lived in London. I remember going into the kitchen to make tea and he followed me in and asked about her. I almost thought he was attracted to her, but after that evening he didn't mention her again. It was about that time that he stopped coming around as often. I assumed he was spending more time with his friends at uni."

"And his behaviour?"

"As I said, he seemed distracted. I suppose I thought he was just busy with his course and his social life, like any other student his age, especially once term started up. Is this kind of information really helpful to you?" Anna Foster looked from Ava to Neal, a puzzled expression on her face.

"Ms Foster," Ava said, gently, "Was Simon really here with you all night when Amy was murdered?"

It was so silent in the room that Neal imagined he could hear the Big Issue vendor across the street dripping in her doorway. From downstairs, muffled by the thickness of the building's old walls, came the sound of the chimes ringing to admit a customer and Maya's cheery greeting. Anna's reply was so soft that Ava had to ask her to repeat it.

"No."

"Are you sure this time, Ms Foster?" Ava asked, clearly trying to keep the eagerness out of her voice.

"Simon wasn't here. I don't know where he was. I'm sorry I lied to you." The words tumbled out punctuated by sobs. Anna Foster had wasted police time, but Neal couldn't find it in his heart to blame her. For one thing, he couldn't be sure how far he would go to protect Archie if he were in trouble, something he didn't like to consider too deeply. Besides, he was uncomfortably aware of his urge to comfort the woman before him. He cleared his throat.

"We'll need you to formally confirm that you've changed your statement, Ms Foster. I must ask you; do you know of Simon's current whereabouts?"

"I don't know where he is. I'm sorry. There's only the postcard I gave you on your last visit, otherwise I've heard nothing from him."

Neal and Ava waited without speaking as Anna Foster made a list of Simon's friends. When she was finished, she handed it to Neal, her hand shaking. Neal wanted to tell her that Simon was no more of a suspect than he had been before, but he knew it wasn't true. Simon Foster had just moved up a notch on the list. Instead, he said, "We'll find your son," in a voice that was, he hoped, more reassuring than ominous.

Downstairs, Maya was saying goodbye to a customer, a regular it seemed, for she addressed him by name. "I'll look out for Punch books coming in, Mr Dalton, and let you know if there are any from your list."

"That was Mr Dalton. Lovely old boy," she said to Ava and Neal, when the elderly man had left the shop, umbrella at the ready. "He collects Punch books and Anna always alerts him when we get some in. Have you come about Simon?"

"Do you know Simon?" Ava asked.

"Of course I know Simon! I work here, don't I?"

"We still don't know where he is. How well did you know him?" Maya's blush brought a hint of pinkness to her white-powdered face.

"I . . . not that well . . . I don't think he even noticed me."

She's not exactly hard to miss, Ava thought.

"Was there someone he did notice?" Ava asked less casually than she meant to, Neal thought.

"You mean the dead girl, don't you?" Maya said. "Simon didn't do that. It's not in his nature. He's a very gentle person."

"So we've heard. Do you know where Simon is, Maya?" Neal asked, watching her closely for tell-tale signs of lying. The girl shook her head, but she also turned away.

Neal left the shop in frustration: at Anna for taking so long to confirm what they had long suspected; at the mystery of why meeting Nancy Hill had so affected Simon; at the weather which was still chucking cats and dogs down from a seemingly limitless rescue home in the sky. As they walked past the bedraggled Big Issue vendor still sheltering in a doorway, Neal bought a soggy copy of her magazine out of pity and a kind of solidarity with her mission.

There was no conversation until they reached the shelter of Neal's car.

"Anna Foster claims she spoke to Nancy about Simon's reaction to meeting her, and Nancy told her she had no idea why Simon would recognise her. To her knowledge she'd not met Simon before and she's lived in Shelton for years, long before Simon arrived. Perhaps she just reminded him of someone?" Neal said.

"That's probably it. Or, maybe he'd been following Amy and seen her with Nancy? Seeing Nancy in his mother's flat would have given him a jolt, especially if he felt guilty about stalking Amy. He might even have been worried that Nancy knew about it."

Eyes fixed on the road ahead, Neal nodded his agreement. He said, "I still have a feeling that Anna Foster knows more than she's telling us. I'll have PC PJ talk to her, just in case she's able to give us any more information."

He didn't feel confident that this would push the case forward, but things were moving so slowly that they were obliged to pursue the slimmest of leads. Neither said anything for a couple of miles. It was late afternoon and already growing dark, daylight having given up the ghost in deference to the overall gloom.

"I'll drop you at the station," Neal said. "I'm going to pick Archie and my sister up. We're going bowling."

"I love bowling," Ava said.

"Come with us," Neal found himself saying, without having meant to. Nothing had been further from his mind than inviting his colleague along to a family outing, but he was aware that he and his sergeant had not bonded on anything other than a professional level, and he was a believer in cops forging strong relationships. Like soldiers, they needed to know that they had each other's back. He could hear the hesitation in Ava's voice when she answered.

"Are you sure? I wasn't fishing for an invite. I don't want to intrude on your family time."

"Maggie's keen to meet you. I'm pretty sure you two will get along. And Archie won't mind at all."

"In that case, sure, I'd love to come along. Thanks, sir"

* * *

Maggie and Archie were good to go as soon as Neal pulled up outside his house. He noted Maggie's amused, questioning look as she jumped in the back seat, and he introduced Ava, noticing a grin spread over his sister's face as he referred to Ava as his detective sergeant. Archie strained forward as far as his seatbelt would allow, to give Ava a high five.

For a heartbeat, Neal worried that his forthright son would ask if Ava was his girlfriend. Neal had been extremely discreet when he dated women, to the point that Archie had never even met any of the few he'd gone out with recently. He didn't want his son to become attached to anyone who was not likely to be around for a while.

By the time they arrived at the bowling alley, Maggie and Ava were well on the way to becoming friends. It never ceased to amaze Neal how women seemed to have the knack of connecting so effectively and quickly on a personal level. Sometimes he envied them that skill. Neal caught a glimpse of his son in the rear view mirror and saw Archie looking sideways at Ava in admiration. Not yet, Neal thought to himself, though he knew that his son was fast approaching that moment when girls are suddenly at least as interesting as football.

At the bowling alley, they teamed up; boys against girls. The girls won by a narrow margin, and Neal and Archie had to endure a round of sisterly high fiving before the victors calmed down and they all settled into a booth for a post-match carbs boost. Over burgers and fries, Ava and Maggie exchanged contact details and arranged to meet up to go clubbing together, making Neal a little uneasy. He would need to have a tête a tête with Maggie about the need for her to be discreet. All he needed was a direct gossip line between his private life and the office.

Neal dropped Ava back at the station where she could pick up her car.

"She's nice," Archie said, as they drove home. "Why don't you ask her out?" Nothing like being direct.

"She's a colleague, and I'm her boss," Neal answered quickly.

"So? What difference does that make?" Neal glanced at Maggie for support but to his annoyance, she was staring pointedly out of the window.

"Our relationship needs to stay professional, not personal. It wouldn't be appropriate," he said, at last, "Even if I wanted to — which I don't." This time Maggie did look in his direction, her eyes full of amusement. As for Archie, he'd caught sight of a new registration Porsche in his side window and his interest switched to cars.

Sleep eluded Neal that night. He lay awake going over the morning's meeting with George Lowe in his head. Lowe was a reasonable boss, but there were pressures on him too. An investigation that threw up so few leads as this one was frustrating for all. It was a relief that media reports about Amy's death had been so low-key. She was just the sort of victim journalists liked to hype up — young, white, attractive woman. It could so easily become a high profile national case. Lowe was eager to avoid this happening.

To her credit, Nancy Hill had shunned all publicity to the point of becoming a semi recluse. Just how long their luck would hold out on this was a matter for concern, and Lowe had made it clear that he wanted results. He'd been particularly critical of Neal's failure to track down Simon Foster. Hence the trip to London. Just what interviewing Simon's father would accomplish, Neal was not certain. From what Anna Foster had told him, Simon had never contacted him, but parents don't always know what their offspring are up to. And children sometimes keep secrets in order to protect their parents.

As always, thoughts about other people's children led him to his own. Archie was a great kid at the moment, doing well at school, no behavioural issues, a little on the quiet side but that wasn't a bad thing. Neal wasn't fool enough to think that it was all his doing. He had seen too much in his line of work to be naïve about the lasting effects of good parenting. Was he even a good father? His job often meant long hours away from home and he was a single parent. No, not going there, he thought, mindfully redirecting his thoughts. Eventually Neal worried himself into a restless sleep. Outside, it was still raining.

Chapter 15

Ava's mobile vibrated against her thigh and she pulled it out of her trouser pocket to check her latest text. Christopher Taylor. Again. He had texted her countless times since their date two days ago, and as yet she had not responded. To tell the truth, she was at odds with herself over how to proceed with their relationship.

That she had been attracted to him in the beginning was forgivable; the man was gorgeous to look at, but right from the start, he had caused alarm bells to sound in her head and Ava feared that she might have exercised bad judgement in going to bed with him.

It was not that she felt guilty about exploiting his attraction to her, nor did she regret their night of passion; it just made her uneasy to think that she was the kind of person who was ready to use another as a means to an end. Then there was the fact that she had no really concrete evidence that he was guilty of anything but vanity and arrogance. Most of all, she wondered that she could have sex with a man who both attracted and repulsed her in equal measure. Whichever way you looked at it, her behaviour appeared shoddy, particularly for a police officer.

Since her visit to the community centre in Sheffield, Ava had tried unsuccessfully to track down Rohina. Stromford did not have a large Asian population, and Ava had made some enquiries, but so far she had drawn a blank.

It had occurred to her that Rohina might be a student at the university. She might even have known or been in contact with Amy Hill. If so, there was a possibility that she was in danger. And there it was again, a line drawn in Ava's mind between Amy's death and Christopher Taylor, even though he had been out of town the night Amy died.

If Rohina believed Taylor had killed Amy, she might have gone into hiding. She might also have been the sender of the anonymous note alleging Taylor was having an affair with Amy.

Ava's mobile felt hot against her leg and she took it out and placed it on the table in front of her. Camden flexed a lazy paw and flicked it as though it were a mouse he was too tired to toy with. Tutting at the cat, Ava caught the phone as it skidded towards the edge of the coffee table. This time she read the message. Why hadn't she been responding to his texts? Could he see her again? Call him soon. Ava put the phone down and got up to make herself a drink.

It was dark outside and the only noise was the familiar patter of rain against her kitchen window; the sounds of small nocturnal creatures going about their business in the woods around her cottage were undetectable to the human ear. Usually, in the peace of her own home, Ava could work or read uninterrupted for hours, but this evening Taylor was so much inside her head that she couldn't concentrate.

Camden had followed her into the kitchen and begun winding his lithe body around her legs. Ava scooped him up and held him against the side of her face, feeling his soft fur on her cheek and listening for a few moments to the contented purring that seemed to come from deep within his being. Then, he wriggled free and jumped out of her arms to land sure-footedly on the tiled floor. A moment more and he was gone, out through the cat-flap and into the night, driven by some primal instinct to prowl the darkness, like the predator he was.

"Traitor!" Ava called after him. "I feed him and fuss over him and what happens when I want a little comfort in return? He's off like a shot."

Just then, her mobile vibrated again, but this time it was a ring tone she recognised.

"Hi bro'," she said, pleased to hear from Oliver, her younger brother.

"Hey, sis," Oliver said in a breezy voice, "What's up? Got time to talk?"

"Always got time for you, you know that. Actually your timing couldn't be better; I was feeling a bit sorry for myself, and Camden doesn't want to know."

"I keep telling you to get a dog. They're more empathetic."

"It wouldn't be fair, leaving it cooped up indoors all day while I'm at work. Cats are independent, they can look out for themselves."

They had had this debate countless times, of course; it was almost a convention of their telephone conversations to banter on about the relative merits of canine versus feline. It served as a warm up; and this evening, the topic was dropped more quickly than usual. Ava had detected a note of unhappiness in her brother's tone.

"Is everything okay?" she asked, knowing that with Ollie, things were seldom okay. There was a silence that told her he was deliberating.

"What's happened, Ollie? You being bullied again? If it's that bastard, Jack Anderson, I—"

"It's not Jack Anderson. He's been expelled for doing drugs in the playground. I don't have to worry about him anymore." Ava waited.

"Can I come and stay with you for a while, Ave?"

That took all of two minutes, Ava thought. They had been here before. Ollie was fifteen years old and emotionally immature in many ways, but intellectually, he was something else again. Gifted and talented they called him at school. Borderline autistic, the psychologist had told their parents when they had sought a professional opinion on their son's combination of high intelligence and low social skills. Clever, geeky, a bit clueless about the kinds of things other kids his age took for granted or just seemed to know about, Ollie was an easy target for bullies. And until recently he had been small for his age, poor kid, although that was definitely changing. On her last visit, Ava had been amazed to see that he had grown two inches in a month, and he was refusing to tell her how much he had grown since then, so she suspected a lofty surprise when she saw him again. *What's worrying him*, Ava wondered, suspecting she already knew the answer.

"Take your time, bro, tell me what's worrying you."

"Mum's got a new boyfriend and I can't stand him." So that was it. Their parents, Carla and Steve Merry, had divorced years ago and Steve had moved to the States with his new woman, an American high school teacher he had met on a school exchange visit. Carla had been single for a couple of years, but recently she had run through a succession of men, some less savoury than others.

Ollie needed order and routine, not the constant disruption and chaos that accompanied a new partner in his mother's life every few months. Then again, Ava thought, wasn't her mother entitled to a life after divorce? Six months ago her brother had come up with the idea of coming to stay with her, and he had been pestering her about it ever since.

Ava's objections had been similar to those she gave for not wanting to have a dog. She often worked long hours. She couldn't be there for him. Moreover, she couldn't be there to sort out Ollie's problems at school . . . the list went on.

"Ava?" Ollie said, waiting, no doubt for the usual excuses and explanations but Ava was having an unexpected rethink.

Ollie was going to be sixteen in a couple of weeks. He had just started on his A-level work at school, but he was bright enough for a short disruption to his studies to make little difference. There was a good FE college in Stromford. What was the problem?

"Okay," Ava replied. There was a silence on the other end of the line, "Olllie? You still there?"

"Do you really mean it?"

Ava could hear the doubt and hope in Ollie's voice.

"Yes. When do you want to move in?"

"This weekend?"

Ava laughed, "It might take a bit longer than that to sort things out, but we'll need to move quickly to avoid disrupting your school work any more than necessary. I take it you want to continue with your studies? I can call the college in town in the morning and find out if they'll take you. Is mum there? Can you put her on?"

Oliver was ecstatic. Ava could hear him calling their mother at the top of his voice, and she knew he would already be upstairs packing the contents of his bedroom. She almost felt sorry for Carla.

"Ava? What's this all about?"

"Ollie's moving in with me. Can you take care of all the arrangements at your end?"

It did not surprise Ava that her mother did not protest for long. It disappointed Ava, but in the years since her father's departure, she had come to realise that neither of her parents had been particularly suited to child-rearing. Her dad had abandoned his family at the earliest opportunity and her mum's heart had never been in it, though she had done her duty by her children, more or less. Ava had been under no illusions when she left home that only Ollie would miss her.

Of course, Oliver, coming along ten years after Ava, had been an 'accident.' Ava could still remember her mother's dismay at finding herself pregnant with a second child after a one-night stand with her ex-husband on one of his transatlantic stopovers. She had been only too happy to hand little Oliver over to Ava whenever she could. That was the reason why the bond between Ava and Ollie was so strong. The loving relationship that grew between brother and sister had compensated for what their parents failed to provide.

It had broken Ava's heart to move away. After school, she had gone to university in her home town so that she could live at home and be there for Oliver but, after her first year, she had decided to drop out; all of a sudden, studying a subject that had no relevance or importance in the grand scheme of life seemed wasteful and indulgent. She had felt she could employ her talents better elsewhere, in a career where she could make a difference, and when she met the detective in charge of investigating a friend's assault case, she had suddenly found her vocation.

For a couple of years she had managed to stay within commuting distance of home, but sooner or later she knew that if she were to advance in her chosen career, she would have to move further afield. Her transfer to the Stromford force, and her subsequent promotion, had meant that she managed to return home less frequently, but she and Oliver emailed, skyped and texted regularly.

What have I done? Ava asked herself after she put the phone down. To tell the truth, it had not been an entirely random decision. She had been considering the possibility of Oliver coming to stay for a while; meeting Neal's family had nudged her a bit closer, seeing how well it seemed to work, all of them together in their slightly unconventional household.

Ava poured herself a drink and stretched out on the sofa, TV remote in hand. For a while she flicked idly through the channels. Her mind was occupied with all the plans and arrangements that would need to be made prior to her brother's arrival. But as the alcohol began to relax her, she found her thoughts drifting back to Christopher Taylor again.

At least the local news hadn't mentioned Amy Hill's murder investigation. That was strange, given that Amy had been a student and the autumn term had just started, but it was something to be grateful for. How much longer the story would stay out of the papers was anyone's guess, but Ava would have bet money that it was only a matter of days. Then it would be open season for reports of police incompetence.

She was still convinced that Taylor was somehow involved. The only way to investigate him further was to resume her relationship with him, though she had all but promised herself that wasn't going to happen. On a sudden impulse, she picked up her phone and speed-dialled the professor.

"Ava! What a pleasant surprise. I was wondering if you were ever going to answer my texts."

"I'm sorry. It's been hectic at work for the past week, what with the murder inquiry and other stuff. I've had to put my personal life on hold."

"I understand, Detective. But everyone needs to take a break sometimes, unwind. I think I could help you unwind and release some tension. How did I do last time? You rushed off without even saying goodbye."

Was he asking her to rate his performance? Ava felt a flush of embarrassment creep over her.

"Sorry, work again. It gets in the way of pleasure. You're right; I really do need to unwind."

"I'll tell you what I'm going to do." Taylor spent the next couple of minutes describing exactly how he would relax her, and Ava was shocked to feel a thrill of excitement shoot through her, as well as a shiver of revulsion. She slipped her phone back into her pocket having arranged to meet him at his place in an hour, distinctly uneasy about the dark side to her character that seemed to be emerging of late.

There was little time to get ready; Ava was grateful that she could look good in practically anything. This was not vanity, but long experience of how others reacted to her looks. Sometimes she dressed down, underplayed her looks, other times she used her attractiveness to her advantage, and this was one of them. There was a low-cut clingy red dress in her wardrobe that she knew looked sensational on her.

Ava wiggled in front of the mirror, trying to make the skirt cover a bit more thigh but it simply wasn't designed for modesty. Red lipstick and a pair of killer heels, which made her ankles ache before she even put them on, completed her look. A short black cashmere jacket and she was ready to go.

* * *

Exactly one hour after her conversation with Taylor, she was parking her car outside his town house and experiencing a sudden stab of nerves that made her feel physically sick. Then, just as suddenly, it passed.

Taylor had evidently been looking out for her. His door opened inwards before she could ring the bell and his eyes travelled over her in appreciation, lingering on her breasts, making Ava feel like a cheap prostitute.

"Aren't you going to invite me in?" she asked.

"Oh Ava. You are very welcome to come in," Taylor answered, taking her hand and kissing it gallantly as she stepped onto the Escher runner in his narrow hallway. With one hand, he closed the door behind them, and with the other, drew her to him and kissed her until she half fainted in a rush of danger and delight.

Two hours after speaking to Taylor on the phone, Ava was lying in his bed, feeling the inevitable mixture of sexual satisfaction and guilt. No matter how she looked at it, this relationship could not end well. Even if Taylor turned out to be innocent of any ill deed, she would still have to live with the knowledge that she had had sex with him when she had thought him guilty of having sex with an under-age girl. What did that make her?

"Are you feeling relaxed, Ava?" Taylor asked, his tone playful.

"Oh, yes," Ava answered, and it was the truth, at least in a physical sense. "You're wasted as an English professor."

"And you are wasted as a police officer, although I wouldn't mind seeing you in uniform."

"Flat loafers, knee-length woollen skirt, blouse buttoned up to the chin. Very sexy." Ava answered.

"I'm getting hard just thinking about it, Sergeant." Incredibly, he was, and that took care of another half hour.

* * *

"I can't stay the night," Ava told him. She had showered and was sitting on a barstool at the breakfast bar in Taylor's stylish but un-homely kitchen. "I have to be up early to take a train to London with DI Neal."

"The dashing Detective Inspector Neal," Taylor said, placing a coffee in front of her."

"Jealous?" Ava asked, smiling.

"Why wouldn't I be? He gets to spend a day in your delectable company and I get to give a lecture on Chaucer to a bunch of half-witted pimply eighteen-year-olds."

"I saw the way those girls were drooling over you in the cafeteria that day at the university. Any man would be flattered by that much attention from attractive young girls." Ava said, choosing her words carefully, but still feeling that she was hinting unsubtly at paedophilia.

"Occupational hazard," Taylor joked, "Young girls continually throwing themselves at my feet."

"Still, you must be tempted," Ava persisted. "Surely any man would be."

"Professionalism aside, there are a lot of reasons why dating your students wouldn't be a good idea," Taylor answered.

"You said Amy Hill had a crush on you, set you up on a date. It could have got you into a lot of trouble if you hadn't had a sound alibi for the night she was murdered." At last, Taylor's face betrayed the slightest hint of irritation.

"Amy Hill was a most persistent young woman," he replied, "I could have reported her for what amounted to harassment."

"But you didn't?"

"I tried to deal with the matter sensitively, *Sergeant*. I had no wish to see a young girl being sent down from university on my account. I thought she would eventually get the idea if I did nothing to encourage her. Which, I am sure would have been the case had the poor child not been murdered first."

It was impossible to tell if his regret over Amy's murder was feigned, but his irritation was obvious. *Tread carefully,* Ava cautioned herself.

"I'm sorry," she said, stroking his hand. "Too many questions. Once a detective . . . I remember having a crush on my science teacher at school. I must have made his life a misery, but he never put a foot wrong. I can appreciate now how difficult it must have been from his point of view. He was married with two kids. I used to post love letters through his letterbox. Imagine what his wife must have thought."

None of this was true, but Ava hoped it would dispel any suspicions the professor might be nurturing.

"I never taught in a school. I worked in a community centre when I was doing my doctorate, teaching English to young Asian women, mainly. Recent immigrants. A lot of them were very young but already married with children. It's a different culture."

191

This much Ava already knew. But they were moving in the right direction.

"That must have been rewarding work. Do any of your former students keep in touch with you?" The question seemed to catch him off guard, and he stared at Ava for a moment. She could tell that she had rattled him, even though he quickly recovered his composure. His eyes were wary.

"No," he replied, dryly, "Not my Asian ladies, but I receive postcards from graduates from time to time letting me know how they are getting on."

"That must be nice." There was nothing else she could ask him without raising his suspicions further, but Ava felt that she had got what she came for. No evidence, not the slightest word wrongly placed, but she had seen it in his eyes. He had something to hide. *And now you know I know it too,* she thought, smiling at him as she grabbed hold of his tie to pull him to her for a lingering kiss. The spark that usually crackled between them was absent.

"It's late," she said. "I have to go." He did not try to dissuade her, and when they kissed again by her car, he bit down on her lip drawing blood.

"I'm sorry," he apologised, wiping the thin trickle from her lip. "Got carried away."

"I'll call you," Ava said, pretending to be unaffected by his sudden violence. As she drove off down the hill, she licked her lip, still tasting blood and feeling violated. "I'm onto you, Professor," she whispered. "You've got a dirty secret and I'm going to find out exactly what it is."

Chapter 16

Living in an isolated county such as Stromford had its advantages, but getting out of it quickly wasn't one of them, Neal thought. He was standing on the platform at Harmsborough station having driven forty minutes along the A15 just to get to a station with a direct link to London.

There were only a couple of trains a day that did not involve multiple changes and these never seemed to be at convenient times of the day. Catching the seven o'clock to King's Cross had necessitated a five o'clock rise, and Neal was not at his most alert. Glancing at Ava making her way down the platform towards him with her trademark Costa coffees, Neal was irritated to see that his sergeant was looking as radiant as ever. Of course, she was an early riser. Years of getting up to train at the pool had conditioned her to jumping out of bed first thing in the morning. She wouldn't have had time for a swim or a run today, but Neal was ready to bet she had done at least a hundred sit-ups before breakfast.

He wasn't the only one to notice her radiant good looks. Male and female heads alike turned as she walked past, and eyes lingered. And she wasn't even looking her best, Neal noted, seeing the shadows under her eyes even from this distance.

Ava's glorious hair, usually pulled back when she was on duty, tumbled over her shoulders, making her look like a cover girl for a glossy magazine, and she was wearing more make up than usual, although it did look as though it had been applied the night before, Neal thought. She was wearing her trademark Levi's with brown Ugg boots and a brown suede jacket layered over a red cashmere jumper. As she approached him, Neal felt embarrassed, aware that he too had been staring at her in a manner that was not exactly neutral.

"Here you go, boss. I got them to stick an extra shot in — you look like you need a caffeine boost this morning." Neal muttered his thanks; he'd told Ava before that strong coffee gave him the jitters but she seemed to keep forgetting. He did not mention that she looked more in need of a caffeine boost than he did.

They stood sipping their coffees, watching the early morning travellers walk up and down the stairs from the bridge connecting the station's two main platforms. A skeletal woman with limp straggly hair bumped a wheeled suitcase down the steps, her coat billowing open to reveal of stretch of white thigh tattooed with numbers and symbols; a middle-aged man with a gut bulging over his trousers, who leered at Ava as she took a step backwards to let him pass; a group of schoolgirls dressed in old-fashioned plaid skirts and blue woollen blazers, the uniform of the town's expensive private school. A cross section of a typical early morning commuter crowd. Was it because he was a police officer trained to observe and catalogue that Neal found himself scrutinising his fellow travellers so closely, making judgements and sorting into categories that were probably more stereotype than reality? A glance at Ava confirmed that she was doing the same. People-watching with a purpose, looking for the unusual detail, the small anomalies that might signify something significant. On guard and alert. They had both done their share of surveillance duties, and old habits die hard.

The train was running ten minutes late, and when it arrived most of the carriages were half full.

"We have reservations," Neal said, unnecessarily, as they had already checked their tickets and positioned themselves at the appropriate place on the platform.

"I've had a couple of bad experiences with trains," Ava said, mysteriously, as she stepped aboard. Neal had already observed that their reserved seats were occupied.

"These are our seats," Ava pleasantly but firmly informed the two young lads who had settled into their seats.

"So? We were here first. Go find yourself somewhere else to sit."

"I think not," Ava answered, discreetly showing them her badge. Immediately their swaggering attitude disappeared.

"We didn't know you was coppers," one of them said sullenly.

"What difference does our being coppers make?" Ava retorted, but the lads didn't wait around to reply. Instead of shifting into the two facing seats, they moved to another carriage, to Neal's relief; he didn't relish sitting opposite their sullen faces for the next couple of hours.

"Subtly handled," he congratulated Ava.

"My pleasure, sir." They couldn't talk about the case with a potential audience all around, so Neal took out his Kindle and Ava her smartphone. Whenever he glanced down at her screen, Neal saw his sergeant engaged in a strange game that seemed to involve a huge catapult launching a succession of colourful birds at a pig. *Must be the game Archie and Maggie were enthusing about last* week, he concluded, *Angry Pig, Angry Bird? Something like that.*

Archie often accused him of being out of the technological loop, but that was not the case. He merely didn't see the point of a lot of the uses people put it to.

Digital books were something that he could relate to and enjoy, although he did find himself still buying hard copies of books he had read and admired on his e-Reader. The device was, he had concluded, a convenient means of storing and transporting his reading material, but he still preferred to run his fingers along the spines of the volumes on his bookcase, the sense of touch stirring memories of the pleasures within.

"What kind of 'bad experiences' have you had with trains, then?" he asked Ava after a while, when the clickety-clacking of the wheels were beginning to make him feel drowsy.

"Flashers, mostly. When I was a student, travelling late in the evening. I remember one kid plonking himself down opposite me in an empty carriage, unzipping his trousers and just staring at me, terrified."

"What did you do?"

"I suggested politely that he put it away and go to the next carriage. Which he did. I think of the two of us, he was the more embarrassed. He couldn't have been more than fifteen or sixteen."

"And you were what? Eighteen, nineteen? That would have been unsettling for some young women." Ava shook her head.

"He was just a kid, and it wasn't my first experience of that sort of thing. The first time I was fourteen and the bastard was at least forty. That was unsettling. I didn't even report it, I was so shocked and ashamed."

At that moment an elderly woman settled into the seat opposite them and Neal felt it inappropriate to continue with the conversation. He had noticed that Ava's expression had hardened as she recalled the earlier incident, and wondered if there were more to it than flashing. He also knew that he should not ask, even at an appropriate time.

The journey passed quickly. Neal became engrossed in his book as soon as the train picked up speed and hardly noticed even when they stopped at stations on the way. Ava put on some headphones and was soon tapping out a beat with her fingers.

"Must be a good book," Ava commented as they pulled into King's Cross. Neal knew that his sergeant's literary tastes did not match his own, and he simply agreed and left it at that. Archie's mother had not been much of a reader either, nor had any of the women he had dated in recent years. Anna Foster was a book lover; he thought of how pleasant it would be to spend an evening in her company discussing their favourite books and authors.

At King's Cross station, Neal and Ava headed for the tube station. Neal had been on trips to London, mostly with Archie to visit museums or other attractions, but he didn't know it well and truth be told, he was always glad to leave it behind. To him, Stromford was a city on a human scale, and it was possible to be in the countryside within ten minutes of leaving its centre. He wasn't sure that he could cope with the size and scale of a larger city.

Heading west on the tube, Neal tried to be surreptitious as he surveyed his fellow passengers. In crowded places like this, he was always hyper alert and he knew that Ava was too, just as they had both been on the platform in Harmsborough. If someone had asked him later how many passengers had been in his carriage, whether any of them had stood out, how many were male or female, black or white, he would have been able to answer with near one hundred per cent accuracy. Being observant was hard-wired into his brain, a skill that he had no desire to switch off.

* * *

"You coppers?" the cabbie asked as Neal and Ava climbed into the back seat of a taxi, after Neal had given their destination as Wormwood Scrubs.

"Or relatives of an inmate?" None of your business, Neal thought, not wanting to answer for fear of being drawn into conversation with their driver. Ava answered, and there followed an exchange of views on the British criminal justice system during which Neal and Ava were left in no doubt about the cabbie's opinion of what should happen to terrorists, murderers and repeat offenders.

Neal refrained from making any comment and, after a few more moments of enduring the man's Draconian views, he began speaking to Ava in a low voice. The cabbie must have got the message because he slid the partition shut and tuned his radio to some kind of discussion programme, the sound of which was mostly muffled by the glass between them.

"The Scrubs is a category B prison, isn't it, sir?" Ava asked, though Neal suspected she already knew the answer. He nodded.

"Bolan's serving a life sentence. Model prisoner by all accounts. He's always denied harming his baby daughter, but he had a rough time of it in the early days because he was regarded as a child killer. His young son, Simon, told some weird tale about his sister being rescued by an angel, and it was probably this that prompted Bolan to claim that Emily must have been abducted. There was a huge search, but the conclusion was that he had killed her and disposed of the body."

"Bolan claimed that Debbie Clarke was alive when he left her, didn't he?" Ava asked, "And wasn't it proven that she didn't die for some time after Bolan left her?"

"A couple of hours. By then, she'd taken a truckload of painkillers. Bolan's lawyer tried to argue that she would have lived but for that. The autopsy was inconclusive, but Bolan eventually went down on both counts. He's always argued that he was wrongly convicted, of course."

"The Jury must have been convinced," Ava mused.

"There was no doubt that he beat Debbie X severely and left her for dead," Neal said, adding, "whatever else he was guilty of." He stared out of the window for a few moments.

Looking back on his cases, he could say with utter conviction that he had been convinced of the guilt of everyone he had been responsible for bringing to justice over the years, but even so, the very thought that some innocent man or woman had been deprived of their freedom as a result of shoddy or dishonest detective work, or any other fault in the legal process, filled him with horror. He had to believe that the system would get it right; otherwise he would not be able to do his job at all.

"If Simon does turn out to be Amy's killer, you could call it bad genes," Ava said. "Like father, like son."

Neal made a face that he hoped told Ava exactly what he thought of that observation.

"Don't look so disapproving, I wasn't being serious. Simon was an abused child, wasn't he? Could have sustained damage to his pre-frontal lobes through injury, or his emotional development might have been impaired by neglect. He could have grown up having a lack of empathy leading to behaviour patterns consistent with a sociopathic personality."

"You've been doing some reading," Neal commented. A couple of weeks ago he'd told Ava about a book he'd been reading that suggested sociopaths and psychopaths should be regarded as damaged rather than inherently evil. It had made him uncomfortably aware of how easy it was to dismiss violent offenders as inhuman monsters.

He and Ava had argued about the moral consequences of accepting such a supposition, and both had concluded that the only sensible way to deal with such offenders was to lock them up and throw away the key for the protection of others in society.

"Simon has a loving mother now. You have to hope her influence would balance out his earlier neglect," he said.

"'Ere we go," the cabbie called cheerfully when they reached their destination. "That'll be ten quid. I expect you'll want a receipt for that?" Neal paid him, adding a generous tip. "Say 'allo to my mate, 'arry Saunders while you're in there," the cabbie said, as they stopped, "doin' three years for GBH. Always 'ad a temper on 'im 'arry did."

"Come on, let's get this over with," Neal said.

* * *

They had both been in prisons before, and one is very much like another in terms of internal arrangement and décor. Still, Neal was struck by the starkness of this one, the sense of oppression and confinement that pervaded its walls. Ava summed it up,

"I always feel like I should take a breath when I enter these places, and not let it go until I leave."

The interview room was cold, ill-lit and depressing. Wade Bolan sat opposite them, a middle-aged man in good shape; evidently he spent a lot of his time in prison working out. He was a tall man, and defiant; even sitting down, he owned the room. Neal had to remind himself that it was he and Ava who would be walking out of the room and into the outside world when the interview was over.

From the moment they entered the room, Bolan's eyes were riveted on Ava. Neal had no doubt that his DS was used to being appraised by men, but there was nothing subtle about Bolan's look, and his gaze lingered a long time on her breasts. To her credit, Ava remained unruffled. It was Neal who was annoyed.

"I know you've been told why we're here," he began, "so let's get to the point. We're looking for your son, Simon. Has he been in contact with you?"

"I don't have a son," Bolan answered, finally looking from Ava to Neal, "He was adopted years ago. Haven't you done your research?" His mocking tone grated on Neal, and he did his best to ignore it.

"My letters are opened, my phone calls are monitored, and I'm not even allowed to receive emails directly. You

200

know all that. Why waste your time coming 'ere to ask what you already know?"

"You and I both know that there are ways of getting around the system." Neal said, patiently.

"What's he done then, my boy? He in some kind of trouble? Chip off the old block is he, eh, Sergeant?" Bolan said, winking at Ava, who smiled at him good-humouredly.

Neal continued, "He's gone missing. We need to question him in relation to a case we're investigating."

"Why would 'e contact me? 'E don't know me from Adam."

"You have contacts on the outside. Is he staying with any of them?" Bolan seemed amused by the question, leading Neal to suspect that he was genuinely surprised they thought Simon might have been in touch with him.

"I told you already. I don't 'ave a son. 'Ad one once. Weird little sod, 'e was. Clever, like 'is old man, only more so. I had a little gel too; don't know what became of 'er neither. Tell you what though, 'er disappearing, that had nothing to do with me. Least you can't accuse me of killing this Simon. Got the perfect alibi this time, ain't I? I mean it's not as if I can just nip out any time I like and bump someone off, is it now?" No hint of amusement now, only anger, and defiance. It seemed almost as if Bolan were challenging them to contradict him.

"Simon isn't dead, Mr Bolan. Not that we're aware of and, like I said before, there are ways of getting around the system."

Bolan shook his head in evident disbelief, but there was no mistaking that his anger was rising, "You lot are incredible, you are. Trying to pin something else on me when I'm already banged up inside. It's a fuckin' outrage."

"No-one's accusing you of anything," Neal said.

"Like I said, 'e ain't been touch an' whatever 'e's got himself involved in it's got nothing to do with me," Bolan repeated.

With Bolan's tone changing from mocking to aggressive, there seemed no point in persisting with the interview. Clearly, he was not going to cooperate.

Neal and Ava followed another guard back down the corridor to the exit. "He doesn't get many visitors," he told them, "but the ones who do come are mostly regulars. Most of them have done time themselves. A bad lot. Did have one non-regular a few months back. Young lad, not the one you're looking for, though, doesn't fit the description." Neal thanked him. All in all, they seemed to have gained nothing from the visit.

Ava exhaled exaggeratedly as they cleared the prison gates. Neal smiled. "Letting go?" he asked.

* * *

The train was cancelled. There had been an incident outside one of the stations on the main line, and long delays were expected.

"Isn't it always the way?" moaned a woman in the crowd of passengers all looking up at the electronic notice board.

"Bloody inconvenient. It's parents' evening at Archie's school. I haven't a hope in hell of making it now. Maggie'll have to step in as usual," Neal said, sounding bitter.

"I'm sorry. I know you don't like letting him down."

Neal's fingers moved furiously over his mobile as he texted his sister. Almost as soon as he had finished, the phone buzzed, and his face lightened considerably as he read Maggie's text, "It's been cancelled," he announced, "at least three of the teachers at the school have come down with food poisoning. Come on, let's have a drink."

They made their way through the press of disgruntled early afternoon commuters, most of whom seemed to be either texting or speaking on mobiles. The real trouble would start as the rush hour approached and hordes more people found themselves stranded or forced to make alternative arrangements for their journey home. Neal found himself sympathising with the station staff; they would no doubt bear the brunt of the frustrated commuters' short tempers.

In a bar a couple of streets away from the station, Ava connected to the free Wi-Fi to check the news on her smart-phone, and review their travel options.

"There's been a derailment. Just a goods train and no-one injured, but all trains to the north and northeast are cancelled until further notice," she informed Neal.

"Fucking hell," he muttered into his beer. He rarely swore. It was the thought of the wasted time that bothered him most.

"It's bound to have a knock-on effect. There's going to be a huge amount of disruption," Ava continued. "We might be better off finding a place to stay for the night before everything gets booked up."

It was a thought that had already occurred to Neal. At least he did not have to worry about Archie; Maggie had already assured him that she would be home all evening. Another thought occurred to him.

"As long as we're going to be stranded in London, we might as well make use of the time. Let's make a visit to the estate Simon lived on as a child. I'd like to see where he came from."

"Aw, boss, can't we just go shopping?" Ava moaned, adding quickly, "Just kidding."

They booked a couple of rooms in a Premier Inn near King's Cross and took a cab to Bethnal Green. Their driver dropped them at the estate where Simon Foster had begun his life under a different name and in very different circumstances.

* * *

There was a housing office near the estate, which served the Trafalgar and a couple of neighbouring estates. A young Bangladeshi woman greeted them at the reception counter. Neal and Ava showed their ID cards and asked if they could take a look at tenancy records from eighteen years ago. They were invited to wait while the woman consulted her manager.

They stood away from the counter to allow other clients access. A frustrated tenant complained about his leaking toilet and the number of appointments the contracted plumber had missed. He left with another appointment and was replaced by a mother of three small children who complained about the state of the communal staircase. The housing officer promised to inform the caretaking team. Then, an elderly man approached the counter to complain about his neighbour's dog, and the person after him in the queue had a grumble about the family living above him who made too much noise.

"Bloody hell," Ava whispered, "Makes me grateful for my own little cottage in the woods." Neal nodded. He would have said that he thought Ava's little cottage was a bit too isolated for his liking, but it was none of his business, and, besides, at that moment, a door behind the counter opened and the Asian girl returned, accompanied by a harassed-looking man in a grey suit.

"Please come through," he said to Neal and Ava. Both were aware of the looks coming from the other people in the reception area, as the girl lifted the counter gate to let them through into a back office. What had they done to warrant special treatment by the housing manager, no less?

"I'm Jack Hammond, housing manager. What can I do for you, Officers?" Neal explained again that they would like to look through some records for background information on a case they were investigating involving a young man who had previously lived on the estate.

"I remember the family," Hammond said to their mutual surprise. "I was a newbie housing officer at the time. It was a terrible tragedy the death of that young mother and her daughter."

"How well did you know the family?" asked Neal.

"Debbie Clarke was one of our 'heart-sink' cases," Hammond answered, "You know, the ones who keep coming back. They make you feel inadequate because there's really nothing you can do for them. Or, more precisely, whatever you do will fail because you can't change some people." He looked suddenly guilty. "Not supposed to say that, I know, but I've been doing this job for twenty years now and I've lost all my youthful idealism. Maybe it's time for a career change."

Neal nodded patiently. He knew so many people working in public services like housing and social work who were similarly disillusioned. Those in his chosen profession were not immune either. He knew all about 'heart-sink' cases: the repeat offenders, drug users and dealers, serial rapists, paedophiles and psychopaths. In his darker moments, he saw his role in terms of rounding up the bad guys, in some cases locking them up and throwing away the key, instead of rehabilitation and reform. He was not yet as disillusioned as Jack Hammond, but he was no longer under any illusions either.

"This is where we keep our archived tenancy records," Hammond said, leading them into a room full of shelf files. "They're arranged alphabetically by the name of the block or street, then numerically by house or flat number. Debbie Clarke was in Admiral House, number fourteen. Here we are." He removed a thick cardboard wallet from a suspended file and handed it to Neal. "You're welcome to sit in here and browse. Give me a shout if you need any help or assistance."

"Cup of coffee would be nice," Ava said wistfully, after the housing manager left the room.

"Take a look through some of the files for neighbouring flats," Neal instructed her, "see if there're any references to Debbie in any of them. Complaints about noise nuisance, domestic disturbances, anything."

Some files were bulkier than others. Many of the blocks had been built in the 1930s by the old London County

Council and in some cases tenancies had changed hands several times. Not surprisingly, Debbie Clarke's file was substantial, bulging with letters and reports from social workers and housing officers. Neal adopted a systematic approach, reading everything in date order: beginning with the housing officer's comments — recorded after every contact with Debbie — then those of the professionals involved with her and her children.

It made for depressing reading. Forms and reports from her previous tenancies attested to the fact that she had been rehoused by the Council several times before arriving on the Trafalgar estate. There was a history of domestic violence going back several years, involving more than one partner.

Before Wade there had been a Darren and a Vince, but Wade was recorded as the father of Debbie's two children, Peter and Emily and Debbie had been moved twice to 'escape' him. According to Jack Hammond, the housing officer at the time, Debbie had 'repeatedly informed her abusive ex-partner of her whereabouts and permitted him access to her home.' Neal wondered how she could possibly have avoided Wade Bolan, as the flats she had been allocated were all located in the same borough; sooner or later, they were bound to collide. In any case, it seemed that Bolan had been permitted occasional supervised access to his children.

Still, as Jack Hammond had hinted, Debbie had been unable to change, to escape the cycle of abuse.

"Oh my god. This guy has got to be the neighbour from hell," Ava said, looking up from a bulging file. "These are all letters from other tenants complaining about his anti-social activities. Spitting and swearing at little kids, noise nuisance, letting his dogs use the walkways as a toilet, minor vandalism, racist language, the list goes on. ASBOs, god rest 'em, were invented for people like this." Neal did not comment. "Boss?"

Neal was aware that Ava was speaking to him, but her words had faded to background noise. He was staring at the record sheet, where one name leapt out from the page. He had almost missed it — a short entry recording a complaint about a leaking soil stack outside Debbie Clarke's flat.

"Ava," he said quietly, "come and take a look at this."

Chapter 17

Nancy had not seen Richard for two days; he had remained true to his word, and left her alone. She had been grateful for the time and space to think. Over and over, the events leading up to the night when her action had changed her life forever, played out inside her head. She was like the Ancient Mariner, under a compulsion to retell her story, in hope of release.

It was early afternoon; she had eaten nothing since breakfast the day before, and had barely stirred from bed, except to relieve herself; hardly moved at all except to kick the duvet off when she grew too warm and pull it over her again when she began to shiver.

Her phone buzzed; a text. Nancy stared at the message from Anna Foster with a feeling of defeat. *I know about Emily.* For nearly nineteen years, she had kept her secret; from her friends, from Richard, even in recent years from herself, as she gradually adopted the habit of questioning the reliability of her own memory of those distant events.

Hadn't she read that when questioned about events in their past, people very often had a distorted view of what had actually happened, and in some cases, their memories were completely false? The past is so often not what we remember, she reminded herself, but what we choose to forget. The very word sums it up. Past. Passed. Over and done with. Except it wasn't.

The past, or more precisely one particular part of it, had been uppermost in Nancy's mind for days, plaguing her waking hours and haunting her dreams. Her fingernails, which for years now had been long and polished, were once more bitten down to the quick, just as they had been throughout her teenage years. Her eyes, when she stared into them in the bathroom mirror, were portals, focusing her thoughts inwards and backwards twenty years and more until the present became strange and dream-like.

More than anything, Nancy had been looking for the love that had gone from her life after her parents died. And what love she had found! An abundance of it, all in one small, beautiful child. There had been only one problem. Emily was not hers.

She had already decided to move away. She had become too embroiled too fast in Debbie Clarke's affairs after their first meeting in the park. Wade frightened her. Ever since the night he had touched her, she had felt violated. That night when Debbie came knocking on her door seeking refuge after Wade had beaten her, Nancy had not wanted to let her in. She had feared for her own safety, and the knowledge had made her ashamed.

After that night, Nancy's instinct had been to extricate herself from the situation altogether. At first, approaching Debbie in the park with her naïve offer of help had given her a warm glow inside; made her feel that she was a good person again, like before. Four years of foster care had not, after all, stripped her of her humanity. The values her parents had communicated to her throughout her childhood were still alive inside her; she would recover the kind of love she had basked in as a child through her kindness to others. How speedily she had become disillusioned. Did she even have the right to judge how

Debbie chose to live her life, how she brought up her children? These were big questions and at twenty-one years old, Nancy did not have the answers.

She had never asked herself what she would have done had the events of that night been different. The first time she held Emily/Amy in her arms, she had been suffused with a love that shocked her with its intensity. It was a feeling that was wonderful yet frightening and possibly dangerous, for Nancy quickly realised that there was little she would not do for this child.

Had she subconsciously been plotting all along to snatch Emily? Nancy had never permitted herself to admit that possibility — until now. Now it was all she could think about.

At the time, she convinced herself that her actions that day had been dictated by circumstance; the need to act. Adrenaline-driven. She hadn't planned, could not have foreseen, the course of events that led to what she ever afterwards referred to in her own mind as, 'Amy's rescue.' It was instinctual; a primal response.

Perhaps if Nancy had simply walked away, Amy would still be alive. She would have been fostered, adopted even, perhaps by a nice family. Babies were easy to place, weren't they? Not like a twelve-year-old.

Who would want to kill Amy? Nancy had gone over this time and again until her head was bursting. Someone who knew her and had a motive? Or some psycho who killed indiscriminately, selecting his victims at random? Which was worse? Did it even matter when the end result was the same? Amy was never coming back.

* * *

For the umpteenth time, she went over the events of that night. Nancy had been writing her letter of notice to her landlady and was thinking of having an early night, finishing her book, when the phone rang. Debbie. Asking her to baby-sit again, threatening to go out whether Nancy came round or not. This had happened a lot lately. Knowing that Nancy feared for the children's safety, Debbie was taking every advantage.

Instead of going to bed, Nancy had pulled on a fleecy top and a pair of boots and headed off to Debbie's. As she approached the block, a voice behind her made her jump. Swinging around, her hand already balled into a fist, she recognized the Bangladeshi man who lived two or three doors along from Debbie. Despite the nip in the air, he was dressed in a loose white shift and open sandals.

"You know Debbie, yes?" He asked, grinning at her, baring uneven, khat-stained teeth. Nancy nodded.

"Her boyfriend very bad man. He frighten my wife and my childruns. All very frightened. Why they let bad man live here? Very bad man. I think he drink very much, beat Debbie and childruns."

"Wade." Nancy whispered.

"Yes. Wade. Very bad man." Her companion repeated excitedly. "Mr Wade. Very bad man."

"Yes," Nancy agreed. A thought struck her, "Is he at Debbie's house now? Have you seen him there?"

"Yes, here today. Gone now. Much noise and very bad language."

With that, the man said goodbye and Nancy could hear him muttering to himself as he walked away, "Mr Wade, very bad man . . ."

She had been in two minds whether to go round to Debbie's after that. The man had said Wade was gone, but was he really? She should have turned back, but she didn't.

* * *

Nancy had already made up her mind before she read Anna Foster's text. The message only served to strengthen her resolve. Now that Amy was dead, all her justifications for acting as she had were exposed for the lies and pretence they truly were, and she knew what she had to do to punish herself for what she had done.

211

Nancy tossed her mobile to the floor and rolled off the bed. She walked into the luxurious bespoke en-suite bathroom that Richard had designed and fitted for her a couple of years ago. She ran her hand sadly over the shiny antique gold-finish taps, remembering how delighted she had been when the room was completed and she had taken her first bath there, feeling like a princess. Richard had strewn rose petals across the floor around the free-standing tub and poured her a glass of Prosecco before leaving her to luxuriate in a foaming cloud of rose-scented bubbles.

Leaving the bath to fill, Nancy brought a portable CD player from the bedroom and placed it on the lowered toilet seat cover, resting the remote control on the side of the bath. Then, she undressed slowly and before stepping into the tub, reached for one of Richard's razor blades and laid it beside the remote control. All she had to do now was step in and let the hot water soak away her pain.

She pointed the remote control at the CD player and lay back listening to Jessye Norman's achingly beautiful voice singing the last of Richard Strauss's 'Four Last Songs.' With her head resting on the rim of the bathtub, and the razor blade poised over the blue-veined skin of her left wrist, Nancy gave the bath taps a last lingering look, thinking that if she had any regrets about what she was about to do, they were all for Richard.

Chapter 18

It had been a long day, and Neal was relieved to see the floodlit cathedral looming up out of the window on his left as the train slowed on its approach to Stromford station. They had not, after all, spent the night in London, but hitched a ride in a patrol car out to one of the suburbs and caught a train home from there. Beside him, her head resting on his shoulder, Ava was asleep as she had been all the way from the outskirts of London. A sweep of golden hair cascaded over his shoulder, staticky silken strands clinging to the lapel of his jacket. For the past half hour, Neal had been experiencing an almost irresistible urge to stroke his sergeant's head, and he was sure that she would not have stirred, so deeply was she asleep. Only his stern professionalism stood between him and the satisfaction of this urge. Instead of finding out if her hair was as silky as it seemed, he gave Ava a poke in the side to wake her up, and then looked out of the window to save her embarrassment.

"Bloody hell. We home already? How long was I out, sir?"

"Only the best part of two hours. Glad the latest development in the case hasn't kept you awake and fretting."

"I suppose you've been mulling it over all the way back?"

"Actually, no. I've been listening to some podcasts. Radio 4. Melvyn Bragg's 'In Our Time.'"

Ava made a face, "Bit intellectual for me."

"Why do you do that? Neal asked, curious.

"Do what?"

"Pretend you're less intelligent than you are. I've noticed you do it a lot. You got good results in your A levels, went to university . . ."

"And dropped out," Ava reminded him, "I didn't even make it through the second year."

"Not through lack of ability, I suspect?"

Ava didn't answer. Sensing it was a touchy subject, Neal let it go.

"So what happens now?" Ava asked, "Do we question Nancy or just arrest her outright for kidnapping?"

"Well, it won't be difficult to establish Amy, or should I say, Emily's true parentage," Neal answered. "If it's proven that Nancy abducted her from the scene of Debbie's death, then she will have to face charges of child abduction. We still have no idea who killed Amy, or why, but this revelation certainly has the potential to open up the case."

"Simon Foster still seems the most likely suspect. Now that we know he and Amy were brother and sister. What with his continued disappearance . . ." Ava said.

The train juddered to a halt and Ava, on the aisle seat, stood up immediately. Neal was right behind her, but he stopped to help an elderly woman with her suitcase, and they both had to wait on the platform while she thanked him from the bottom of her heart.

At last, through the barrier and outside the station, the elderly woman safely in a taxi, they were able to resume their conversation.

"So Simon's reaction to meeting Nancy Hill at his mother's book group makes sense now," Ava began, "if he recognised her as 'the angel' who took his sister Emily it must have been a shock, not just to see that Nancy was flesh and blood, but to learn that his sister was still alive."

"Amy. Emily. Nancy didn't change the name much. It's highly likely that the two-year-old Simon pronounced Emily's name as 'Emmy,' and that's where Nancy got the idea. All seems so obvious when you start to join the dots, doesn't it?"

"Bit of a coincidence, isn't it, brother and sister ending up in the same city, their mothers being friends, don't you think, sir?"

"That does bother me," Neal commented, "makes me wonder how much of what both Nancy Hill and Anna Foster have told us is the truth." He glanced at his watch. "Too late to deal with any of this tonight. I'll have Nancy Hill brought into the station in the morning. Should scare her into telling the truth."

It had been a long day. He wanted to get home and say goodnight to Archie. Neal could not have known that by morning, Nancy Hill would be beyond all questioning.

* * *

As soon as she walked into the station the following morning, Ava could tell that something was up. Neal didn't even thank her for the coffee she plonked in front of him when, unusually for her, she showed up ten minutes late.

"Where have you been?" Neal asked irritably, "leave your coat on; we need to get to Nancy Hill's as soon as possible."

"I thought you said we were bringing her in?" said Ava. She had half thought that Nancy Hill would already have been picked up by a couple of constables and be waiting to be questioned. Neal glared at her, though she could not possibly have known what he was about to say.

"Nancy Hill is dead. Our uniforms found her when they called to pick her up. When she didn't answer the door they looked around outside the property and discovered the back door unlocked. Found her in the bath with her wrists slashed."

Ava did not dare take the lid off her coffee cup. Neal had not so much as glanced at his, and his urgency and vexation were palpable.

"If that damn train hadn't been delayed . . ." he began.

". . . We wouldn't have gone to the Trafalgar estate and discovered that Nancy had a big secret. And we wouldn't have had a reason to call on Nancy. The outcome would still be the same; Nancy would still be dead," Ava said bluntly. Still, she understood that part of Neal's anger stemmed from his frustration at not having brought Nancy in the evening before, thereby saving her life. "I know that, Sergeant," Neal snarled, then, less irascibly, "look, I'm bloody frustrated about all of this . . . just when we seemed to have a chance to move the case forward, this happens. Four deaths now. At the rate the bodies are piling up, we'll have exhausted all our suspects soon."

Ava had seldom seen him so wound up. She did not share his sense of guilt. Neal was feeling bad because he had failed to save Nancy. It caused Ava a moment's concern that she did not seem to care as deeply as Neal, then she dismissed the thought; it was not that she did not care enough, but that sometimes, her Chief cared too much. Perhaps she was learning professional detachment after all. She felt sorry for Nancy's terrible loss and for the despair that led her to take her own life, but that was all. No doubt one day there would be a case that would get to her and unravel her, but she was determined it wouldn't be this one.

* * *

It took less than half an hour to drive out to Shelton. The village was one of a cluster that lay within a six-mile radius of the city, and was popular with families because of the good schools and easy commuting distance from Stromford. Ava drove. Only ten minutes from town, they were already in open countryside, but now, off the A-road, it felt as if they had left the city a hundred miles behind. The road was lined on either side with fields, ploughed over at this time of year, brown and flat and stark, and in many areas, still flooded with water from the recent rains. The bleak November landscape was relieved by hedgerows and copses and the odd farm building, and crows flapped their scrawny wings over ridges in the fields, looking for food.

"Ever thought of moving out of town, sir?" Ava asked as they neared the village and a radar speed sign flashed out a warning to her to reduce her speed. "Nice cosy cottage in a place like this?" Shelton was postcard picturesque. As Ava spoke, they passed a pretty fourteenth century church on their right and the restored village pump on the green to their left. A cluster of traditional cottages surrounded the green, all topped with orange pan-tiled roofs and built out of the same cream-coloured local stone. It made Ava think of chocolate boxes and jigsaws.

"Quite happy where I am for the time being, and Archie's settled in school. Besides, Stromford isn't really a city, is it, more like a big town? I hear you're a bit of a country girl?"

Ava smiled, "Not exactly. I'm a bit out in the sticks but I'm only three-and-a-bit miles from town. And of course, there's a hamlet about half a mile away."

"Doesn't it feel a bit isolated?" Neal asked.

"I have neighbours. Sort of. Nearest one's about five minutes' walk away."

"Is your place alarmed?"

Ava snorted, "You're kidding, aren't you? My landlord's a bit on the tight side to say the least, but the rent's low — mostly because there are few amenities nearby. I do have Camden — he's as good as any guard dog."

Neal did not comment; they had arrived at Nancy Hill's cottage.

* * *

A uniformed officer stood by the door. He said good morning to Neal and smiled at Ava, self-consciously puffing himself up as she came close.

"Hi Ava — I mean, Sergeant." A friendly voice greeted her inside Nancy's small hallway.

"Hi Dan," Ava answered, "How's life?"

"Busy," Dan said, his smile instantly transforming him from geeky to handsome. "This one's straightforward enough, I think. Obvious suicide according to Hunt." Ava nodded soberly.

"Partner's in the sitting room. He's in a bit of a state."

Ava cringed, recalling Nancy's distress when she'd received the terrible news about Amy. It seemed like there was no end to the fallout of grief and tragedy from Amy — or Emily's — murder. With a feeling of trepidation, Ava entered the sitting room where Neal and a police constable stood over a bewildered-looking Richard Turner. Richard was slumped in a chintz armchair, head in hands. He looked up at Ava as she entered the room and shook his head, saying, "I can't cope with all this now. You'll all have to come back later. All I can think of is Nancy lying in that . . . that . . . bloodbath."

"Mr Turner," Neal said gently, "we understand you are upset but there are a few questions we need to ask. I'm sure Nancy would want you to cooperate with us in our investigation into her daughter's death." Neal signalled to the police constable to make some hot, sweet tea. He sat down in the other armchair and Ava took a seat on the sofa feeling awkward and voyeuristic.

"What about Nancy? Who's going to be looking into her death?" Turner asked in some confusion.

"Mr Turner, it seems very likely that Nancy took her own life," said Neal.

"Why would she do that? She would have recovered from Amy's death given time and with my support. A couple of nights ago she asked me to marry her. Why would she do that if she intended to . . . to . . . kill herself?"

Neal sighed, "Grief makes people act irrationally sometimes. They don't know their own minds. Nancy was suffering from a reactive depression. Another evening she might just have picked up the phone and called you. Last night, she responded to her feelings in a tragic way. It makes no sense to a rational mind, but Nancy wasn't thinking rationally when she stepped into that bathtub. I'm so sorry for your loss, Mr Turner."

Ava mumbled her own condolences, and she did feel for Richard Turner, but at the same time, she felt impatient with him for holding things up. She wondered how Neal was going to proceed. Was it possible that Richard Turner had no inkling that Amy was not Nancy's natural born child? To her surprise, she saw her boss nodding at her to take the lead. She cleared her throat,

"Mr Turner. We have recently discovered that Nancy may not have been Amy's birth mother. Were you aware of this?"

Richard Turner's astonishment dispelled any doubt. Ava would have bet money that he was as shocked as she and Neal had been to discover that this was the case.

"That's preposterous," Turner said. "Why would you even suggest such a thing? Is this some kind of sick joke?" Anger had temporarily replaced grief. For a moment, Ava thought him capable of striking one of them.

Evidently, the constable preparing tea in the kitchen had the same thought, for he appeared suddenly in the doorway, asking, "Everything alright in here?"

"Quite alright, constable," Neal assured him, "Mr Turner has just received some disturbing news." With a look that questioned what could be more disturbing than to discover your partner in the bathtub with both wrists slashed, the PC returned to the kitchen.

"Please be calm," Neal said to Richard. "We wouldn't be asking this if we didn't have a good idea that it might be true. It may be important in finding Amy's killer. Take your time and think; did Nancy ever give you reason to suspect that Amy wasn't her flesh and blood daughter?"

"Of course not!" Turner exclaimed, but his face said otherwise. It was as though a penny had suddenly dropped and he had found the answer to something that had been puzzling him for a long time.

"Mr Turner . . ." Ava prompted. He had suddenly gone quiet.

"I . . . I . . . Amy wasn't conceived in this country. Nancy had a . . . had more than one sexual encounter whilst living in France and Amy was the result, or so she claimed. She said she didn't know for certain who the father was and registered Amy under her own name when she was over a year old. She . . . she said she gave birth to Amy by herself and kept her hidden for a while to avoid what she perceived at the time as the shame of not being able to name the father."

As he spoke these words, it was obvious from Richard's face that he realised how improbable they sounded. Ava resisted the urge to ask him if he had ever questioned Nancy's version of events. Turner put his head in his hands again,

"She was always so protective of Amy, over-protective. She wouldn't let me in, wanted to keep Amy to herself. I always suspected there was something she wasn't telling me, something big that stopped her accepting my proposal. She was going to tell me, I think. After the funeral, when she asked me to marry her, I felt that there was something else she was on the point of saying but changed her mind at the last moment. I was too stunned by the proposal to question her."

They were interrupted by the constable bringing tea. Ava gazed enviously at the steaming mug, thinking of her coffee, left untouched, back in Neal's office.

"I'll take that," she said, stepping forward. She placed the mug on a heart shaped coaster on the coffee table in front of Turner. "Mr Turner, try to have a sip of this. It might help."

Turner gazed up at her in bewilderment. "The love of my life has just killed herself. How could a cup of tea possibly help?" he asked.

"I'm sorry," mumbled Ava, "I can't begin to understand what this must be like for you."

It was obvious that Turner was in no fit state to be questioned further, and the fact that Nancy's death seemed to be a textbook suicide suggested that there was little to be gained from continuing.

"Mr Turner," Neal began, gently, "If there is anything about Nancy's past that you think might be relevant to our investigation, please give me or my colleague a call. Even if it seems insignificant, don't hesitate."

"Nancy didn't talk about the past. It's as if her life began when she and Amy moved to the village. She was barely twenty-three then. Before that she lived in France, before that, London and before that she was in foster care for four years. Her parents were killed in a car accident when she was twelve." Neal nodded, and Ava jotted down some notes.

"Thank you, Mr Turner. Like I said, if you think of anything else, let us know."

Ava felt her head clear as soon as they walked out the door of the cottage into Nancy's small front garden. "That was intense," she commented. "So much emotion in one room."

"Ours is often a sad business," Neal said, quietly. He was, she noted, looking around the garden. Neal was known to have green fingers. The small plot would have looked pretty in the summer, she thought. There was evidence all around that Nancy had been a keen gardener, but already the garden was showing signs of neglect. Soggy brown leaves lay un-raked on the grass and across the path, roses un-pruned and plants that should have been moved indoors before the first winter frosts stood withering in their pots. Only a cheerful fuchsia and some flourishing winter jasmine hinted that life goes on.

"I'll check information on Nancy's background now that we know it may be relevant," Ava said.

"Right," he answered. "I want details of her foster carers and any foster siblings. It shouldn't be that hard to ferret out. In the meantime, I'm going to pay Anna Foster another call, see what she has to say about any prior ties to Nancy."

* * *

They drove back to the station in near silence. Neal had popped a disc into the CD player, some kind of Celtic music that he was fond of playing, melancholy and plangent, that did nothing to lift the mood. Ava's ankle was aching and she squirmed in her seat trying to find a comfortable position. It was bothering her a lot lately. Perhaps she should take Neal's advice and see a 'proper' doctor.

At the station, they went their separate ways.

PC Polly Jenkins caught Ava the moment she walked through the door. "Have lunch with me. I've been on desk duty all morning and I'm itching to get out of here."

"I've just got back," Ava said, though just at that moment her stomach rumbled audibly, reminding her that she hadn't eaten since six that morning.

"So what? You've been working, haven't you? And I heard that racket — you need carbs — now. Don't fight it."

"Let me just . . ." Ava began.

"I said now. I know you, the minute you sit down at that computer of yours you won't stop 'til you faint from hunger."

Ava laughed, "You win. Just give me five minutes." Before Polly could moan, she pointed and whispered, "Ladies' room."

"Five minutes and I come in there and haul you out."

"Five minutes and you won't have to."

Three minutes later, Ava was rubbing her hands together vigorously under the dryer when she felt her mobile buzzing in her pocket. A text. She looked at it quickly, intending to reply later, but when she saw the caller ID, she felt a thrill of excitement. It was from Rukhsana Begum from the community centre in Sheffield, saying that she was in town and that she wished to speak with her about Rohina Ali.

"Is it that obvious?" Ava said to Polly apologetically as she emerged from the women's loo.

"I know that look," Polly said, dejectedly. "I shouldn't have let you get past me."

"I'm sorry, PJ. I've just had an urgent text. Could be a lead. Some other time, okay?"

"Oh, yeah. Like you're available twenty four seven, aren't you?" Polly called after her, but Ava had no time for more apologies. She had already texted Rukhsana back and agreed to meet her at the train station, and she had precisely eleven minutes to get there.

* * *

Rukhsana was standing near the door of her train, glancing nervously at her watch, when Ava, sprinting along the platform, caught sight of her. The connection to Sheffield was due to leave in a couple of minutes. Whatever she has to tell me, Ava thought, she'll have to talk fast.

"I have an address for you," Rukhsana said as Ava approached, her lungs exploding from the sprint.

"Rohina Ali?" Ava gasped. Rukhsana looked around as though she was afraid they would be overheard.

"Here, take this," she said, pushing a small envelope into Ava's hand. "In case the whistle blows — there's not much time to talk." At that very moment, the guard put his whistle to his mouth and motioned to the two women to either get on or off the train.

"Thank you," Ava mouthed through the window. Rukhsana nodded solemnly, her face already blurring as the train moved slowly down the platform.

Ava ripped the envelope open, tearing the note inside in her haste. She stared, astonished, at the address on the slip of paper; it was right here in the city. Rohina Ali was a student at Stromford University.

Chapter 19

For the first time in weeks, the temperature was beginning to drop and the sky did not look overcast. Perhaps soon there would be the first real frost of the season, a welcome change after so much rain. Neal parked his car at the bottom of the Long Hill and walked up, admiring the partial view of the cathedral straight ahead. As part of an ongoing programme of repairs and restoration, much of its magnificent west front was obscured by scaffolding, but at this distance, none of that was evident; only its jutting towers were visible, piercing a startlingly blue sky, and they were flawless.

Perched at the top of the Long Hill, the gothic structure could be seen from miles around. Soon after moving to Stromford, Neal had realised that, whenever he drove towards the city, he began searching the skyline from as far away as twenty miles, looking for the familiar towers to guide him home. Years before, pilots returning from bombing missions in Germany had done the same, using the cathedral as a beacon to guide them to the airfields in the flat countryside surrounding the city. For almost a thousand years the cathedral had stood as a symbol of hope, a manmade edifice that seemed to embody the permanence of a natural landmark.

Anna Foster's shop was a short distance ahead across the cobblestone street, as Neal reached the hill's half-way mark. A few afternoon shoppers, pausing for a break in their ascent of the relentlessly steep hill, looked in the window then continued on. The shop seldom seemed to be busy, but as Neal drew closer, he could see that there were one or two customers browsing the shelves nearest the door.

Reluctant as he was for Ms Foster to lose precious custom, he was going to request that she turn her 'open' sign to 'closed,' so that he could be sure of conversing with her free of interruptions. Neal pushed open the door and breathed in the alluring scent of books old and new, full of knowledge and wit, facts and fantasies, beginnings and endings.

"Good afternoon, Inspector," Anna Foster greeted him from her desk. Today, he noticed, she looked her age. Dark circles underscored her eyes; her hair was caught up carelessly in a ponytail held in place by a scruffy blue scrunchy, loose strands hanging limply around her face, which was paler than usual. To Neal she still looked attractive — delicate and vulnerable, as though she needed looking after, and it troubled him slightly that he was drawn to her.

Ava teased him that he had a weakness for damsels in distress, and he feared that she might be right.

"Is Maya here today?" he asked, still hoping to save Anna from losing custom.

"Maya doesn't work here anymore. I had to let her go."

"Then I'm sorry but I must ask you to shut up shop for a bit. I need to speak with you."

"More questions, Inspector? I've nothing new to tell you. I haven't heard from Simon."

Neal nodded at the door, "If you wouldn't mind."

Anna Foster took a set of keys from her desk drawer and locked up, having first ushered out the remaining disgruntled browsers. From across the street, the Big Issue seller gave her a wave.

"I usually take her a cup of coffee and a sandwich around now," Anna explained. "She's a dear girl. Romanian. I'd offer her a job, but things being as they are — well, you can see business isn't exactly booming. Shall we go upstairs?"

Neal followed Anna Foster up the creaky winding staircase to her flat above the shop, the property's age evident in the exposed timbers and heavy stone walls. Being on the historic Long Hill, her premises, like others located there, was a listed building and few alterations were permitted that would accommodate modern standards of comfort or style, but the period features more than compensated for their lack.

While she fixed some coffee, Neal looked out of the window at the street below. It was a quiet morning, not really the time of year for tourists. The Christmas market would change all that; it attracted coachloads of visitors every year, giving a much-needed seasonal boost to local businesses. Already preparations were underway with strings of festive lights stretching across the narrow cobbled street of the Long Hill, leading up to the cathedral and castle.

At the beginning of December some local celebrity or other would be called upon to do the honours and switch the lights on, instantly transforming the Long Hill into a twinkling hub of festive commerce.

Looking down, across the cobbled street, Neal saw the Big Issue seller shuffle from foot to foot in an effort to keep warm. She really needed her cup of warming coffee, he thought, guiltily.

"Half a teaspoon of sugar, no milk, that's right, isn't it?" Anna Foster asked, a little too breezily, Neal thought. Perhaps her nerves were on edge. She handed him a dainty china cup and saucer with a pretty floral design; the handle was one of those fancy loop-shapes that made it hard to slip your fingers through, especially if, like Neal's, they were on the large size. They sat facing each other in Anna Foster's mismatched, worn leather wing chairs.

"I haven't come to ask about Simon — well, not directly anyway," Neal began. "I need you to be honest with me now, Ms Foster. You've lied to us before and I must caution you that hindering a police investigation is a serious offence."

Anna Foster nodded, holding her poise though her teacup rattled tellingly in its saucer.

"I would like you to tell me what you knew about Nancy and Amy Hill, particularly what you knew of them before moving here, and whether their residing here had anything to do with your decision to move to Stromford."

"First of all," Anna Foster said quietly, "apart from giving Simon a false alibi, I haven't lied to you about anything else."

"But you have withheld information."

"Only because I didn't think it relevant to the case."

"That's for us to decide, Ms Foster. Tell me what you know, even if it seems irrelevant. When did you first suspect that Simon and Amy were brother and sister?"

"I suppose that was going to come out sooner or later."

Anna Foster leaned back in her chair as if she was making herself comfortable before beginning on a long tale. But really she was deflating, letting go of pent up anxiety. Neal had witnessed guilty people react in just this way, as though telling the truth at last would free them of their oppressive burden of guilt — or in some cases simply give them an opportunity to share the burden.

"I always knew that Simon had a sister. Once or twice, a woman, not the children's mother, brought them into the library and read to them. We used to chat a little but I never knew her name. She was young, pretty. She was very

228

fond of the children, especially Simon's baby sister, Emily. Besotted with her, really."

"This was Nancy?" Neal prompted.

Anna Foster nodded, "She looks very different now, of course, put on a lot of weight and changed her hair colour. I almost wouldn't have recognised her, except for the fact that Amy was so like her mother — her birth mother, that is. I'd seen her picture in the local paper at the time of her death. Of course, you must know that there was some mystery surrounding Emily's whereabouts? Nothing was ever proven, but it was commonly believed that the father, Wade Bolan, was responsible. If nothing else, he was guilty of beating his wife to death. Simon was found cowering in the bedroom cupboard but there was no trace of Emily. It was assumed that Bolan killed her too, though he denied it and no body was ever found."

"Was Simon a witness to his mother's death?" Neal asked.

"He was three years old, Inspector; it wasn't possible for him to give a coherent account of what happened. He did tell the police and social workers that his father had hurt his mother."

"And Emily? What did he know of what happened to his sister?"

"It was the strangest thing. He said that an angel took his sister to heaven."

Neal stared at Anna Foster, puzzled. "Was anyone able to make any sense out of that?"

"He was questioned by the police and by child psychologists but that's all he would ever say. It was suggested that the trauma of witnessing his mother's beating caused him to block the memory of what took place. And, of course, he was very young — who knows what was real or fantasy to him?"

"You told my colleague and me that Simon reacted strangely to meeting Nancy Hill at your book group. Do you believe that he recognised her?"

"I believe that seeing her stirred some kind of memory in him. You have to realise, Inspector, that Simon remembered nothing of his mother's death and the disappearance of his sister other than the 'angel' vision — a kind of protective fantasy.

I was advised by child psychologists who worked with him that Simon might be permanently affected by his early childhood trauma — and there were difficult behaviours to deal with in the early days, as I've already mentioned. I like to think that it was because my late husband and I gave him such care, such love, that he has grown into a wonderful young man."

Anna Foster's voice trembled, her eyes tearing up, and Neal resisted a strong impulse to comfort her. For all he knew she might be manipulating him; he had to remain detached.

"You're probably thinking that Simon's early experiences damaged him, predisposed him to some kind of psychopathic behaviour — that's what people think nowadays, isn't it, that mistreated children grow up to be monsters?"

"That's a kind of populist view that has been given credence by misleading accounts that skew the facts," Neal said. "It's a much more complex issue really, Ms Foster, and believe me, I would not suspect Simon of murdering his sister on such a basis. Besides, as far as I have been able to ascertain, Simon's birth mother, though not a model parent, was not cruel to her children, only neglectful to an extent."

"But you do suspect Simon, don't you? That's what this is all about, isn't it? All these questions? You've decided he's guilty without even giving him a chance."

"Ms Foster, our investigation into Amy Hill's death is on-going. Simon's continued disappearance does not necessarily point to his guilt, but he can't be excluded from our investigations until we have questioned him. He was quite possibly the last person to see Amy alive."

"Allegedly," Anna hissed.

"You gave him a false alibi for the night of Amy's murder. Did you ask him where he really was?" Neal asked, beginning to feel frustrated.

"He wouldn't say, just got angry that I even needed to ask him to justify his whereabouts; then he disappeared. I let him down, betrayed his trust in me. It should never have entered my head that he might have had anything to do with Amy's death."

"Ms Foster, why did you track Nancy Hill down after all those years? How did you even find out where she was?"

"I told you I'd seen her in the library with the children. I knew the estate the family lived on; it was in all the papers. For some time I'd been obsessed with Simon's past. I thought if I tracked down some of the people who knew him back then I could piece together some of his history for him.

I had a friend who worked at the Council and she had access to old tenancy records that were being scanned and digitised. I went through his mother's records and came across Nancy Hill's name twice — once in connection with a repair that she'd reported, and once when she'd asked about moving Debbie Clark to keep her safe from Wade Bolan."

Neal nodded, acknowledging her skilled detective work and remembering the records she was referring to.

"Of course, there were other names in the files, which I followed up, but eventually, clutching at straws, I came to Stromford, and the minute I walked into 'In Stitches,' I knew I'd found Simon's 'angel.' Of course, I was astonished when I met Amy and realised what her resemblance to Debbie Clark must mean." Anna paused, as if expecting a question from Neal, but he nodded for her to continue.

"Simon was studying for A levels and considering universities. I persuaded him to apply to Stromford in the hope that he might run into Amy and get some kind of closure."

Neal snatched a look at his watch as though symbolically assessing how much Anna Foster had delayed the investigation by not telling him all this to begin with.

"Even the smallest things can be relevant in a murder investigation, Ms Foster. This is pretty huge. Did it really never occur to you to tell us any of this before?"

Anna Foster stared at her untouched coffee. Her answer was so quiet that Neal had to lean forward to hear it.

"I was protecting Simon." She looked at him defiantly. "You have a son, Inspector. How far would you go to protect him?"

Her words irritated Neal. He looked at Anna Foster with sudden clarity, wondering why he had ever felt attracted to her. For the first time, he realised that what he had taken for vulnerability was really a kind of armour, and that maybe she was tougher than she seemed. Then, just as suddenly, his anger dissipated. The answer to her question was obvious. Of course he would defend Archie to the ends of the earth, but if his son were guilty of a heinous crime, how far would he then be prepared to go to protect him?

"To the extent that the law would allow," he answered. "For his own protection and that of others."

"How very noble of you, Inspector," Anna Foster said, her voice replete with sarcasm, "I sincerely hope that your son never gives you cause for doubt."

Ignoring her comment, Neal pressed on. "You encouraged Simon to apply for a place at Stromford University and you took out a lease on this place so that you could stay near him, and so that you could make a connection with Nancy and Amy Hill."

Anna Foster nodded. "Simon needed to confront his past. He's always suffered from anxiety and bouts of depression, mood disorders, a kind of PTSD, I suppose. I thought that seeing his sister alive and well might help lay some of his demons to rest, so to speak."

Neal thought but did not say that, far from being laid to rest, Simon's demons might just have jumped out of the box with the shock of seeing Nancy and Amy. He realised suddenly that Anna Foster had no idea that Nancy Hill too, was dead.

"I'm sorry to have to give you more bad news, Ms Foster. Nancy Hill took her own life last night." For a moment, Anna did not react at all and Neal wondered if she had heard him.

"Ms Foster? I'm sorry, that was a bit abrupt. It must be a terrible shock for you. I know that you and Nancy had formed a friendship."

All of a sudden, Anna Foster's face crumpled, all her defiance and bravado wiped out by Neal's news.

Neal felt himself stir, begin to stand; confusingly his feelings for the woman before him were rushing back, urging him to go to her and take her in his arms. With a force of will, he rooted himself in his chair and watched, as Anna Foster wept.

"It's all my fault," she said, "I should never have moved here with Simon."

"Ms Foster . . ."

"No, don't say anything. I should have told you everything. It's not true that I didn't think any of it was relevant. I just didn't want to make things look worse for Simon, and now two people are dead and it's all my fault."

"Please don't distress yourself. None of this is your fault."

Neal remembered how he had laid a comforting arm on Nancy Hill's shoulder when she was bereft over the news of her daughter's death. Why did he feel the need of such restraint when faced with Anna Foster's grief? Because he feared that if he touched her, it would not end with a gesture of comfort? Neal did not enjoy feeling conflicted.

He left her then, conscious that she had given him as much information as she could for the time being. She saw him to the door, and closed it without changing the sign. The Big Issue seller looked across, hoping, perhaps, for that cup of coffee at last, but Anna Foster seemed not to notice her.

Hesitating for a moment outside the shop, Neal slipped into a nearby tearoom and bought a large coffee to go. The woman was much younger than she had first appeared in her shapeless long black skirt, headscarf and oversized grey wool coat that had obviously come from a charity shop. She thanked him, her pretty round face glowing with gratitude, and he felt obliged to buy a copy of her paper.

"You are looking for Simon, yes?" she asked, as he was about to walk away. Neal looked at her in surprise.

"You know Simon Foster?"

"Not so well. His mother is very kind lady, and I know his girlfriend a little. She volunteers some evenings helping with English at hostel." Neal stared at her, in amazement. Why had it never occurred to him to speak with her before? She stood on this patch of the hill every day; of course she would be familiar with all the comings and goings.

"Simon has a girlfriend?"

"Oh yes, Maya. She used work for Ms Foster sometimes." Neal tried to suppress his excitement,

"Are you positive they are in a relationship?" he asked, "not just friends who work together, colleagues?" The Big Issue seller snorted indignantly, giving Neal a patronising look.

"Is obvious when young people more than good friends: holding hands, kissing, know what I mean? Mrs Anna not know. I think she not like Maya so much. Maybe she worry Maya turn Simon into Goth like her."

"I'm sorry, I don't know your name," Neal said.

"My name Ileana. Ileana Vasilescu."

"Pretty name, Ileana," Neal said and was rewarded with a beaming smile.

"Ileana, what evenings does Maya work at your hostel?"

"Only Wednesdays, but I know where she live. Sometimes she give me extra lessons, help with my English. I want to stay here, find good job one day." It took only a second for Neal to learn Maya's address. He said goodbye to Ileana, thinking that for the price of a cup of coffee, he might just have gained the biggest break in the case so far.

Back in his car, Neal texted Ava and requested that she meet him at the address given to him by Ileana. Then he put his car in gear and headed towards it with his first feeling of optimism since the sad discovery of Amy Hill's body several weeks ago.

* * *

Around the time that Neal was interviewing Anna Foster, Detective Sergeant Ava Merry was driving northwards in the direction of an estate on the outskirts of the city. Once owned by the Council, it was now partly privatised as a result of 'right to buy' legislation, and those properties still classed as social housing were now managed by a local housing association simply named Stromford Homes. Rohina Ali lived in a three bedroom privately owned house that was being rented out as a student let and managed by the university accommodation office. She shared with two other women, both postgraduate students at the university, as indeed, was Rohina herself. All this, Ava had established with a quick call to the station.

It was hard to say who was more startled when Rohina opened her front door to find Ava standing before her holding up her police ID. Presumably Rohina was surprised to see a police officer on her doorstep; for Ava it was the shock of coming face to face with a Rohina who was utterly different from the newspaper picture. So different was this woman's appearance from the shy-seeming Asian girl in traditional sari and headscarf that, at first glance, Ava was convinced she had the wrong address, or at least the wrong flatmate.

"Rohina Ali?" she asked uncertainly, staring at the spiky pink- haired girl in front of her. If ever there was a classic punk look, Rohina fitted it to the letter: drainpipe tartan leggings and Doc Martens, studded leather jacket, piercings and tattoos; she had the lot.

"I prefer 'Roxy,' these days, the girl answered, finally taking her eyes off Ava's badge and looking her steadily in the eye. If Rohina had appeared reserved and submissive, there was no hint that her alter ego was similarly afflicted. Everything about her was kick-ass.

"Can I come in?" Ava asked, intuiting that Roxy would respond better to a non-authoritarian approach. Roxy shrugged,

"Place is a mess."

"That's ok, I'm not here to inspect your domestic standards," Ava answered, smiling, "You should see my place."

In fact, the lounge that Roxy led Ava in to was far tidier than she would have expected the average student flat share to be. It did smell of stale cigarette smoke and the carpet looked like it hadn't seen the vacuum cleaner for some time, but it was otherwise orderly and a bit sparse. Obviously Roxy and her flatmates would spend a lot of time in their own rooms, using this one mainly for socialising.

"What's this about then?" Roxy asked, guardedly. Ava came straight to the point.

"Roxy, I think it was you who sent an anonymous letter to the police tipping us off that Professor Christopher Taylor was having an affair with Amy Hill, the girl who was murdered and found on the South Common."

Roxy took out a roll-up and lit it. "Say it was me, would I be in some kind of trouble?"

"Not really. It's not a particularly serious allegation to accuse a lecturer of messing about with one of his students. Did you send the letter, Roxy?"

"Have you told Taylor about it?"

"He only knows that an anonymous letter was received. He denies any sort of relationship with Amy Hill. I should tell you that he does have a rock solid alibi for the night she died."

"Why am I not surprised?"

"Do you have reason to suspect that Taylor was involved in Amy's murder, Roxy?" Ava watched Roxy closely for signs of hesitation. The girl took a deep drag on her cigarette and the cuff of her long-sleeved tee-shirt rode up slightly revealing a cluster of scars just above her wrist. She must have caught Ava looking, for she tugged her sleeve down, hastily tucking the cuff under her fingers.

"I don't do that anymore," she said.

No, Ava thought, you're tarring up your lungs instead. But you're still punishing yourself. What for?

"It's okay. I'm not here to judge or to pry," she reassured the girl. "If you have any information about Professor Taylor that you think might be relevant to our investigation into Amy's death, that's all I want to hear about."

"How did you find me?"

Ava explained about her enquiries in Sheffield.

"I could walk past the women in the community I used to be a part of and they wouldn't give me a second glance. Except Rukhsana, of course." Ava nodded.

"You mean they wouldn't recognise you?"

"That's right, just like he didn't have a clue who I was when I stood right next to him in the queue in the diner in my first week at the Uni."

"I take it you mean Professor Taylor?"

237

"He was plain old Mr Taylor when I first knew him. 'Call me Chris,' he used to say and we called him, 'Mr Chris.' We were so bloody polite. Of course, it had been four years since he last saw me, and my appearance had changed just a bit," she said wryly. "My own mother wouldn't have known me. And believe me, compared to how I looked when I was eighteen, I'm a conservative dresser."

Ava did the maths. Roxy was a postgraduate student, so around twenty-two or twenty-three. "You were fourteen when Taylor was your English tutor?"

"Only just."

"Did he behave inappropriately towards you?" Ava asked, carefully.

"Yes," Roxy answered without hesitation. "For a long time I felt — and was made to feel — that what happened was somehow my fault. I know better now." She looked at Ava defiantly. "Right?"

It wasn't the first time that Ava had come face to face with a victim of sexual abuse, but it was the first time she had encountered one so defiant. Then she thought of the scars, the makeover, saw the way Roxy was holding herself rigidly against a sudden lapse of self-control. On a sudden impulse, Ava leaned over and touched the thin Asian girl on the arm; just the lightest touch but it dissolved the tension between them. That's how easy it was then, Ava thought, to be spontaneously compassionate, just like Neal could be.

Roxy asked, "You're sure his alibi is watertight?"

"He was in London on the night of the murder. With a bunch of students who all testify that he went to the Globe Theatre with them, then on to a nightclub until three in the morning. There's no way he could have killed Amy."

"Then why are you here?"

Ava sighed. She had asked herself time and again why she was pursuing this angle, when Taylor's alibi eliminated him so definitively from guilt. She looked at Roxy. The girl's eyes were heavily made up with shades of grey and black kohl, two flicks like wings at the outside edge of each eye giving her a look that was both exotic and classically punk. Still, she looked startlingly young. In the photograph of her at fourteen, she had looked prepubescent.

"Even if he didn't kill Amy, I couldn't shake the feeling that he's involved somehow, and now at least I know he's guilty of something."

"You want me to tell you what he did to me, don't you? You want me to make a statement and go to court and have him charged with being a paedophile." Roxy's dark brown eyes challenged Ava to deny it.

"You're probably not his only victim, Roxy. If you come forward, others might follow. We can get him the punishment he deserves."

"You've fucked him, haven't you?" Startled by the directness of the question, Ava could only nod.

"Maybe the good professor's predilection for young girls has changed. Or, maybe he's still too clever to get caught. He had a girlfriend in her twenties when he was fucking me, just for show, I suppose."

"He raped you."

"That's one way of putting it. There were some who saw it somewhat differently."

"You were under the age of consent. It was rape."

"I brought disgrace upon my family." There was an edge to Roxy's voice.

"No, Roxy, you didn't"

Roxy laughed, "You're fucking right, I didn't. Do you know how many hours of counselling it took for me to start believing that? And that was after I'd run away from home because my family saw me as unclean and wanted to send me off to a country I'd never visited to stay with relatives I'd never met and marry a half-witted second cousin with a face like a rat's arse."

"Don't you want Taylor to pay for what he did to you, for taking your life away from you, making it so hard for you to find a way to survive? I know I would."

"It's more complicated than that."

Ava waited for an explanation. It was all she could do to contain her frustration. She wanted results and she wanted them quickly.

"Plenty of people have told me I should do what you suggest, go to the police; expose my abuser for what he is. I never revealed his identity to anyone before. I never thought you'd be able to track me down from an anonymous note. You're obviously in the right job, Detective."

Ava accepted the compliment with a nod.

"I could have ruined his career, his reputation, stopped him from getting to other young girls."

Ava's patience was tipped over the edge, "Why didn't you?"

As if provoked to vent her anger, Roxy rolled up the sleeve of her T-shirt and revealed the scars that zigzagged all the way up to her elbow. Despite herself, Ava flinched from the sight of such terrible self-mutilation.

"Like I told you, I don't do this anymore, and I know I'm not to blame for what Taylor did to me. I'm not the same person I was and, do you know what, I'm glad of that. I've got a new life now; I'm in control, I'm in charge, no-one tells me what I can and can't do. My family did me a big favour telling me they were ashamed of me; it allowed me to discover things about myself that I might never have known: what I could achieve, who I might love. And I have found someone to love, you know? Her name's Tanya and my family wouldn't approve of that either."

Ava was confused. Was Roxy trying to say that Taylor had done her a backhanded favour by releasing her from the expectations of family and culture? As if reading her mind, Roxy said, "And no, it's not what you're thinking, that I owe him for setting me free or anything like that. These hideous scars are a daily reminder of just how much he damaged me. Fuck, I'm not going to say something pathetic and corny like, 'the scars inside are still there,' but that's pretty much what it amounts to. Selfish or not, I've no desire to revisit what happened to me, let alone stand up in court and announce it to the whole world."

Ava was silent for a few moments because she genuinely did not know what to say, then she leaned forward and forced Roxy to look her in the eye.

"Did you know Amy Hill, Roxy? Did you warn her what Taylor's like?" There was no doubt that the question unnerved the truculent, vulnerable woman in front of Ava. She looked like someone whose guilty secret had just been exposed.

"Have you been keeping a watchful eye on him? Is that why you chose to study at Stromford, the last place on earth you'd be expected to choose, given Taylor's presence here? You're not selfish at all, are you? You've been trying to protect other potential victims from a sexual predator." Ava leaned back, convinced she'd hit the nail on the head.

"You're good," Roxy conceded. "But there's a slight twist in Amy's case."

"Go on."

"Taylor started seeing her when she was fifteen. Amy wasn't naïve like I was; Taylor wasn't her first sexual partner, although I think he was the first who wasn't of an age with her. She was besotted with him. What girl wouldn't be — you fucked him, right? Never did anything for me, mind, but then my tastes lie elsewhere as I've said.

Yes I warned her off him, but she laughed me off, told me she knew exactly what she was doing and she considered herself old enough to give her consent whatever the Law maintained."

Ava said, "I take it his interest in her was short lived?"

"Yes, and he must have realised how stupid it was of him to have picked a local girl."

"How did Amy react?"

"She was furious. She came to me with a plan, saying that she was going to blackmail him and that she would use my name — my former name — as leverage. I warned her not to be stupid, but Amy was a stubborn girl. The most I could do was beg her not to reveal my new identity or whereabouts, which she agreed to."

Something Anna Foster had said about Amy Hill's selfish behaviour towards her mother popped into Ava's head. Richard Turner had hinted that Amy was 'on the wild side,' not easy to control, that despite Nancy's having tried to keep her on a very tight leash, she had rebelled and spent evenings, sometimes whole nights, away from home. In her own way, she too had been straining at the restraints of family and convention, and when the story of her murder was told, if her killer were caught, she too would be judged harshly and her status as victim diminished as people judged her by her behaviour. The two cultures were not so different after all.

A current of anger shot through Ava. At the same time she felt exasperated. If Amy had been blackmailing Taylor for money to pay for designer clothes and visits to beauty spas, that gave him a possible motive for murder. He might have feared an escalation in her demands, particularly as he was set to become considerably richer if his boasts about publishing houses bidding for his novel had any substance. Damn the man and his perfect alibi.

The intensity of their conversation was broken suddenly by the sound of the front door banging and a cheery voice calling "Roxy! You home?" A punky young woman strode into the room.

"Fuck's sake, Rox, haven't you got the fire on? It's as cold as a witch's tit in here."

"It's been condemned. Bloke came this morning to do a service. He's going to get in touch with the university accommodation office and let them know."

"Who's your friend?" the woman asked, noticing Ava for the first time.

"This is Detective Sergeant Ava Merry. She's investigating Amy Hill's murder." Turning to Ava, she said, "This is my partner, Tanya. She knows everything."

Tanya said, "Are you going to arrest that bastard professor?"

"He has an alibi," answered Roxy.

"Then have you come to your senses at last and decided to report what he did to you to the police?" Roxy shot her girlfriend a look that required little interpretation. Ava decided to take her leave. "You have my card," she said to Roxy, "Stay in touch." It was Tanya who showed her out.

Chapter 20

Neal was still sitting in the driver's seat waiting for Ava twenty minutes after parking his car in a side street close to the address Ileana had given him for Maya. He had texted Ava straight after leaving Anna Foster's shop, and half expected her to be at the meeting point before him. She was only coming from the station, after all. From his radio, he knew that there had been no incidents to hold up the traffic more than usual. This was the second time Ava had turned up late; last time it had been a bogus emergency dental appointment. What would be her excuse this time, he wondered?

As he was wondering and drumming his fingers unconsciously on the steering wheel, he saw a flash of red in his left wing mirror and as he looked over his shoulder, Ava's Ford Escort pulled into the space behind his. "At last," he muttered under his breath, stepping out of the car.

* * *

"Explain later," he said, as Ava joined him on the pavement, mouth open to speak, expression apologetic.

"I've tracked down Simon Foster. Follow me." His voice was stern, but driving here, he had been in the grip of an excitement he had not felt so far on this case: the familiar buzz of knowing that finally he had a lead that just might open the whole thing up. As they descended the two terraced streets to Maya's address, he explained about his conversation with Ileana outside Anna's shop. He had hoped the news would prove as thrilling to Ava as it had to him, but she seemed distracted, her only comment being that it was a 'solid lead.' Perhaps she was feeling guilty about her tardiness. *Well, with good reason.*

They were heading for a mid-terrace house in an area of town that was populated by an eclectic mix of students, recent immigrants and low earners unable, in the present climate, to get a foot on the property ladder. The houses had been bought up by the dozen a few years before the recession hit, when the university was still in its planning stages and prices in the county were below the average for the rest of England — as indeed they still tended to be. Neal thought of his own comfortable house in the more sought-after Uphill area, which would have been out of his price range in many other parts of the country.

Despite the paucity of architectural styles (every street looked the same, row after row of terraced houses) and the lack of landscaping (not a tree in sight), numerous interesting, small, independent businesses were thriving. A Chinese supermarket, Polish and other Eastern European food shops and an Indian takeaway were testimony to the growing diversity of the city's burgeoning population.

"Here it is," Neal said, pausing outside the number he had been given by Ileana. Net curtains at the window obscured the room within, but Neal thought he caught the shadow of a figure moving. Or was it just his eager imagination playing tricks? After knocking three times and receiving no response, they slipped round to the back of the house, via a narrow passageway, to a small backyard that offered a view through the kitchen window to the living room beyond.

Ava said, "Two up, two down. Think he's hiding upstairs?" Rather optimistically, she tried the door handle, forgetting for the moment that they had no right to enter uninvited. Above them, the upstairs curtains were open, but there was little light on this side of the house this late in the afternoon and besides, unless Simon stood by the window and waved, there was no way of knowing if he were inside. Neal gave a frustrated grunt.

"He's in there, I'm sure of it," Neal called out, looking up at the bedroom window, "Simon! Open the door, or I'll have this place surrounded and be back with a warrant."

Neal looked around, amazed that his yelling had not produced an army of nosy neighbours across the walls marking out the boundaries between the back yards. Then it hit him; of course, to a lot of people in this area, the police weren't friends and protectors. Some of them probably had good reason to fear or at least be suspicious of a police presence so near their back door. He wished he could reassure them, but the truth was, arrests in this area tended to be more numerous than elsewhere in the city, and besides, today he was not on a mission to bolster police and community relations.

"Sir!" Ava's cry jolted him, despite his already heightened tension. "Round the front!" Neal didn't stop to question how his sergeant had heard the front door open and close; he was hot on her heels as she bolted past him.

Back out front, ahead of them, a young lad was racing along the pavement, not stopping to look back. They took up the chase, Ava in the lead before she started to drag her left leg. Before long she was limping outright. Neal ran past her when she was forced to stop, catching a flash of the pain and anger in her eyes.

Foster was fast, Neal gave him that, but Neal was faster; he did not carry his fitness routine to extremes like Ava, but his running and trips to the gym kept him in shape. Simon had soon slowed to a virtual halt. Neal could hear his laboured breathing long before the boy doubled over, gasping for breath.

Out of puff himself, Neal stopped alongside him and read him his rights, cuffing him as he did so. Walking Simon back along the street in silence, Neal saw Ava, still red with anger (and possibly shame), struggling to her feet.

"Leave your car here. You can't drive on that foot," Neal said, no hint of pity in his voice. He was about to order her to have her ankle seen to by a properly qualified practitioner, when he caught the look of pain on her face and checked himself. Leading Simon Foster by the arm, he could offer her no assistance as she limped back to his car.

* * *

Back at the station, Simon was placed in an interview room while Neal briefed Ava on his conversations with Anna Foster and Ileana.

"It seemed a bit too much of a coincidence that they ended up in the same town," Ava commented. "Did Simon find out about his sister before Anna had a chance to discuss it with him and Nancy?"

Neal said, "Nancy turned up unexpectedly at Anna Foster's book group on a night that Simon just happened to be there. She didn't expect Simon to recognise her, but seeing Nancy again must have awoken some long-suppressed memory in him."

"Amy looked upon him as a kind of benign stalker according to Becci. She felt no sense of threat from him. Maybe she felt a kind of bond with him, even though she had no idea he was her brother," Ava speculated, but Neal looked sceptical.

"Bit weird, I know, but strange things do happen."

"Like a ten minute journey stretching to half an hour?" Neal remarked.

Ava coloured, "I can explain, sir. I was following up a lead on Christopher Taylor. Sir, he was being blackmailed by Amy Hill."

Taken aback, Neal stared at her. "That's an interesting piece of information, Sergeant, and I'm looking forward to your explanation of why you've obviously been investigating Taylor when his alibi is rock solid. I realise your feelings towards Taylor are complicated, but he's not our killer and he's not what we should be focusing on right now."

"But, sir, it could be relevant. Taylor had motive."

"And that can explain how he came to be in two places at once? "Neal's back was up. *If she's going to continue working with me, she'll damn well have to shape up,* he thought. *Her complicated feelings about Taylor are undermining her objectivity.* Cutting off her reply, he said, "Save it for later. We have a suspect to interview. And by the way, Sergeant, straight afterwards I want you to make an appointment with the police doctor. I need to know that you are physically fit for duty."

The atmosphere between them was strained as they entered the interview room where Simon was sitting waiting. He had said nothing on the journey to the station, only stared out the side window, his head bowed, perhaps ashamed to be seen in the back of a police car, even though it was unmarked. He did look up briefly as they settled in the chairs opposite him, running his eyes discreetly over Ava. Men tended to do that when Ava entered a room. But Simon was politer than most — his eyes did not linger.

Neal took the lead, "You know why you're here Simon, don't you?" Simon Foster nodded. It was not enough. "Simon?" Neal prompted.

"You think I killed my sister," the boy said. He looked Neal straight in the eye. There was a keen intelligence in his gaze, no hint of defiance or challenge.

"No-one has accused you of anything yet Simon, but taking off the way you did wasn't very clever. Care to explain?"

Simon Foster was a good-looking boy with the kind of symmetrical features that would make him strikingly so as his lingering acne cleared and his features matured. He was in need of a more flattering hairstyle than his mop of shoulder length thick, dark hair. At least his glasses were trendy; perhaps Anna Foster had helped him choose them, or one of those assistants at the opticians who were good at that sort of thing. There was a certain vulnerability about him also, not weakness, just a sort of 'little boy lost' look, like that celebrity physicist who was always on TV that Maggie and most of the women at the station were always drooling over.

It was easy to be misled by a face like this, Neal knew. He had been in the room with convicted psychopaths who tugged at your heartstrings with their sweet expressions and sincere assertions of innocence. It was their gift, just another tool in their box that they could employ at will to appear normal. A skilful interviewer learned to use another set of tools to expose them for what they were: cunning dissemblers with no heart or conscience.

"I know that now," Simon answered, quietly. "I went a bit crazy for a while. I was going to come to you when I got my head sorted out. But it's true, isn't it? I wouldn't be sitting here now if you thought I had nothing to do with Amy's death."

"Did you have anything to do with Amy's death?"

"No. God, how can you even think that? I'd only just worked out who she was — might be. It was all so mixed up and I kept having these sort of flashbacks. I thought I was going mad. I felt this need to look out for her, keep her from harm just until I could get my head round it all."

"When did you last see Amy?"

"The evening she . . . she . . ." Simon couldn't bring himself to say it, ". . . disappeared."

249

"Had you been following her all day?"

Simon hung his head in shame.

"I saw her in the morning, going into a house up the hill. She'd been there a couple of times before and I'd checked who lived there. It was a professor at the university."

Neal pointedly avoided looking at Ava, but he was aware of her leaning forward in her seat, and the sudden shift in Simon's gaze to Ava's face confirmed that she had reacted.

"Did you find out the name of this professor?" Neal asked, pre-empting his sergeant.

"I can't remember now, but I think he teaches English at the uni. That's what Em — Amy was studying. I assumed she was either involved with him or getting extra tuition from him, or something. She only stayed about twenty minutes or so."

He has an alibi, Neal reminded himself, sensing Ava's excitement. "Where did she go after leaving her professor's house?" he asked.

"She went shopping on the Eastgate."

Ava gave Neal a knowing look. Neal knew exactly what she was thinking. The Eastgate was where the town's most exclusive shops were located; designer boutiques and brand names abounded. He'd heard Maggie bemoan the fact that she didn't earn enough to shop there. If Ava were right about the blackmail, the professor must have been paying handsomely for Amy's silence.

"She had a lot of shopping bags," Simon continued. "In the middle of the afternoon, she went to the new patisserie on the Long Hill."

It was a favourite of Amy's; the same one Nancy had taken her to for lunch a few days before she disappeared, Neal remembered.

Again, Simon looked down, "I followed her in. I sat down at a table near the one she'd chosen. She came over and joined me."

The silence that followed Simon's words was electrifying. Ava was not just leaning forward in her seat now, but practically jumping out of it. Neal made a mental note to talk to her later about the need to contain her emotions.

"You spoke with her?" Neal asked; his voice steady.

"I thought she was coming over to tell me to fu . . . to get lost," Simon said, "but she wasn't annoyed at all; she was amused. I can remember the exact words she used, 'why don't we have a coffee and a nice pastry and you can tell me why you keep following me?' I almost got up and ran out, but she seemed . . . so okay with it that I just agreed."

"Did you tell Amy about your suspicions that you were brother and sister?"

"No. I was going to but at the last moment I bottled out. I told her she reminded me of my sister who'd died when I was very young, that following her made me feel close to Emily."

Neal saw Ava roll her eyes. Needless to say his sergeant would never have fallen for a line like that. He asked Simon, "And she believed you?"

"I think she felt it too," Simon answered, then perhaps picking up on Neal and Ava's questioning looks, he added, "The bond between us. I think she kind of sensed it. I know she wasn't scared of me. I know she didn't feel any sense of threat from me."

Neal had to admit that Simon did not fit the profile of a typical stalker. He had never had a romantic relationship with Amy, nor did he crave one. He simply wanted to know if she were his sister and to keep her safe. Maybe he felt partly to blame for her disappearance.

It was at that moment that Neal doubted they had found their killer. He had done the training, learned about aspects of deviant behaviour and psychopathy. He knew there were manipulative and charismatic individuals out there who could dissemble to a spectacular degree, but in

251

his heart of hearts, he just did not believe that Simon Foster was one of them. Yes, he had issues relating to his early childhood abuse and would probably benefit from some hours on a psychologist's couch, but he was no killer. He said, quietly, "Simon, we know you weren't with your mother the night Amy died. She told us so. Care to tell us where you were, really?"

Simon looked as miserable as a person could look. Looking like a man about to damn himself, he said, "I was following Amy, but only until around seven thirty. She met a girlfriend outside the cinema. I hung around for a bit, wondering whether to go in, then I just left."

"And where did you go?"

Simon looked completely miserable, "I bought a bottle of vodka and drank it sitting on a swing in the little kids' playground off Friary Lane. It was deserted at that time of the evening."

Neal nodded. He knew the park Simon was referring to; he had taken Archie there often when he was younger. It was near a school in the Uphill area and wasn't frequented by the usual vagrants and junkies because it was kept locked at night.

"How did you get in?" he asked Simon.

"I climbed the fence. It wasn't that hard."

It was believable. Your everyday vagrant wouldn't think it worth the effort, but for a young, fit lad like Simon, it would present little difficulty.

"And you stayed there all night — in the rain?" Ava asked.

"I drank half the bottle and passed out in a little playhouse."

Neal sighed. He remembered bumping his head in that playhouse whilst chasing Archie through it. No one would have seen Simon in there; small as it was, he could have lain curled up inside without his feet protruding. He said, changing tack, "Simon, are you aware that following Amy

252

in the way that you were doing could be construed as stalking?"

"That's what Maya said, but I didn't see it that way at the time. I was kind of obsessed by her, but I wouldn't have harmed her, I swear. I just wanted to look out for her and learn more about her. I wasn't the only one obsessed with her either."

Neal and Ava exchanged glances. Neal frowned, thinking of Becci's remarks about someone else besides Simon stalking Amy. "How so?"

"I was in the Union bar one day and I got talking to this bloke — he wasn't a student at Stromford Uni — he was studying elsewhere but was visiting his dad for the weekend. Anyway, we'd had a few beers and got talking; we were looking out the window . . ." Simon paused, colouring, "Seeing if any hot girls were walking by, and he got all kind of puffed up at one point and pointed out a girl standing outside the library. When I looked over, I saw it was Amy. He told me he used to fancy her, but I got the impression he still did. We'd both had quite a few pints by then and I started telling him how I thought Amy might be my sister who'd disappeared years ago after my father killed my mother. He was really taken by the story, wanted to know all the details, where my father was doing time, when and where it all happened. I made him swear not to tell Amy about all this."

"And what makes you say he was obsessed with Amy?" Neal asked.

"Because he was following her too. He was in Stromford all that week and I saw him watching her and her friend, the skinny blonde one, on more than one occasion. Then he just disappeared. I assumed he'd gone back to uni."

"You spent — what — a couple of hours chatting over beers. Did you exchange names, contact details?"

Simon shook his head, "We kind of just called each other, 'mate.'"

"Can you describe him to us?"

"He was a big guy — I mean not particularly tall, just kind of . . . overweight," Simon answered tactfully, "not being mean or anything but he wasn't really god's gift — I doubt he was the type a girl who looked like Amy would go for. Even if he had a great personality, which he didn't, really." Simon paused, embarrassed, perhaps, at his honesty.

"Go on," Neal said. A picture was forming in his mind, but he needed to be more certain. Ava, he noticed, was leaning forward in her seat again. Did she share his suspicions?

"He had light brown hair, very short, spiky really, like he'd shaved his head and his hair was just growing back. Sorry, I don't remember much more about him. After that first time, I only saw him from a distance."

Neal turned to Ava, "Get PC Jenkins to bring a picture of Bradley Turner from the file." He and Simon sat silently while they waited for Ava to return, which she did after less than two minutes, carrying a brown file, which she handed to Neal. He opened it, removed a photograph and slid it across the table to Simon, rotating it until it was the right way round for him to see.

"Is this the person you were just describing?" he asked. There was no hesitation.

"That's him. Who is he? Did he kill Amy?" Simon seemed to suck a big breath in and forget to let it go, then he did let go but the next breath came as a laboured gasp and within seconds he was struggling to breathe.

"Simon. Do you have asthma? Where's your inhaler?" Ava said, sounding a little panicky.

"It's not asthma, it's a panic attack," Neal said, recognising the symptoms. "Get a paper bag, quickly." As Ava dashed out the door, Neal pulled his chair to the other side of the table so that he could sit next to Simon.

"Okay, take it easy, son, just concentrate on breathing." Simon Foster was twenty years old, but at that moment he seemed younger than Archie. Neal pushed the comparison out of his mind, reminding himself that Simon was still a suspect in a murder investigation. The boy's attack appeared genuine enough, but even if it were, how could Neal be sure that it had not been somehow self-induced?

Ava re-entered the room carrying a brown paper bag. Before passing it to Neal she turned it upside down and scattered pastry crumbs all over the table, explaining, "Sykes had a Cornish pasty for lunch, he dug this out of his waste paper basket."

"It'll do the trick," Neal said, placing the bag over Simon's mouth and nose and instructing him to breathe in and out, repeating the words, "in and out," over and over to help the lad focus on something other than his alarming symptoms. Within minutes, Simon's breathing steadied and he signalled for Neal to remove the bag.

"Okay, Simon. Here's what's going to happen. Detective Sergeant Merry here, is going to contact your mother and ask her to come down to the station to collect you. She will take you home and you will stay there. No more running, understand?"

Simon nodded, still recovering. Ava gave Neal a quizzical look and left the room to call Anna Foster.

"Get one of the PCs to bring Simon a glass of water," Neal called after her.

In less than forty minutes, Anna Foster had collected her son and taken him home. Ava had explained the circumstances over the phone and when Anna arrived at the station, she greeted Neal and Ava with a chilly look and no exchange of pleasantries. All she said was, "Where is my son? What have you done to him?" Clearly, she was of the opinion that Simon's panic attack had been the result of mistreatment whilst in police custody.

"She should be grateful we're letting her precious son walk," Ava commented, after the Fosters' departure.

"For now," Neal reminded her. Frustrating as it was, they had no real reason to detain Simon; he had bolted, but there was no evidence to tie him to Amy's murder. Despite Neal's feeling that Simon was not a killer, the lad did lack an alibi and he was still a suspect.

"How's the foot?" Neal asked Ava. He'd noticed she was still limping.

"Better. I'll make that appointment."

"See that you do, Sergeant." There was an awkward pause, but the previous tension between them had evaporated. Neal asked, "Fancy a bite? We can discuss Bradley Turner and you can tell me about this idea you have that Amy Hill was blackmailing Taylor."

"I'm famished," Ava admitted. Then, perhaps sensing that Neal was no longer angry with her, she added, "It's more than an idea, sir. I have proof."

At a secluded table in the nearest pub to the station that served decent food, Ava related how she had spent her morning, and her suspicions about Taylor, leaving Neal with a sense that there was something she had left out. There was an edge to her voice when she talked about him that hinted at something — what? Neal couldn't put a finger on it. An idea flashed in his mind and was cursorily dismissed. There was no way his sergeant was involved sexually with Taylor, was there, even as she sat in front of Neal, accusing the professor of having intercourse with underage girls?

At first, Neal made no comment, only concentrated on working his way through the best steak he had eaten in a long time. Or was it just that it had been a long time since he had eaten?

Taking a slug of cold beer, he said, "It seems that you've been carrying out your own investigation, Sergeant." His voice was stern, but he wasn't certain how he felt about Ava's behaviour. Was she a bit of a loose cannon, or a person who acted on her own initiative and got results? He would not give her any indication that he approved of her running a parallel investigation into a man who wasn't even a suspect.

"How do you even know if this Rohina or Roxy or whatever she calls herself is telling the truth? You say she admitted herself that as a young girl, she fancied Taylor. What if, as he claims in Amy's case, he turned her down and she resented him for it?"

Ava was shaking her head in frustration.

"I'm sure she was telling the truth. The man's a monster." The words came out with such vehemence that Neal was startled.

"I know his alibi is cast iron, sir, but even if he didn't kill Amy, his relationship with her was far more than he admitted to."

Neal had had enough. He said, "Taylor did not murder Amy Hill. If he's guilty of having sex with underage girls, then that's a whole separate investigation. And what do you have? Look at it from the point of view of a jury. At best, one possible victim's word against that of a respected academic. At worst, a spiteful girl getting her own back on a man who spurned her."

Ava was staring at him, looking a little stunned.

"I didn't take you for the kind of man who dismisses allegations of abuse against women so casually," she said, "I know that kind of attitude is still prevalent amongst lots of cops but I didn't have you pegged as one of them."

"What are you talking about?" Neal answered, astonished at his sergeant's interpretation of his words. To his annoyance, his next words were even more inflammatory, the more so for being untrue. "And I hadn't pegged you as one of those women who carry a huge chip around on her shoulder."

To say that Ava was provoked was putting it lightly; she was practically turning purple and emitting steam from her ears, but she managed to keep her mouth shut. To his shame, Neal realised that, as his lower ranking officer she was obliged to show respect, and not answer back or undermine his authority. He was in the position of power.

She was holding back because she couldn't trust herself to speak.

"Look, Sergeant — Ava — your initial assessment of me was the correct one. I'm not the kind of cop who takes issues of violence against women lightly. I know it takes courage for girls and women to come forward and report abuse and that their actions often encourage others to come forward against the abuser. I would never make an assumption that such matters should not be properly investigated and I apologise if that's how I came across. I was playing devil's advocate, trying to make you see you can't jump the gun in police work. It's about more than just clever deduction and matters of right and wrong. It's about putting a solid case together that won't fall apart the minute we walk into court.

I know we're still finding our way as partners and that we have to earn each other's respect, but I need you to be sure what kind of man I am, and what kind of police officer. And, to be frank, I'm a little disappointed that you don't know me better than that."

Ava's demeanour seemed to revert to something less reminiscent of a raging bull. Her complexion faded to a healthy pink and her shoulders relaxed. In a low tone, she said, "Yeah, I do know you better than that. And, if I'm carrying anything around, it's not exactly a chip." She cleared her throat, "I have some . . . personal experience of this kind of thing."

Neal waited, but she didn't elaborate. What kind of thing was she referring to? Sexual abuse? Assault? He thought again about their conversation on the train, but he would not press her to reveal more than she was willing to share. Ava spoke again, but this time, it was the Ava he was more familiar with,

"Okay, I accept I don't have much to build a case around, but do you object to my carrying on looking at Taylor, if it doesn't interfere with the main investigation?"

You had to admire her tenacity.

"Alright," he agreed, "See what you can dig up and make sure you can back any allegations up with reliable evidence or credible witnesses. The last thing we need is for lives — and that includes Roxy's — to be ruined by press coverage without evidence. He wondered if the word 'credible' would be taken the wrong way, but Ava didn't challenge him on it. Unhappily, he sensed the chill in the air between them hadn't quite thawed. He said,

"We need to talk about Bradley Turner now that we can prove he was following Amy. Even though we have only Simon's say-so on that."

"His flatmate provided him with an alibi," Ava said.

"Simon's mother provided him with an alibi," Neal replied, guessing that his sergeant was silently bemoaning that a total of fifteen students, and not an individual, had provided Christopher Taylor with his alibi.

"PC Jenkins interviewed the flatmate — Josh something or other. Confirmed what Bradley said — they'd been out drinking all afternoon, got home and crashed out. They were both sick as dogs the following morning."

"Go through her interview with a nit comb, interview the flatmate and Bradley again, if necessary. Make sure Jenkins follows up on the pubs they'd been to, possible witnesses to their presence there," Neal said, "see if you can find a loophole in the story that PC Jenkins missed."

"Yes sir," Ava replied, a little wearily.

"Thoroughness, remember?" Neal said, picking up on her lack of enthusiasm, "Attention to detail, that's what solves cases. That, and catching a break," he said, sounding a bit weary himself.

"Ava," he said, as an afterthought, acknowledging his own tiredness. Her first name had slipped out and felt comfortable on his lips, "Tomorrow will do. Go home, rest that foot and get some sleep. It's been a long day."

* * *

Simon was so quiet and still on the short drive home that Anna feared a regression to the closed-in state he had been in when he first came to her, broken and traumatised by witnessing his mother's death. Now that he was returned to her, she felt ashamed of her earlier feelings of wanting to reduce him to a state of dependence, so that she could keep him safe from harm forever. Now, all she wanted was for her son to be whole again, even if that meant she would have to release him into the world to take his chances with everyone else.

Back in the flat above the shop, Simon did not go immediately to his room and close the door as Anna half thought he might. Instead, he sat down in his favourite chair, the one that, as a small boy he had curled up in with her to listen to her read a seemingly endless number of books. His thirst for stories had been insatiable. The first day she saw him in the library she had known he was a child who loved books. He had chosen a book about giants immediately, and settled down on a beanie cushion in the children's library not stirring until the teacher called time on the rest of her unruly class.

He was still sitting in the chair when Anna returned from the kitchen with two mugs of coffee and a packet of chocolate digestives.

"Thank you," Simon said, quietly as she placed his mug on the coffee table before him. It was his favourite mug, the one with Spiderman on it, that he had received one Easter years ago with a chocolate egg in it wrapped in red foil, Anna recalled. Funny the things to do with your children that stick in your memory.

"You're welcome," Anna said, smiling at him.

"I don't mean just for the chocolate — and the biscuits — and the mug," Simon said, solemnly. "Thank you for adopting me, for looking after me, for loving me all these years."

Tears shone in Anna's eyes, then rolled down her cheeks. She wiped them away with the back of her hand, reached into her sleeve for a tissue, and dabbed her face.

"I'm sorry I caused you worry. I thought you'd let me down. Now I know that when you gave the police that false alibi before I even had a chance to speak or explain where I'd had been, it wasn't because you thought I'd killed Amy — it was because you wanted to buy me time, hear my story first so that, if necessary, you could make sure I didn't incriminate myself. I know you never wavered in your support for me."

Anna wanted to ask him why he had disappeared, but she waited, hoping he would open up further.

"All I could think after the evening when we bumped into that police officer was how everybody was going to think I killed Amy because I'd been . . . following her." He looked at Anna and she nodded to show that she knew about it. "I would never have hurt her; I wish I'd waited outside the cinema, seen her safely home, but it was then I had the . . . flashback."

Anna felt suddenly faint with the thrill that pulsed through her, a mixture of trepidation, excitement and hope. Was it possible Simon was at last dealing with the traumatic event in his past that had been so long suppressed?

Over the years there had been intermittent fallout: the nightmares he had suffered in his early years with her; the aloofness followed by clinginess; the mood swings in his early adolescence, the worrying signs that he was succumbing to depression as he entered young adulthood; could they now be consigned to the past so that he could embrace his future unencumbered by the baggage from his childhood? That dreadful, over-used cliché of a word was what he needed now. Closure. "Go on," she encouraged.

"I was standing on the pavement outside the cinema wondering what to do. I decided to go back to my flat at the uni, maybe see if Gary or Ric or one of the others fancied going out. I started walking home, thinking of Amy and Nancy. I'd just turned into Tanner's Close — you know where I mean, just off the bottom of the High Street, near the river." Anna nodded. She knew exactly where he meant. A narrow close of steep steps that led down to the river, where it ran between the backs of buildings fronting the high street. It was a gloomy, dank spot known locally as 'Tanner's Hole,' which people tended to avoid after dark, even though it provided a convenient short cut to the university. It made her shudder to think of her son facing the horrors of his past in such a lonely, unwholesome spot.

"Thinking of the two of them, Nancy and Amy, set something off — something like a panic attack, I think. I couldn't breathe properly and I was sweating and shaking all over. I managed to get to the bottom of the steps without falling over, then I sat down and suddenly all these images started exploding in my head. Things from before I came to live with you: places and people's faces and the sound of my baby sister Emmie crying in the background, a man shouting, my mother's face — so like Amy's." Anna placed a hand on her son's arm. It had begun to tremble as he spoke, and under her touch it steadied. She took his hand and held it as he went on talking.

"All the images, flashes really, finally came together in a single moment, a single place, and I remembered when and where it was. I was in my mother's bedroom. The man shouting was my father and he had been hitting my mother. Now she was lying on the bed, sobbing, Emmie was crying and I was hiding in the wardrobe, afraid he'd come back. Afraid to go to her and see if she was all right." At this, Simon withdrew his hand from Anna's and buried his face in both his hands.

"Shh," Anna whispered, "You were three years old. You had a right to be afraid and there was nothing you could have done."

"I just stayed in there, with my mother sobbing on the bed and Emmie screaming her head off until . . . until my mother suddenly went quiet. I looked over at the bed and she was lying there very still. I thought she was dead. Emmie was still crying but not loudly anymore, just a kind of tired grizzle."

"How long were you in the wardrobe, Simon?" Anna asked, quietly, remembering that the police had found Simon there several hours later.

"I don't know. It still feels more like a dream than a memory. I was so young. Could have been minutes or hours, I don't know. After a while I heard a noise but I was too scared to come out, even though I recognised the woman who came into the room."

"Nancy Hill?"

"Yes. She looked after us a lot. She took me to the library sometimes," he said, looking at Anna, who nodded at her son, noting the feverish excitement in his face.

"It's the clearest image of all. My mother was still alive. Nancy shook her and she made a noise and moved. Then Nancy . . . Nancy made her swallow some pills . . . a lot of pills, then she took a pillow from the bed and held it over my mother's face until she stopped moving."

The words gushed out, too vivid to be untrue. For a moment, Anna wondered if she could have misheard. In complete shock, she stared at her son, lost for words.

"Nancy Hill killed my mother."

"She took an overdose," Anna said, forgetting for a moment that she had left that part out when she had told Simon that his father murdered his mother. "There was an empty bottle of pills. And it was claimed at her trial that she could have died of her wounds anyway if they had gone untreated for as long as they did."

With mounting horror, Anna began to appreciate the enormity of what Nancy had done. "She could have saved her," she said. "Nancy could have saved your mother if she had called for help, but she didn't." And it hadn't just been a sin of omission. That would have been hard enough to bear; Nancy had not just let Debbie Clarke die, she had sent her on her way. Anna realised that she was covering her mouth with her palm. "Do you remember anything else?" She asked Simon, afraid of what more he might reveal.

"I remember what she said when she took Emmie. She said, 'She wasn't fit to look after you, Emily. She can rot in hell for putting you in danger. I'm your guardian angel and where I'm going to take you will be heaven compared to this place.'"

It was what the three-year-old Simon had repeated over and over when he was questioned after his mother was found. *An angel took my sister to heaven.*

Everything else had been wiped from his memory and his words had been interpreted as the ramblings of a confused and frightened little boy who had witnessed his father beat his mother to death. Allowing Nancy to disappear with Emily. No one had suspected her; no one even mentioned her, and Simon's father, Wade Bolan, had gone down for a murder that, technically, he did not commit.

Chapter 21

Ava could find no loopholes in Bradley Turner's story. She had been going over PC Jenkins's report hoping to find some scant evidence to prove he might have been in Stromford on the night of Amy's murder. PJ had visited Sheffield and interviewed Bradley again, along with his flat-mate and drinking partner, spoken with other students and with bar staff at the pubs Bradley had been drinking in that evening. Everywhere she had drawn a blank. Yes, the other students she spoke to had seen Bradley at the pub watching the match that afternoon. Yes, most of the pubs they claimed to have visited had at least one member of staff who remembered them being there. Yes, the waiter at the Indian takeaway recognised their photos and remembered they had been in his restaurant the evening after the match — he was a fan of the winning team and remembered talking to them about the result.

It was evening now and she was going over her notes and the findings again, staring at the writing, bleary-eyed, until the words seemed to dance across the page in a sleepy unfocused blur. Camden was lying across her lap, a heaving ball of tortoiseshell fur, his soporific purring causing her eyelids to droop.

She had read the report so many times she almost knew its contents by heart. PJ had been thorough. Bradley and his mate, Josh Hogg, had been memorable during their drunken spree; bar staff remembered seeing the lads because they stood out, both dressed in identical T-shirts bearing the slogan, 'don't mess with me . . . I'm a furniture restorer.'

The lads claimed to have arrived back at their flat around eight in the evening. Their drinking spree had begun with 'pre-drinks' in their flat before they set off at midday to watch a football match in the student union bar in the early afternoon.

Spurred on by their team's magnificent four-nil win, they had embarked on a mammoth drinking binge that took them to seven pubs in less than four hours. According to Josh, they had been, 'totally rat-arsed' by the time they returned to their flat with their takeaway chicken vindaloos, which they stayed awake long enough to eat before crashing out for the night. Bradley, Josh claimed, had still been asleep when he knocked on his door at eleven o'clock the following morning.

Ava speculated that, had Bradley not been as drunk as he seemed, he could have driven to Stromford, located Amy Hill, strangled her, and been back in his room before his flatmate awoke the following day. It would have meant a four and a half hour round trip — easily doable in the time. The theory would need to be checked out — if Bradley's car had been on the road between Sheffield and Stromford that night, it might have been caught on a camera somewhere along the route. An echo of Neal's words about thoroughness rang in Ava's ears like an unwelcome attack of tinnitus.

She sighed. She felt like crashing out herself, though it was still early evening. "Sorry, Cam," she said, pushing the warm, fluffy mass off her lap, ignoring her pampered cat's disapproving meow. The bag of peas she had draped over her ankle earlier was beginning to thaw; there was a bag of sweet corn somewhere in the freezer. It was time to swap them over.

"Bloody foot," she muttered as she limped into the kitchen, remembering her shame at having to give up the chase earlier in the day. What if Neal hadn't been there, or if he'd been similarly indisposed? He'd had a right to be ticked off at her; fitness was a prerequisite of the job; she'd had problems with her damn foot for weeks now, and she had to concede the various treatments and therapies she was trying weren't working.

Despite the lingering ache in her foot, Ava couldn't settle. Camden looked at her expectantly as she approached the sofa again, but instead of sitting down and inviting him back onto her lap, Ava paced restlessly around the room. There was a lot on her mind, uppermost of which was her conversation with Roxy earlier in the day.

Christopher Taylor had a predilection for young girls, of that she was convinced. Frustratingly, of the two women who could prove it, one was dead and the other refused to come forward. Instead, Roxy was behaving like a kind of benevolent vigilante, keeping a watchful eye on Taylor and warning off his potential victims. It was a system that worked for Roxy, but it did not satisfy Ava's sense of justice. She wanted to see the professor brought to account for his actions. Supposing his boast about his forthcoming novel was true? He was set to become a very wealthy man and, along with greater wealth would come more opportunity and less chance of being caught.

Ava picked up her smartphone. There were no fewer than five texts from the good professor, all unanswered. She had to admire his brazenness, courting a police detective when he had so much to hide. Was he really attracted to her, or was he playing a game, deflecting suspicion by dating a grown woman and a police officer to boot? Perhaps he was a risk taker, the kind who derived satisfaction from the proximity of danger, for surely, he understood the threat she posed him? Such was the man's arrogance that Ava doubted it was even that. He simply refused to believe that he could be bested.

Her fingers hovered over her phone pad. Camden yawned, urging her to make a decision. Taylor answered on three rings.

"Detective Sergeant Merry. It's a pleasure to hear your voice. I thought you were avoiding me — all those unanswered texts."

"Yeah. Sorry about that, I've been busy," Ava said, hoping that her voice betrayed nothing of the loathing she felt for the man, "I was wondering if you'd like to come over . . ."

* * *

Only one hour later, Taylor's sleek red Porsche was crunching over the gravel in her driveway. Ava had been busy in the hour since her phone call, changing from comfy, baggy sweats into a tight-fitting red dress and sheer black tights. She had showered, washed her hair and applied just enough make-up to hide her tiredness. Standing in front of the mirror in her bedroom she approved of what she saw. As a concession to her still painful foot, she considered eschewing her flattering high heels for a pair of glossy black ballet pumps, then changed her mind.

The entrance to Ava's cottage was via a wooden porch and her front door opened straight into a flagstone-floored living room divided into two halves, separated by a staircase leading to the bedrooms and bathroom. One side of the room was the living area, with mismatched comfy chairs and sofa, TV and end tables, the other served as a dining-room-come-study-come everything else. A single, wide, stone step led into the kitchen from the dining area.

Ava's pride and joy was a long oak table that doubled up as a dining table and work space. More often than not, it was, as it was now, piled up with papers and books, some relating to cases she was working on, some articles that she was intending to look at or was already some way through. It didn't bother her that it looked untidy; to her it represented her work and leisure and the two were intertwined.

She had, in fact, never used the table for entertaining; the kitchen was big enough to accommodate a drop leaf table that could sit up to six at a pinch, and Ava could count on one hand the number of occasions when she had had that many guests in her home at once. Perhaps when her brother moved in, she would make more effort.

Ava opened the door before Taylor had a chance to knock; she noticed how he took everything in as he stepped over the threshold and kissed her on the cheek, handing her a posy of red roses, tied with a velvety red ribbon. They didn't look like they'd been bought in a supermarket or a garage. How had he managed to conjure them up after the shops had shut up for the night, she wondered; perhaps he kept a supply at home for emergencies.

"If you haven't already eaten, I've sort of cooked," she said, after making just the right amount of fuss over the flowers.

"Sort of?"

"Marks and Spencer's — dine in for two. Main course and dessert. All ready to pop in the microwave."

"Wine included?"

"Of course."

He followed her into the kitchen and she showed him where to find a vase for the roses, while she took two meals from her freezer and set the microwave timer, and laid the table for two. All the while she was aware of Taylor in her peripheral vision moving, quiet as a cat from cupboard to sink, to table, where he placed the posy in a cut glass vase.

"Pretty," Ava said, hoping that the loathing she felt tingle through her whenever he was near wasn't detectable. Despite her utmost resolve to act normally, she stiffened as he slipped an arm around her waist and pulled her to him. Then she found herself responding to his kiss, a little shocked and dismayed that she was actually feeling aroused by his touch.

Even though she had prepared for his arrival, psyching herself up, telling herself that she was working undercover, doing her job, practising detachment, compartmentalising the man and her feelings for him, her assurances now seemed hollow. What she was really doing was justifying the means to an end and it made her wonder what kind of a person she was, that she'd been willing to go so far in the line of duty.

Shimmying out of Taylor's amorous embrace, Ava said, "Let's eat first." It was at that moment that she realised she had absolutely no intention of having sex with Taylor again.

"I'll pour," Taylor said, picking up the bottle of red wine that had been part of the meal deal. "It's a little chilly in here, isn't it?" he said.

"Sorry," Ava apologised, "heating's on the blink. I've let the landlord know but he can't get anyone round 'til Friday. We can eat in the other room if you like. I'll put the fire on."

Taylor touched the cold radiator, then moved to where the wall-mounted boiler was fixed to the kitchen wall. He said, "In here's fine. You know, I could take a look at that boiler for you. I know this model; in fact I could probably tell you exactly what the fault is without even taking it apart. It's one my father recommended not to buy when I fitted mine recently."

"I thought you said your dad was a plumber."

"Plumbing and heating engineer. Boilers, radiators, gas fires. He's pretty versatile, and never out of work. Real work, as he calls it. He doesn't regard a career as an academic and a writer as a proper man's job. Always hoped I'd go into business with him; I was his weekend apprentice when I was a kid. Boring as hell but it taught me the value of money, saving for university. And the skills I picked up come in useful from time to time, of course."

Ava thought she detected a hint of bitterness in his tone. Clearly, Christopher Taylor was contemptuous of what he obviously regarded as his lowly background.

It was such a mundane conversation that, for a moment Ava nearly forgot that she was almost certainly in the room with a sexual predator of underage girls. That was good. One of the reasons she had invited him to her home was to regain his trust. He had been suspicious of her questions the last time they had been together. She needed him at ease with her again, playful, teasing, but she also needed to be careful . . .

"I'll wait for my landlord's bloke if you don't mind. He probably wouldn't approve of anyone else fiddling with his appliances, and besides, we can't have the great professor and soon-to-be celebrated author getting his hands dirty." The microwave pinged a second time and Ava took out their meals and gave them a stir.

Whilst they waited the requisite five minutes for their food to finish cooking and cool, they clinked their wine glasses together and sipped, and Ava encouraged Taylor to talk about his novel. He didn't need much, and was still droning on about it when she brought out their dessert, her favourite chocolate mousse pudding.

It sounded unutterably dull, she thought; one of those tedious, plotless, overlong or too-short tomes that seemed to win all the literary prizes. The sort of thing Anna Foster and her friends discussed at her book group, no doubt. No wonder Neal fancied her; his bookshelves were full of that kind of thing too.

Ava's mind began drifting to the case, as Taylor droned on and on about his 'work.' Careful to smile and nod approval at Taylor as appropriate, she sifted through the layers of facts and information relating to Amy's murder. For some reason an image of Amy's pale, stick-thin friend,

Becci, kept popping up in her thoughts, feeling puzzlingly like a warning.

The deaths of Becci and Gary had been a tragic accident, but not suspicious. An examination of the gas fire in their bedroom had revealed a slow, insidious leak, undetectable and deadly.

Taylor's voice droned on, ". . . Booker longlist . . . Not bad for a lad whose prospects, if his parents had had anything to do with it, would have been for him to unblock sinks and toilets and fit gas fires and central heating boilers for the rest of his life."

Ava was on the verge of pointing out that making an honest living in that way would be attractive to a lot of people when the words suddenly stuck in her throat, and she experienced one of those revelatory moments that pretentious people sometimes referred to as an epiphany.

Once, reading a book about psychology, she had come across another word, synchronicity, and she wondered if that, along with the epiphany was what she was experiencing right there and then. A sort of double whammy of intuition and serendipity. At around the very moment that she had been picturing the tragic sight of Becci and Gary curled up together in front of their poisonous fire, Taylor had mentioned fitting gas fires with his father.

Ava's senses prickled with a top-heavy rush of excitement and fear. Taylor had her full attention now. As she caught his gaze across the polished surface of her Ikea table, Ava was certain she was looking into the eyes of a killer. Taylor had tampered with the gas fire at Amy's flat and, instead of killing Amy, it had killed the hapless Becci and Gary.

All thoughts of regaining Taylor's trust, or putting him at ease were forgotten. Ava stood up clumsily, spilling red wine across the pretty white broderie anglaise tablecloth that had belonged to her grandmother, "S . . . sorry," she stammered, trying to be calm but suspecting her dinner guest had already seen the sudden terror in her eyes. At that moment, she caught sight of Camden curled on the floor at her feet.

"Camden startled me," she said, simultaneously giving her poor cat a kick that brought him, squealing and startled, to his feet. Camden darted out from under the table and streaked across the kitchen, a whiz of black, white and orange fur disappearing out the cat flap. To her intense relief, Taylor laughed.

Ava's thoughts were racing. How could she prove it? Amy and Becci themselves had put off the service appointment arranged by their landlord which might have alerted them to the danger.

It had been an uncommon but not impossible fault that had been found in the appliance. Someone with the appropriate knowledge and skill would have been able to make deliberate tampering look like a tragic accident. Was this enough to build a case for circumstantial evidence around? If Roxy could be persuaded to come forward, if Amy's extravagant spending the afternoon after Simon Foster had seen her entering and leaving Taylor's flat could be cited as evidence that she was blackmailing him. So many ifs when what she needed were certainties . . . Ava was paralysed with doubt and indecision.

Above all, it was important to remain calm. Ava's instincts were screaming at her to get Taylor out of her home immediately, but how to oust him without raising suspicion?

It didn't even occur to Ava that she was in any personal danger from the man sitting opposite her at her kitchen table. So utterly absorbed was she in working out how to expose him for the detestable killer that he was, that she almost missed what he was saying to her as she creamed dark, velvety chocolate mousse across her plate with the back of a silver dessert spoon — another hand-me-down from her grandmother. Slowly, on the back of her delayed processing, his chilling words insinuated themselves into her consciousness and she looked up.

". . . so how should I dispose of you, Ava? Another dodgy gas fire would look far too suspicious so soon after the regrettable deaths of Amy's young friends. And I doubt whether your dashing Inspector Neal could be convinced that you're the sort of woman who might stick her head in the oven. That still leaves me with plenty of other options, some more practical than others, that wouldn't point the finger of suspicion in my direction."

Ava stood up abruptly, her chair legs screeching on the flagstone tiles of the kitchen floor. Almost simultaneously, quick as a predator, Taylor was on his feet. Ava rounded the table and made a dash for the opening leading to the other room, Taylor right behind her.

The killer heels were a mistake but there was no time to kick them off. Ava made it as far as the doorway before her ankle suddenly gave way and she went down with a thud, looking up in time to see the satisfied grin on Taylor's face as he grabbed her arm and deftly twisted it behind her back, a move that she had executed on others so many times that she knew it was useless to struggle.

From her undignified position on the kitchen floor, Ava looked up into the amused eyes of a cold-blooded killer.

* * *

Jim Neal laid his mobile phone on the desk in front of him, staring at it as though it had been the phone itself that had conveyed Anna Foster's shocking news to him some hours ago, "*Simon remembers what he saw the night Amy's birth mother died and his sister disappeared. His father beat Debbie up, but he didn't kill her. It was Nancy. Nancy Hill forced a load of pills down her throat and held a pillow over her face until she stopped moving.*"

Neal and Ava already knew that Nancy had abducted Amy, but the thought that she might have been Debbie

274

Clarke's killer had not crossed his mind for a single moment. An old mentor of his had once cautioned him never to think of the past as 'another country' when it came to a murder investigation. Always go back to the beginning, had been his refrain, and Neal had lost count of the times throughout his own career when the old man's axiom had been vindicated.

The explanation for Amy's murder reached far into the past and involved long kept secrets and hidden lies. Amy's death was the end result of something that had been set in motion years before.

With a flash of insight, Neal pictured Wade Bolan, heard his protestations of innocence, his sneering words about having the perfect alibi for the night of Amy's death. He was serving a life sentence for murdering his wife; he had been suspected of abducting and killing Amy, an accusation that he had always denied. He had admitted to beating Debbie, but insisted that the injuries she sustained at his hands could not have resulted in death, maintaining, ironically, that he had beaten her enough times before to know how far to go.

It had been the overdose that killed her, but had the pathologist overlooked signs of smothering? Neal knew that homicidal smothering was not always easy to detect. The empty bottle of pills together with her injuries might have seemed like proof enough to a tired, overworked or downright negligent pathologist.

In the hours since Anna Foster's revealing phone call, Neal had been busy, making calls of his own, forming hypotheses and trying to think outside the box whilst remaining grounded in solid detective practice. He had also been in touch with Ava Merry for an update on her follow up interviews regarding Bradley Turner and his movements the night of Amy Hill's murder.

Five minutes ago, he had received a phone call from a contact in the Met who had provided some vital information that was helping him to piece the puzzle of

Amy's murder together. Something had been niggling away at him since his visit to Wormwood Scrubs. It had to do with something the guard had said when they enquired if Simon had been to visit his father.

No one fitting Simon's description had visited, but the guard mentioned that Wade had recently had a visit from someone who was not a regular visitor. On a sudden impulse, or perhaps because Bradley Turner was so much in his thoughts, Neal had faxed a photograph of Bradley to his contact, who had shown it to the prison guard and received a positive identification. He had used his mother's maiden name, Henry, which had not sounded any alarm bells.

Earlier in the day, Ava had texted him with the suggestion that Bradley might have had time to drive to Stromford, kill Amy and be back in bed in his flat-share in Sheffield in the window of time when his mate was asleep. The pub crawl could have been a carefully constructed alibi.

Neal sighed. His old mentor's words about the past impacting on the present kept hammering away in his head. Bradley Turner had a role in Amy's death, of that he was convinced, but was he the killer? Of that, Neal was less sure.

Another explanation for Amy's death was taking root in Neal's mind; on the surface it seemed preposterous, too far-fetched to be real, but nevertheless . . .

He needed to speak with Ava, get her slant on things, but he had been calling her number repeatedly over the past hour, and she hadn't answered. Ava wasn't the kind of person who switched off her phone on a day off, or let it go unanswered; she was far too conscientious for that. The only time she was likely to part with her mobile, was when she was in the pool and, even then, she would follow up missed calls immediately after retrieving her belongings from her locker, of this he was certain.

Still, she had let him down on two occasions recently. Neal looked at his watch. It was still early evening. Archie and Maggie were due back from the cinema soon. If he had not managed to contact Ava by the time they arrived home, then he would swing by her place and the pair of them could talk it through.

* * *

Taylor smacked Ava hard across the face, bringing tears to her eyes. The force of the blow jolted her neck painfully sideways, but she turned immediately to look him in the eye, with, "Whatever way you play this, Taylor, you're finished. What's it going to look like if I suddenly turn up dead? Don't you think no-one else knows of my suspicions about you?"

"Shut up, bitch!" Taylor said, jerking her to her feet, shoving her towards a chair, forcing her to sit down, "You're not in any position to give me advice."

"You tampered with the gas fire in Amy's room and didn't even bother to go back and repair it after she — so conveniently for you — turned up dead. You killed Becci and Gary."

"I didn't know her stupid little flatmate was going to swap rooms before Amy was even in the ground." No regret about the deaths he had inadvertently caused, only irritation that things had not gone according to plan, Ava noted.

"If you'd stopped at raping and molesting underage girls, it would have been bad enough, Taylor, but double homicide? That's a big step up," Ava taunted, steeling herself for the inevitable blow.

"Shut it!" This time Taylor used his fist, and the force of the impact of his hard knuckles on her face sent her senses reeling. Ava tasted copper in her mouth and felt warm blood trickling down her throat. Perhaps she would do well to stop antagonising him. Reluctant as she was to follow his order, Ava kept her mouth shut, considering her options, except her head was still befuddled from the blow, and she couldn't think of a single one that made any kind of sense in the circumstances.

* * *

By the time Maggie's cherry-red Ka pulled into the drive, it was gone eight o'clock and Jim Neal was more than a little irritated at Ava's failure to get in touch. It wasn't that he begrudged her a bit of off time, just that she should know that he would not call her at this hour if it were not something urgent. He felt let down again. The door slammed and Archie and Maggie burst back into his life.

"Dad! Guess what Auntie Maggie said to Ryan Douglas's mum?"

"I'm all ears," Neal said, with a quick look at his sister, who was lurking by the doorway, ready to make a quick getaway by the looks of it. Never one who could be accused of being subtle in her approach to human relations, Maggie's outspokenness had caused Neal many a blush in front of other parents or even teachers at parents' evenings, to which she always seemed to assume she had an automatic invitation as a sort of surrogate mother figure.

"If they're saying something about Archie, I've a right to know what it is," she had insisted on many such occasions. And Neal couldn't disagree given the significant role that Maggie had been playing in Archie's life for some time now.

"Well, Jordan Prescott tripped me up when I was running for the ball just so he could substitute for me — he didn't 'cos I wasn't hurt that much," Archie said, looking down at a bandaged knee. "His mum said it was my fault even though everyone was saying it was obvious Jordan did it deliberately. Auntie Maggie got into an argument about it and called Mrs Prescott a bloody lying old cow."

As the words left his lips, Archie looked at his dad challengingly, knowing he could hardly be at fault for a direct quotation of his aunt's words. Bad language was banned in the Neal household, and it was usually Maggie who forgot to be a role model.

Neal knew Mrs Prescott pretty well. He had stood next to her at enough football matches and sporting events at Archie's school to know that she was a deeply unpleasant woman and an indulgent mother whose thuggish son displayed early signs of psychopathy on the playing field.

More times than he could count, Neal had felt the urge to throttle the woman with his bare hands, and it was all he could do to suppress an approving smile at Maggie. Instead, he got ready to adopt the stance of shocked, indignant parent, but before he could get a word in, Maggie was off on a rant.

"She was setting a bad example for the kids. Honestly, Jimmy, she had it coming. It was high time someone stood up to her. She's an arrogant, shameless bully and her son's a little shit. If Archie sees me standing up to Jordan's mum, he's more likely to stand up to Jordan and other kids like him. Besides, kids need to know that it's not all right for people to behave like that just because they're grown up. I mean you're a bloody copper Jimmy, you must know what happens to kids who don't learn to look out for themselves." Leave it to Maggie to come up with a justification for almost anything, Neal thought, but in this instance he couldn't disagree.

"Thanks for taking him, Maggie, and for feeding him. And the life lesson." Archie had already told him about the McDonalds, a rare treat, as junk food was usually banned.

"I've told you before to stop thanking me for looking after Archie. He's my nephew and I love him to bits and besides, you know how guilty I feel for living here rent free — surely I can help out?"

"Actually, could you help out a wee bit more this evening?" Neal asked. "Something's come up and I need to go out." Maggie stood on tiptoe and kissed him on the cheek.

"No problem. We'll watch Top Gear and finish that Darren Shan book about the vampire magician at bedtime."

"Thanks, Mags. You're a star. I'll just nip up and say goodnight."

Before leaving the house, Neal tried Ava's number again. As he listened to the ringtone, an image of the photographs she had shown him of her rather lonely cottage flashed into his mind and, for the first time that evening, he felt a stab of worry. Why had it not occurred to him before that Ava might not be answering because she was in some kind of trouble?

* * *

Ava listened to her mobile ring for the third time, wondering why Taylor seemed untroubled by the sound. Ever since he'd punched her in the face, she had kept silent, not wishing to antagonise him further, particularly as he was agitated enough already. If he were as smart as a professor ought to be, he would have forced her to send a reassuring text to the persistent caller (whom she knew to be Neal) but so far this solution did not seem to have occurred to him. He doesn't have a clue how to play this, she thought, wondering how she could use this to her advantage.

She was also wondering why he had not bothered to restrain her. Was he so arrogant that he thought she wasn't capable of retaliation? She wasn't one of his fourteen-year-old girls. Still, there was a need for caution. From her bedroom encounters with Taylor, she was well aware of his physical prowess. Being proficient in martial arts did not necessarily mean that she had the advantage over any opponent. For all she knew, Taylor might be just as capable as she of delivering a handy karate chop.

Looking at him pacing in her peripheral vision, Ava sensed Taylor knew he had made a mistake. He should have played it cool, she thought. If he had reacted with astonishment to her accusing him of tampering with Amy's fire, he could have accused her of being ridiculous, challenged her to prove it (Could she? In these days of CSI, even trained police officers might be forgiven for thinking that the forensics people worked miracles) — and just left in disgust; instead he had a situation to deal with which, whatever way you looked at it, could only bring him more problems.

Taylor kicked over the chair nearest to him in a sudden burst of anger. Ava flinched, seeing the leg break with the force of his rage; she supposed she should be grateful he hadn't chosen to vent his anger on her face again.

The longer he spent trying to figure out what to do, the more time she had to work out how to act, but the ideas just weren't coming. Passivity wasn't an option here, Ava decided suddenly. Besides, it wasn't in her nature.

Then, before she even knew she had a plan, she was launching herself out of the chair, grabbing hold of the splintered leg of the broken chair and lunging at Taylor like a demented cavewoman with a sawn off club.

His arrogance was her salvation; clearly he saw himself as so superior to any woman that he was in no danger. Ava's crude weapon was already crashing down on Taylor's shoulder before he had a chance to shield himself from the blow.

Ava thanked her stars for the hours she'd spent shifting weights in the gym and keeping her body in peak condition. The force of her blow knocked Taylor off his feet. She moved swiftly to deliver another hit, but he grabbed her leg and brought her to the floor beside him.

For a few moments they grappled with one another, with Taylor trying to manoeuvre Ava into a position where he could use his weight to pin her to the floor, but Ava was quick as well as strong, and she wriggled free of him.

Springing to her feet, she concentrated all her energy into delivering a swift kick to the professor's groin area. Pain seared through her foot at the impact but it was gratifying to see Taylor's face turn green and his hands clutch his precious manhood as he yelped in pain.

There wasn't a second to lose. Taylor wouldn't be disabled for long. Ava shot across the floor to retrieve the chair leg and raised it above her head ready to bring it down hard on Taylor's skull, no longer caring how seriously she hurt him; this wasn't self-defence; it was a fight for her life.

Her arm came down at the same time as Taylor roared like a man possessed and ran at her, knocking her off her feet and sending her sprawling headfirst into the sofa, the chair leg flying through the air, narrowly missing Taylor's head as he ducked.

I'm done for, Ava thought as her hands sank down between the scatter cushions on her sofa. Taylor knew it too; he was looming over her, fists balled, a murderous look on his face, lips curling into a cruel, triumphant smile.

* * *

Neal had never visited Ava Merry at her home before, so he didn't know if he should take the private road leading to the cottages, or park his car at the end of the official road. In the end, he parked up and walked the couple of hundred yards to her place, wondering all the way why anyone would choose to live alone in such an isolated setting. He wasn't a die-hard city dweller and he loved to be up in the Scottish hills away from it all, but he also liked a bit of civilisation right on his doorstep.

When he saw the red Porsche parked outside Ava's cottage, Neal was unsure what to think. He recognised it immediately, of course, as Christopher Taylor's — even if Taylor hadn't had a personalised number plate he would have remembered the registration. Most police officers were into noting number plates and Neal had the advantage of an excellent memory.

His first thought was that Ava had been seeing Taylor, and for some reason had been trying to conceal this from him by spinning him a story about her investigating the professor. There was no doubt that she had been attracted to the man, but Neal had gained the impression that Taylor simultaneously repulsed her.

In the end, it was gut instinct, that elusive, indefinable impulse that led him to believe that something was wrong. Later, he would rationalise it as a kind of sixth sense arising from years of experience on the job.

The door was unlocked and he didn't knock — another instinctive act that he could not rationalise later. What if he walked in on Ava and the professor entwined on the sofa in an impassioned embrace, both of them stark naked?

Throwing any such thoughts to the wind, he turned the handle and stepped inside with a police officer's instinctive, cautionary stealth. Professor Taylor and his sergeant were indeed entwined upon the sofa but they were not engaged in any kind of amorous activity. Far from it.

Taylor lay sprawled across Ava, blood spurting from a wound in his neck, his hands clutching at a pair of scissors sunk deeply into his throat. As Neal stood, stunned for a moment at the sight, Ava heaved Taylor off of her. He landed on the floor with a dull thunk, staining the light beige rug crimson as he thrashed about in pain and panic.

"For fuck's sake, sir," Ava was yelling, "call a bloody ambulance before he bleeds to death!"

Chapter 22

The damage to Ava's face was superficial. Her nose had had to be re-set and would never be the same as it had been before Taylor's fist knocked it out of joint, but the slight imperfection, the barely noticeable misalignment added character to what had been a too-perfect symmetry of features, or so the nurse was assuring her patient when Neal came to visit. He hadn't pegged Ava as vain, but then beautiful young people have no need for vanity, he considered, watching Ava turning the hand-held mirror this way and that, the better to assess for herself what Taylor had spoiled.

"I'll do," she declared at last. "Small price to pay for putting that bastard behind bars."

Neal cringed inwardly, wondering how Ava might have felt if the three hour operation to save Taylor's life had gone differently. It was one thing to injure a suspect in the course of doing one's duty, but quite another to cause lasting damage or worse still, loss of life. You had to be able to live with the consequences, and coping with the knowledge that you had killed was not something he would wish on Ava — having lived with it himself.

Fortunately, Taylor's life had been saved by the surgeon's skill and the generosity of the anonymous person who had donated his or her rare blood for the good of mankind.

Neal placed his bouquet of flowers on the table beside Ava's bed, with a guilty glance at the departing nurse. Was it still permissible to bring flowers into a hospital ward in these days of superbugs? Ava was in a room of her own, so maybe it didn't matter so much.

"Thanks, sir," she said. "Pull up a chair."

Neal, who had been about to perch absent-mindedly on the edge of the bed, fetched a chair from across the room and sat down.

"So. How are you feeling?" he asked, suddenly awkward.

"I'm fine. They're discharging me tomorrow, I think. Thank God, the food here's abysmal. Face is on the mend and the cracked ribs are less painful. Oh, and they x-rayed my foot. I'm going to need a small op. to put that right but I'll need to get in line for that."

Neal nodded. "I meant, how do you *feel?*" he asked again. Ava squirmed back against the pillows.

"To tell you the truth, I feel great," she admitted. "I know I should be feeling bad about injuring — nearly killing — another person, but I don't. I'm just glad to be alive, because, I tell you, that man intended to kill me."

"Good." Neal said. He wondered if Ava would always feel this way, or if she would wake up in a cold sweat one night, horrified at what she was capable of. Taylor is alive, he reminded himself. It's not the same.

"I suppose I'm in for a bollocking?" Ava asked, far too cheerfully. Really, she was in such good spirits after her ordeal, Neal couldn't help wondering whether she was going to crash down hard sometime soon. He would make sure she saw the police counsellor, whatever her protestations might be.

"No, actually," he said. "You've been instrumental in apprehending a persistent and dangerous sex offender. I contacted Rohina — Roxy — yesterday and she was so shocked that Taylor had tried to kill you that she said she would reconsider her decision not to come forward and testify against him. I suspect, as did you, that her story will open the floodgates."

Ava started to grin, but he carried on. "However. You were way out of line inviting Taylor to your home like that and putting yourself in danger. That's not how a good police officer operates, and you're damn lucky not to be finding yourself back in uniform. You have me to thank for that. I see your potential, Ava, and I want to carry on working with you, but I need to know that this kind of thing isn't going to happen again. I won't tolerate a lone wolf . . ."

"But I got results, sir."

"Don't say another word, Sergeant," Neal said, an edge to his voice. Her reply had not pleased him, but a conversation about her attitude could wait until she came down from whatever high she was riding on — perceived success or painkillers — best leave her to reflect awhile and see if she saw things differently then. Sooner or later they would need to talk. He even suspected that Ava would seek him out.

"Forensics are all over Amy and Becci's flat as we speak. They'll find something to connect Taylor to that faulty fire. He wouldn't have been stupid enough to leave a print, but you have to be pretty adept or downright lucky to walk away without leaving a trace that these guys can pick up nowadays.

Even if they come up with nothing, there's enough to build a case around. With Roxy's testimony and a little detective work it should be straightforward enough to prove that Amy was blackmailing him, which gives him motive. And your testimony, of course."

Neal stood up, feeling conflicted. On the one hand, he wanted to congratulate his sergeant, tell Ava that she had done good work. On the other, she had acted out of line and they could have been looking at a wholly different outcome. How to play it? To his surprise, it was Ava who spoke first.

"I'm sorry," she said so quietly Neal wasn't sure if he'd misheard, "— for going it alone. I'm not some vigilante. It's just . . . sex offenders like this are kind of personal to me."

Neal stood perfectly still.

"Your experience with the flasher?"

"No," Ava answered quickly, "I handled that. It's not an uncommon experience for young women, you know."

Neal nodded, admonished. She wasn't going to say any more but that was fine with him. Her apology, however low-key, was enough for now.

Ava changed the subject. "Taylor killed Becci and Gary but we're no further forward in finding Amy's killer, are we, sir?"

"I have an idea about that," Neal said. "That's why I turned up on your doorstep last night. I wanted to talk it through with you because it's a bit out of the box." He sat down again, pulling his chair closer to the bed, conspiratorially, and told her how — and why — Amy's death had come about.

* * *

The following day, Neal travelled to London alone. Ava had been discharged from hospital and was expected to be off work for a few days; then it would be light duties until she had the operation on her foot.

A pleasant young constable picked him up at King's Cross and drove him to Wormwood scrubs where he had arranged a visit with Wade Bolan.

The same guard he had met on his previous visit with Ava showed Neal to the interview room, barely concealing his disappointment at not seeing Neal's 'charming young DS' again.

Wade Bolan looked up as Neal entered the interview room. Their eyes met. Bolan's seemed to be insolent and guarded at the same time, and for a brief second, Neal felt with utter conviction that his theory was right, though he might never be able to prove it.

"I want to talk to you about your daughter, Amy," Neal began.

"Who's Amy? My kid's name was Emily. Emmie."

"You killed Amy," Neal said, suddenly impatient. To his credit, Bolan did not flinch. He cocked an eyebrow, a lazy, self-satisfied smile spreading across his face, crinkling the skin around his eyes. On someone else it might have looked charming.

"In case you hadn't realised, they lock us in at night here, you know. Be a bit difficult to slip out and bump someone off, don't you think?"

"At the end of September, you had a visitor by the name of Bradley Turner. He told you what you'd always suspected. Your daughter was still alive. Your son, Simon, told Bradley that in a chance meeting in a pub, not long after he'd made the same discovery himself. He also told Bradley about his past, how his father murdered his mother and how his sister disappeared, and his father was suspected of killing her too, though no body was ever discovered.

He told you Emily, now Amy, was alive and well and living with Nancy Hill, whose name you recognised from the past. Debbie used to offload the kids on her when she couldn't be bothered looking after them herself.

Amazing, isn't it, how Nancy's name never came up at the time? She was so unassuming that no one would have suspected her of being involved, still less being capable of murder and child abduction. No-one ever mentioned her name to the police."

As he spoke, Neal watched Bolan's face closely. Bolan's expression remained impassive but a tell-tale pulse throbbed in the side of his neck.

"I must admit to having a certain sympathy for your plight. You stopped just short of killing Debbie, but you were convicted not only of her murder, but on suspicion of killing your daughter too when you knew you had nothing to do with her disappearance.

You knew you were innocent of harming Emily, but it didn't matter, did it? You went down for it just the same, because how else could her disappearance be explained? Simon's story about the 'angel taking Emmy to heaven?' They thought that was his way of blocking out the terrible truth of what he'd really witnessed." Neal paused, knowing he was on the right track, also knowing he couldn't prove a thing.

"You needed to punish Nancy so you took the thing she loved most in the world. Her daughter."

"My daughter," Bolan corrected him.

"Your daughter. You were serving a sentence for killing her anyway, so why not make it justified? Who did you get to do it for you, Wade? An old mate, a stranger, someone who owed you from the past?"

Bolan leaned back in his chair, appearing to be relaxed, but Neal suspected a lot was going on in his head.

"You can't prove nothing," Wade said at last, and Neal smiled inwardly, satisfied now that he was right, even if, ironically, Wade was also right. He stood up, signalling to the guard that he was ready to go.

"I'm going to appeal, you know. Now it's come to light I never killed Debbie nor Amy, I'm getting out of here with a truckload of compensation for wrongful conviction."

Wade's words stopped Neal in his tracks, "You've spent eighteen years of your life in this place. No amount of money can compensate for that," he said, but his heart was in his shoes. In a perverted way, Wade had served his sentence backwards and he was likely to be well recompensed for his time.

Even if he were guilty of hiring a hit man to kill Amy, Wade Bolan could not be convicted of murdering her twice. It was an unsatisfactory conclusion to the investigation. Even tracking down Bolan's hitman — which might or might not happen at some indeterminable time in the future — would bring small reward. The whole case, like life, Neal supposed, was full of small victories and crushing disappointments.

All the way home, Neal wrestled with his feelings. He thought about the letter Richard Turner had shown him a few days after Nancy's suicide, in which she confessed to feeding Debbie Clarke painkillers and smothering her with a pillow before abducting Amy. Richard had wanted to throw it away without showing anyone, but in the end his conscience had made him take the letter to Neal. This backed up Simon's story, which might otherwise have been dismissed as a false memory.

Richard Turner had also confessed to knowing about Bradley's trip to London to see Wade Bolan. Once Bradley found out that Amy's father was a 'jailbird,' he had wanted to use this information to hurt and embarrass her. He had had no idea that Nancy was not Amy's real mother nor could he have foreseen the tragic consequence that would result from his visit to Bolan. Between father and son, Neal could not decide which was the more pathetic.

He thought also about Nancy Hill and the choices she had made. It had recently come to light that, while she had been in foster care, she had been raped, aged fourteen, by a fifteen-year-old boy, and became pregnant. The child had been stillborn.

Had Nancy seen in Emily Clarke the baby she had lost and now could save? No amount of tragedy in her life could justify what she had done to Debbie, but as Neal so often observed, people who do wrong have very often been wronged themselves.

290

He picked up his mobile and called home. His sister answered on the second ring.

"It's me," he said, "Is Archie home?"

THE END

Thank you for reading this book. If you enjoyed it please leave feedback on Amazon, and if there is anything we missed or you have a question about then please get in touch. The author and publishing team appreciate your feedback and time reading this book.

Our email is jasper@joffebooks.com

http://joffebooks.com

ABOUT THE AUTHOR

Janice was born and grew up in West Lothian, Scotland. After completing an English degree at St Andrew's University, she moved to London where she lived for ten years doing an assortment of jobs.

Her passions are reading, writing and walking in Scotland and the Lake District. She currently lives in Lincolnshire with her husband and two sons. Her second novel DARK SECRET is available now.